The Crystal Tomahawk

The Crystal Tomahawk

Daniel L. Philips

Contents

Special Thanks

I would like to thank:

The National Aquarium in Baltimore
Re: Giant Angelfish
Particularly Joe Harber & Alison Davidson
Joseph, Joan & Joey Hannas
Re: A Crystal Tomahawk
Kathy Philips & Daughter Stefanie
Proofreading & unlimited cooperation
Virginia Hess (Mother)
Proofreading & help
The Becker's
Michael, Debbie (Helen) & grand pop
Joey, Christopher & Steve
The Townsend's
Re: Sean in particular, my guitar instructor
My former co-workers
Especially Ted Barger

List of Characters

The Becker Family

Michael—Dad
Helen—Mom
Joe—Son
Christopher—Middle son
Little Steve—Youngest son

The Townsend Family

Sean—Neighbor-Dad
Jane—Neighbor-Mom
Little Sean—Neighbor-Infant
Greg—Ex boyfriend of Marie
Grand mom—Neighbor-The Townsend's
Shimonock—Native American Father of little one
Little One—Lost Native American child
Father John—assistant to Father Fortune
Father Fortune—
Officer James—Police Assistant
Officer Startfirst—Chief Investigator
Frank—Neighbor on other side of Becker's family
Lady—Run away dog of Frank
James Floyd—Co-owner of an investment firm & a local Forge
Grandmom Floyd—Lady who finds lost winning lottery ticket
Karen—Secretary to James Floyd
Susan Floyd—Wife of James Floyd

Julie Floyd—Daughter of James Floyd

Carol—Girlfriend of Julie Floyd from school]

John Harold—Curator of museum

Donna—Secretary to the curator's office

George—Janitor at museum

Marsha—Sister to George

Arnold Friends—Guest speaker on first floor lectures on topic: "The Existence of Strings."

Chuck—Manager of work crews in museum

Wilma—Physic who visits during a school bus trip with students

Janet—Lady who finds lost daughter—home room mother to school bus trip at museum

Pauline—Johnson—new curator who replaces John Harold

Gary Thomas—Conference member who wants the Eastern Indian display on a National tour

Willie—Friend of Pauline Johnson from the N.Y.C.'s old job

Jeff—Temporary fill in for Joshua, new supervisor for museum work crews

Joshua—coworker helps with chuck and Giant angelfish

Officer George—Rookie Policeman

Rich—Janitor of school—steals tomahawk from Becker family

Jackie—Wife of Rich, the janitor

Barney—Small blue pet fish of Becker family

Old gentleman-unnamed go-between of Rich to Gerald

Gerald—Next owner of tomahawk

Pam—Younger sister of Gerald

Gloria—Gerald's mom

Joyce—Gerald's girlfriend

John Smith—Nightclub owner next to own tomahawk

Jim Smith—Brother to John helps fill in for Skip as bouncer

Joan Smith—Wife of John Smith

Showgirl—Unnamed—also helps run errands for John

Judy—Lone Clairvoyant

Paul Hayride—Retired school teacher & local historian and friend of John

Ron—Magician who performs tricks before music band plays

Sam—Older bartender & private business associate to John

Skip—Bouncer who dies in his sleep

Krista—ex wife of Skip
Joe—Oldest physic group
Gary—Physic in group
Stella—Female physic of group
Trish—Girlfriend of Joshua
Harvey & Greg—Workers hired to support giant Angelfish with driver
    to Baltimore

Chapter One

THE LUCKY FIND

It was early afternoon in mid-August and the sun was becoming very warm. The two brothers, Joe and Chris were walking slowly home after a hard fought basketball game. As they were kicking and bouncing the ball from each other, Joe, the oldest, suddenly came aware of something peculiar. About 100 yards from their back yard, they realize their neighbor's dog, is loose.

Joe looked at Chris in fear and yelled, "Ooops, run!" Dropping the ball as they approach their home, the two enter their fenced-in back yard just in time. Within seconds, the big dog enters the rear driveway and growls through the rear fence.

Their neighbor, Frank. slowly responds, returning "Lady" to her own fenced-in playground. Joe and Chris now remember their forgotten basketball. During the fiasco, the basketball had rolled down over a slight hill, along a wooden fence. A small city improvement in waterlines, had caused a fresh mound of soil, making way for a new extension. Joe and Chris searched for hours without finding the ball. When hopes finally wane and interest lost, Chris finds the ball. Joe, running over to see, notices something peculiar. As he lifted the ball, he unmasks a real treasure. In plain view was this perfect, opaque tomahawk.! Chris, reaching for it, couldn't believe someone else hadn't noticed it before now. Walking casually up the bank to the road, then towards home, Chris held the stone up and yelled, "Mom! Look what Joey and I found!"

Helen, unaware, smiles and says, "Oooh boys, what you find?—Looking Closer, she takes the stone, wow! some kind of crystal thing.

grasping the stone, Helen walks in the back door, "You boys wash up, take off those soiled clothes." Helen walks in sitting at the kitchen table, "This looks like one of those Indian things! Joey stops preparing to walk in the living room.

Chris, wanting the stone back, runs for a shoe box in his bedroom.

Helen laughs, "Don't trust your own mother?" Then adds, Dinner's almost ready."

Dinner well underway, both boys slowly drift back for a closer look at the treasure. Chris watching Joe asks, "Do you think it's for real?"

Joe, placing the stone in the bathroom sink full of hot, soapy water, reaches and grabs the white, clean towel.

Chris, impatient, said, "Let me see!" Grabbing the stone, Chris holds it up to the bathroom light. They could almost see straight through it!

Joe remarked, "We'll show dad when he gets home this weekend."

Their father, a truck driver, was rarely home except on weekends, and once a month, on Mondays. Usually when dad was home, it was party time. Michael, their father, liked to take his family everywhere. Restaurants and bowling alley's were an absolute. Sometimes the games got very competitive, but Helen usually scored the highest. Both boys shared the same History teacher, with Joey, the older brother, attending the morning class.

After receiving permission, Chris brought the stone to school. Mr. Richard was amused and handled the stone very carefully. All at once, Joey popped in during Chris's class and joined in the group's discussion. Joey asked the all important question, "Mr. Richards, were there real Indians around here?" Pausing briefly, Mr. Richards politely handed the stone back to Chris. The suburbs of Philadelphia was the host of several groups, most go all the way back to the beginning."

Joey looked over and asked, "When was that?"

Mr. Richards, noticing the large crowd forming, said, "Native American History can be sketchy; some groups were friendly to settlers," pausing again, "others weren't."

John and Chris walked home that afternoon, soon they forgot all about the stone. All that crossed their minds was dad promising to take them to the Monster Mash at the Spectrum.

When dad finally got home, it was almost too late. Michael and Helen were so busy discussing the new washing machine, that Chris and Joey forgot to mention their new found treasure.

Sunday brought with it the Townsend neighbors, relatives from Lansdowne plus others who never seemed to know when to go home. It was late Sunday night when things finally began to settle down. The treasure had found it's new resting place—in a windowsill facing their parents bedroom.

Michael looked right at the shoe box several times never thinking to ask where the stone came from.

Several weeks passed, and Joey and Chris were eagerly engaging in school work. Somehow the shoe box got shuffled to the master bedroom.

Helen was busy taking little Steve to preschool, picking up kids, grocery shopping, and running errands. Somehow she forgot where she put the treasure.

Monday morning seemed only a few winks away. Joe and Chris went about their routine as little Steve watched dad. Once a month, dad gets an extended weekend. The whole family can't wait. Helen takes the children to school with the normal bustle of things, with usually a "good-bye" chorus, and then silence.

Michael, hearing the door close, started his normal morning wake up. Not much different than any day, but this day, Michael stayed home. Once the showers are completed, the regular day begins. Coffee pot perking, stereo playing music, laundry going, if any and finally an old fashion shave! As he gently removed the single edge blade from the pack, placed it in his razor, Michael heard a giggle and then a running sound. Originally thinking of little Steve, he realized they all had left for school! Michael, walking through the house, dripping all over everything, shouted down the hallway, "Steve is that YOU?" No noise anywhere! Michael ran for the bathroom sink.

Once the shave was completed, and a quick peer down the throat followed by a nasty tooth brushing, he heard a giggle again! But this time followed by the sound of a child darting down the hallway. Michael, bewildered, again, searched the house completely. Finally remembering to call his dad, he settled down with his coffee and the sports page. Sitting in his boxer shorts and robe with coffee in hand, Michael called his dad. Pushing the "auto call", his dad quickly answered. "Hello dad? Yes,"—finally "man that's a real rat race!" What's hot? Talking to dad, he never noticed Helen's quick amazement. Helen, now back from the errands approached the front door. Michael opened it still talking to dad.

Helen, not bothering to even ask, yelled, "Yo! What's this??"

Michael, still absorbed in his call, never looked back at Helen, who was totally in shock.

Michael, subconsciously recognizing Helen's despair, turned toward Helen making a slow advance toward the bathroom. After finally reaching her, after what seemed forever, he quickly dropped his coffee. Looking at Helen, with his shoulders sloughed, and shaking his head, Michael began to explain. "Honey, this is what greeted me this morning," he said as they both stared at the bathroom, now is shambles. Shaving crème in neat, long stretches along the mirror like Christmas garland; aftershave bottle completely spilled.

Helen looked back at Michael, now completely in shock and slowly replied, "No more Strawberry Dacheries for you!"

Once the havoc cleared, Helen and Michael balanced the check book and started the rest of the once a month Monday routine. Michael called his dad back after having hung up on him.

Helen running full speed all morning, started preparing for the afternoon errands.

Michael aware of Helen's plight, begged her to let him finish the errands. He left quickly preparing to pick up little Steve.

It starts out vague looking back, but SIMINOCK, who was an Eastern Native expert in tanning hides, fishing and gathering fruits and berries was to play a big part in the scheme of things to come. He was also an expert in trading with others and notoriously known for his knowledge of wild animals. Some of our people, who traveled extensively in our area, told stories of the mysterious man. The stories ranged from mire strange encounters with others to actual horrible encounters such as:

I started out a survivor of the raid wars. No vengeance ever entered our camp, just immense fear. We didn't trust them and they certainly didn't trust us either, especially toward the end. The others suffered hunger and while we suffered common ailments, they seemed much more apt in dealing with those challenges. We were taught early in our years how to use scrappers which were rocks or stones that helped mold arrowheads, spearhead, and in particular, our number one all round tool—the tomahawk!!

The others had leader, which were later called "politicians." They borrowed the term to describe peace, "bury the tomahawk." During my life it was primarily a symbol of brutality.

After our tribe survived, what they called, "encounters," many moved first south then later west. Subcomponents of nations didn't share the same traits, like customs of gathering food, and rituals were totally different. Our awareness of other nations existence and their deeds, whether good or bad, was never passed along. The others never talked about things to us for they were completely immersed in their own difficulties.

When I was about 14 years old, I was fishing on the outer waterfall, west of Philadelphia. When I discovered a beautiful, almost perfectly clear stone. Our people believe that certain living things posses spirits. I know the stone was made from some spirit to be a tomahawk for it had the general shape even before I finished it. After being completed with a special scraper that seemed to keep the scrape marks at a minimum, I held it up toward the sun. I could feel my face get hot almost instantaneous. Shortly after using it to throw at deer, I realized it had a very special quality to it. This beautiful, clear, stone seemed to be perfectly balanced; always being accurate, even when I wasn't! If souls came back to dance around camp fires, they would definitely want the rock. Other members wanted it badly, too. They offered everything imaginable.

When "little one" was born, we spent a lot of time together as I showed him how to tell the "leaves of three" rules. The difference between common roots, berries, and some mushrooms. When "little one" became about four summers old, we went hiking along the Schuykill River. It's here something mysterious happened. The water became dark around high sun. My boy disappeared. I jumped in the water screaming over and over, but no sign of him. Our nation, even the others that lived locally helped, but found absolutely nothing!!

I left my clothes, along with my tomahawk, on the bank during my screaming fiasco. The clothes were ravaged perhaps by some wild animal—the tomahawk gone!! During several earlier encounters with the others, a "peace meal" which included an offering of tobacco, beads or other rare things had taken place. It seemed trading or even killing for it was not even remotely a possibility!!

The settlers were very busy people. but in most cases, we never crossed paths. They seemed interested in trading, but only when it became necessary. I was taken to the "land of the spirits," by something the settlers called "The Fever." Both sides had suffered casualties, but came to rest outside a well built up community.

Now it seemed, years later, someone found and returned the stone-eons of time later. Our stories forgotten!

The Townsends visit every other long weekend. Their arrival usually meant an upcoming work party with wall painting, plumbing and maybe a weekend pool party. But this time their visit was to bring with it an unexpected, strange mission. Both families have children around the same age with the Townsends having one child a lot smaller. After Michael greets Sean, the fiasco began with Michael mentioning the hard to ask question.

Sean remarked, "Let me guess, it's about money?"

Michael laughed, "No, Sean, it's about a change in plans.

Sean said, "Michael, I need help with the carpet. I got a great deal, but I don't know how to lay that stuff!

Michael laughed, "No problem, Sean, we'll get it!"

Helen, was busy setting dinner, threw out the answer. "Spirits! Super- natural, apparitions, possessions."

Sean was completely ready to laugh, but looked puzzled at Michael.

Preparing for dinner came about in a flash with home made entrées. Once dinner got underway, Michael started out about the truck job.

Sean mentioned a major employer would soon be taking applications. But eventually the subject returned to the unusual.

Helen began by bringing up the morning fiasco.

Sean, completely overwhelmed in interest, suggested a solution. "Michael, what would you say if we hold a spiritual some night? You know, a séance.

Helen and Michael remained frozen in thought. Michael looked to Helen, now giggling, "Well, I know Father John well. If things go wrong we'll just have to have him come do a blessing or something.

Drowning in thought, Sean said, (speaking loudly over the kids), "Come on! It might be fun!"

The kids, now restless, were leaving the table one by one. Sean remained talking with Michael. "How's your job?" pries Michael.

Sean, trying not to laugh adds, "Which one?" Then he smirks, "Greg has a Ouija board. "Did You know that?"

Michael, totally unmoved walks toward the kitchen.

Sean follows Michael as he helps wrap the garbage. Jane couldn't help but notice the cluster in the kitchen workspace.

Helen, putting food in a tray, looked disturbed at Sean's intrusive way. Helen, without pondering interrupts, "O.K. Do it!!"

Sean, who was looking at Michael, giggles at Helen, "I'll be right back." Moments later, while Jane was describing her plush carpet, the door bell starts to ring. Michael Jumps up taking off to answer— Seems the kids were as interested as the adults with Chris pestering in a continuous, "Mom!—Mom!"

Helen watches Sean open the box then shouts, "What Christopher!!!???"

"They're suppose to use a candle,"

Helen holding Little Steve, "How do you know?"

Joey half interested, "Chris and I watched some movie late the other night on "Scary Week."

Helen, looking for Michael's thoughts slowly starts raising her voice, "Scary Week!! Who said you could watch that stuff!!!???"

Michael reluctantly cleared the table noticing the centerpiece still wet from Helen's dish cloth.

Sean lit the candle supplied by Chris

Joey got the light switch and headed for the living room. Sean looking very serious began, "We should all now hold hands. Then he asked Michael, "Do you want to ask the questions?" Michael, still very reluctant suggested, "Why don't you? You seem to understand these things better than I do." Sean said, "Oohh, low blow! This is your house! Your spooks!" Helen laughed and said, "Go ahead Michael!" Michael, holding the hand piece, slowly started the questions. "Are there any spirits in our house?"

The board remained still.

Michael persisted, "Are there any children who like to play in shaving crème?"

Again no movement.

Moments passed, the tension high. Then all at once, Joey dumped his soda.

Helen, alarmed, ran to wipe the spill. As she scanned the room, she couldn't find Joey. She suddenly became frantic! "Joey, where the heck are you?"

"I'm over here, Mom!" Joey said.

She stopped in her tracks, realizing, he didn't cause it.

Joey stood puzzled next to Michael and Sean.

Sean added, "Don't stop now. You made contact. With a frog in his throat and in total fear, Michael continued, "What do you want?"

Suddenly a glimmer appeared on the hallway. First, what appeared to be a fire, then a stampede, all took place in total silence on the giant hallway wall. Everyone saw it, but no one made a sound. A bear, a moose, even a fish seemed to be running along the wall! Without a sound, these shadows continued forming. People were fleeing, some appeared frantic, then total silence! Waiting patiently and quietly, the Townsend's catch the light then finally blew out the melted candle.

Helen noticing the time in a stern voice, "Boy's, let's move it. You got school, unfinished homework." Then Helen reluctantly grins, "I don't know what to think." What do you think that was all that all about?"

Sean and Jane were still preoccupied when leaving the Becker's. Jane remained speechless. Sean silent driving home kept thinking. Jane frowns looking over at Sean "I could never mention any of this, gosh they'd swear I was crazy!" Sean, shakes his head turning into the driveway, but seemed a lot more interested. "I have a friend who has an aunt who does tarot cards. Maybe he'll talk to her about tonight and get some insight."

Jane replied, "Why did we drive over there when we could have walked?"

Sean laughed, "We had dinner! Remember we had food to carry?"

Jane slowly answers, "I'm sorry, I forgot about the food."

Sean, "I'm sure they won't throw any containers with food away." After opening the car door for Jane, Jane hurries into the house "Think I'll give them a call." Sean, making the usual sweep to the kitchen realizes he left his keys in the front door.

The phone ringing; Helen answered. "Jane, yea,—well, this was all Sean's and Michael's adventure. I wasn't crazy about the Oiija board Idea in the first place. It was Michael and Sean's brilliant minds at work." Jane, "Yea, he's right Here, I didn't think we'd get anything to happen."

Helen interrupts, "You know you forgot your plate and bowl?" Jane . . . laughs, "I was so upset, I couldn't think to do anything right." She continued, "I don't even remember why we drove over, when we live next door." Then Sean reminded me, "I plum forgot dinner." Jane looking at Sean thinks about Michael, "Where's the other mastermind?'

Helen giggles feeling interrupted, "He's helping Chris finish his report on "Ancient Mexico. Did you know Tenochtitlan had everything gold?"

Jane curious replied, "Why did they?"

Helen wipes out the sink with a cloth, "Because gold looked cool." Then laughs "How do I know!" Helen, deep in thought, said, "Ask Sean when he wants Michael.

Michael, picking up the bedroom phone said, "I'll ask him."

Helen yawned, "Too much boy talk, I'll call you tomorrow."

Jane giggled, "I'll call when I get back from running."

Helen, being polite, said, "Too bad you can't run a few laps for me."

Michael suddenly interrupted, "Where's Sean?"

The phone beeped just as they began talking. Michael, waiting for Sean, answered the beep, "Dad! Man, I got something to tell you! You ready to hear this?"

Grand pop Becker said, "I guess so.

Michael, collecting his thoughts said, "We had a séance in the dining room!"

Grandpop Becker, "A séance, what the heck for?"

Michael furthers with, "You remember the mess in the bathroom?"

Grandpop Becker, "The Strawberry Dacheries?"

Michael laughed, "I didn't have that many. Helen had more than I did.'

Grand pop Becker said, "Yeah, but she doesn't lose her composure."

Michael, remembering Sean said, "Hold on a minute, dad." Clicking back to Sean, "Yeah, next weekend for sure. Then added, "I'd give you a hand Tuesday but Helen has some parenting school conference." Then he added, "I have dad on the other line."

Sean replied, "I'll call you later in the week."

Michael said, "Sounds good." Clicking back with the phone Grand pop Becker asked, "You going to help with the dog, next week?"

Michael remembering earlier fiasco's, "Well, yeah, I suppose."

Michael looks over, "Last time things go pretty crazy."

Grand pop Becker, You know—this dog was part your idea. You wanted a puppy."

Michael quiet in thought said, "That was when I was still a kid." reminiscing the evening, Michael refrained from letting it go.

Helen exited the living room over an hour before. Michael found himself thinking about work, T.V. late night shows. Then he started worrying about Monday morning. By this time, Helen was fast asleep. Michael decided to go to bed and within moments, all was calm.

The children, taking turns running to the bathroom while their parents door remained closed. Michael started dreaming about the Strawberry Dacheries. Suddenly in a deep sleep, he sees a visitor sitting in the bedroom chair! Michael remained calm. The visitor peered across at them very patiently, never talking or even gesturing. Michael, in the curiosity mind, woke up and peered over at the chair. Falling back to sleep reassured, he starts to dream again! Then Michael notices a bright light coming in the bedroom window. The light from neighboring cars could be seen on the bedroom chair. Then Michael became extremely startled. The figure in the dream was an Indian Brave! Then startled Michael wakes up again and looks over at the chair. Empty!! Wrestling for the covers, Michael has a dream about the séance, the fish, the moose and some people running around then an Indian Brave jumping in a river!

Helen woke up from all his squirming. "Michael, it's 3:00 a.m. What's making you squirm so much?"

Finally Michael settles down. Little Steve enters now crawling in bed. Michael, fast asleep starts to remember the toilet paper fiasco, the giggles, and the little foot prints in the shaving crème. Michael, not knowing that little Steve was in bed, pulled hard at the covers. Little Steve on the opposite end, falls out on the floor! Helen wakes up. "Michael, wake up!" Then louder, "Michael!!

Finally Michael says, "WHAT?"

Helen replies, "What?" It's two to one, can we have our fair side of the bed?"

Michael, finally ready to talk says, "I've been having horrible nightmares!"

Helen, lifting up little Steve into the bed," Please Michael let's go to sleep."

Sean and Jane returning to the world of work. Once again with Jane remembering but, refusing to talk about the séance. Sean opening his field office back door walks through looking for his work acquaintance with a very special aunt. No luck, Sean remembers the Carpet job then gets side tracked thinking about his other home improvement options.

The week days move fast. Sean couldn't wait to see Michael on Friday. Making every conceivable excuse to walk out back, Sean caught a glimpse of

Helen separating trash recyclables. Sean pries, "Did Michael make it in yet?"

Helen, startled looks over, "No, Sean, not yet.

Sean again, "Must be the traffic."

Helen refocuses her attentions keeps separating cans and plastics.

Jane stumbled on a friend from High School at the supermarket. Grand-Mom back at the house grows increasingly impatient. Grand mom attacks Jane entering the back kitchen," Must be really busy on Wednesdays."

Jane frowns, "I got stopped by some guy who use to date Marie."

Grandmom, now really curious, "Marie? Greg? What's he want?" Jane replies, "Nothing really, just wanted to know how Sean and I were doing. Remember you know, I did go to school with him." Grand mom frowns, "Your daughter really remembers old Greg!"

When Michael got through the door, the children were already seated.

Helen quipped, "Take your time, we just sat down." Michael b-lined for the shower and clean clothes. The phone rings with someone knocking at the door at the same time. Little Steve ran to open it. Helen interrupts Little Steve's adventure, "Where you going?" Michael answered the phone while Helen pulls open the front door looking back towards the kitchen," It's Sean."

Michael, with the portable phone looks up around Helen's shoulder, "Let's switch."

Helen smiles grabbing the phone and makes for the table. Sean was flicking the T.V. when Michael returned to the table. Michael curious, "Jane coming over?"

Sean shakes his head, "No, She's caring for her mom back home." "Her Mom's been acting stir crazy for some reason." "She's great helping during the week with Little Sean, especially with Jane running errands."

With everything back to normal, Michael forks a mouth full of food when the phone rings again; this time Chris answered. Chris shouts from the living room," Dad, it's Grand pop Becker."

Michael swallows watching Chris bring the phone. Lifting carefully from the wooden Chair over the family crowd. Michael listens quit. "Can you bring him over here?" Michael looks around before answering. "I'll be over after I'm done catching my breath."

Grand pop Becker asked, "If you want you can eat over here." Michael quipped, "Oh, gosh, thanks dad. Helen's got dinner served and the neighbors are here." As he watched little Steve play in his dinner, Michael looks making a big yawn. Sean rambled on about the weekend fiasco. Helen started off talking about Michael having nightmares.

Sean laughing uncontrollably looks over at Michael Joey comes into the conversation asking about what the Indians were like.

Sean quipped, "It was no picnic, the Indians wanted to trade, but half The time the settlers wanted no parts." The weather, was very difficult back Then." Chris, who arrived in the middle, said, "The Indians wanted their own Hunting lands back."

Michael, who was listening added, "Who knows? That was a very long time ago. Philadelphia in those days had lots of problems, Something like today." Jane looking in a phone book stumbles on Sean's friend Tim's number. Sean grabbing a notepad, picks up the phone walking in the living room. suddenly the phone picks up," Hello Tim, this is Sean from work." looking at Jane, Sean continues," You remember Your Aunt's phone number?"

Helen prepared for the "Teacher's Conference" leaves quietly. Then Joey and Chris walk exiting to the basement.

Sean looks up at Helen, "Tim, You still have an Aunt who does Tarot?"

Michael, listening intently, cleared the dinner table leftovers.

Sean looks at Michael and smiles "How much does she charge? Think she would be interested in making house visit?"

Michael, not hearing the phone talk, becomes increasing curious

Sean looks over again at Michael "How about asking her when she's free to make a visit? Yea, that's right. I'll wait here for her phone call. "Tim, You know the number at the Becker's?" Sean waits patiently, No Tim, The Becker's Phone number." Looking Odd at Michael, then smiles with a giggle, "I almost Forgot it myself." Sean scratches his elbow," It's 123-456-7890. Looking over again with big eyes at Michael, Sean shakes his head at Michael then closes," hey, thanks Tim, I'll be waiting."

Michael peers out the front window, "Helen will go bananas!" Sean frowns, "She's not goin to charge." Michael turns around, "How does Tim know what his aunt will do? Sean jumps up walking to Michael's refrigerator," Tim helped finished some choirs with the lawn a few weeks ago."

Michael still reluctant "I still can't do it if Helen doesn't approve. She's half of this, you know, maybe 7/8."

Sean pours a soda, "If she doesn't like the idea, we'll do it over at my place." Helen who returned early noticed something was up. Tim's aunt was coming and everyone in the house was smiling and quiet. Helen scratches her neck, "I'm half afraid to leave the house. Now what are you two scheming?"

Joey, jumping for the chance to talk, gets cut off by Michael in a quiet deep voice "Sean wants to invite a witch over."

Helen looks around silent, "That ought to be really interesting! What's she suppose to prove?"

Michael looks over at Sean then back at Helen, "Sean's friend from work has an aunt." Helen pulls open the refrigerator door ignoring Sean then stares back at Michael "When's Sean ever going to get his carpet done?"

Michael sits back in the chair watching Helen pass "This is all his idea I've been busy cleaning dishes." Helen looks out the front Bay window towards The Townsend 's Property. Michael waits for Helen's return of thoughts "How was the Teacher's Conference?" Helen looks back at little Steve then walks to the Kitchen holding his hand. "They cancelled it because the school has some Budget problem; can't pay the electric bill or something" Never even Bothered Calling anyone. A whole lot of people were really upset." Jane, ringing the doorbell invites herself in. Looking puzzled at Helen She asks, "Now What's going on?"

Helen smirks, "You really did have to ask," dropping down the towel Walking from the kitchen grabbing the checkbook on the china cabinet. Chris ran out the kitchen just as the doorbell rang. Sean looked at Michael then glanced at Joey and said, "Well?" Michael looked toward the kitchen, laughing he said, "I'll get it. "Hello, are you Tim's aunt, the lady with the special gifts?" The older lady smiles greeting the family," we'll find out soon enough." Sean introduces himself, then invites the lady through to the kitchen.

Judy takes off her coat. "I want you all to know this can be a very difficult to attempt." Most families are very skeptical. To do readings requires a lot of different things to sort of mesh together. Don't get your hopes up and maybe I won't disappoint you. Looking towards the kitchen, Judy looks with a smile "Hello." Helen and Jane stand speechless. Judy pries, "Are you having any trouble here?"

Michael interrupts "Yes, sleeping! Everyone starts laughing. Judy looks across the large living space, "Milk helps a lot.

Chris, totally uninterested, pesters Helen to go upstairs. Leading the way, Little Steve follows.

Sean said, "Maybe we should get started?"

Judy looks back at Sean, "I could use a candle." Michael pushes himself up from a wooden chair, "I'll be right back." Sean cleared the tablecloth. Michael giggles at Sean returning with the large thick candle.

The Becker's remained standing while Sean and Judy start to sitting down. Judy takes the candle, "It's not that scary a medium thing." looking at Michael. "You both can sit down."

Spreading the card on a silken black table cloth, using a card spread, and candle, Judy asks the first question.

Michael looks up at Judy "You have no idea what kind of response we'll be getting?" Judy patiently listens not answering.

Michael spurts out "We literally had shadows jumping all over the walls here" Judy, looking amused glances at Sean, "What kind of shadows?"

Michael excited interrupts "All kinds, moose, fish." then adds "Sean even started losing his composure."

Judy, "That doesn't usually follow a normal reading."

Helen quiet in thought,. "The shadows are so alive! It's something like watching the negative film of some wildlife outdoor sporting event." Judy listening to Helen looks carefully over at Michael, "What about your nightmares?"

Michael laughs, "Some little child was playing in shaving crème." Judy looks over at Michael puzzled. "As in your dream?" Michael shakes his head, "No! In my bathroom." Judy smiles, "Let's try the medium."

Holding hands, with the room darkened, the candle lit, Judy pops the first question. No response. Michael asked, "Are there any children attracted to my shaving crème?" Little Steve and Joey returned, walking down the steps. Moments seemed to fly by. Patience was growing dimmer. Sean relaxed holding hands, begins to yawn. Helen bumps Michael's arm, nodding she smiles "Let's talk in the kitchen."

Judy stops feeling the tension in the air, "This isn't working." Looking over to Helen, Judy reaches for a deck of cards, "These tarot cards might tell us something."

Sean shaking his head looks across asking Judy the all important unanswered questions. "Suppose the Spirits were buried here or gravitated here from some magnetic pull or maybe someone brought something in the house; or maybe the house was made from something which belonged—"

Michael cuts Sean off, "Let Judy think" Judy lifts disappointed from the table rolling up her black table cloth. Chris and Joey run upstairs, little Steve looking bothered starts pestering mother in the kitchen.

Helen looks to Michael, "This is one of those days you wish you'd stayed home in bed."

Michael silent in thought remains quiet. Sean hands Judy an envelope with money then ushers her back to her car. Jane making her return trip back in the house watches Sean, "What was all that about?" Helen smiles, "I'll tell you, but you really don't want to know. Your husband thought we should try a witch." Michael disappointed in Helen's crude comments looks at Sean reentering the house. Sean looks catching the tail end of the conversation Jumping in to defend his pride, Sean Interrupts, "I thought it could help!" Jane turns around weird looking back at Sean, "A witch! Sean looks around noticing all eyes focused on him, "A Tarot reading" Chris returns with Joey, wanting refreshments Michael hears the backdoor open

Sean looks across from the dining area and whispers to Jane, "It's Marie." then Michael jokes to Marie about a missing strange encounter. Marie opens the refrigerator, "I have lots of my own."

Jane looking intense asked, "Everything all right?" Marie, coming right at Jane exploded, "What did you tell Greg?" Jane thinking momentarily, "Nothing. He asked how things were, that's all!" Marie thinking looks around really upset by now. "Mom! He's almost dad's age and not only that—really weird!"

Helen interrupts "Seems like you two have a serious conversation to resolve." By now, the whole kitchen becomes empty. Jane and Judy refocus looking over at Helen then take off for the front door.

Sean looks over at Michael, "Don't we have carpets to examine?" Michael apologetic, "Hopefully it will be laid by my next long weekend."

Jane, moments later enters with Marie from outside. Marie seemingly relieved, smiles once again while All emotions returns to calm. Little Steve casually mentions the shoe strings getting mysteriously in knots. Michael smirks refraining from a laugh then asks "Are you sure you didn't do it?" Jane starts off talking about the errand with Grandmom when the phone rings. Jane and Sean on cue leave to go pick up little Sean. Sean jokes, "I'll see you when your long weekend comes."

The weekend evening seems to end quickly. Helen b-lines first with Little Steve and the other sons follow close, taking turns for the bathroom before Landing In a good night's sleep.

Michael, now alone, began thinking a bout the witch. Then he pondered the Tarot cards along with wondering about the nightmares.

Peace came quickly at the Becker's with phones and doorbells quiet. Michael began snoring. Little Steve rushed to the bathroom and then to the master bedroom. As he passed the night light in the hall, Steve felt like he was being followed. He suddenly stopped. Not sleepy yet, he decided to try some- thing. First, you run, then you stop dead. Steve's shadow stopped. The other delayed. Steve bends over, his shadow bends, but the other stayed standing!! Steve looked again, before standing erect. When finally up straight, the second shadow remained bent over. Little Steve panicked. Running full blast to the master bedroom. "Mommy! Mommy! I got something to show you." Helen moans answering, "In the morning." Little Steve tugs harder. Helen remains fast asleep. Michael, awakened by the fuss, exits for the bathroom. Helen smiles looking over. "Steve wants to show you something." wasting no time in the hall, Michael returns to the bedroom. Little Steve starts pestering harder. Michael shouts, "Behave! Go to your room!" Little Steve becomes frantic!

The crying wakes Helen, "What's going on! Come on! I need to get some sleep, the sun will be coming up soon!" then quickly Little Steve jumps in bed. Once Steve got comfortable, thing's returned to normal. Chris next wakes up looks over for Little Steve Then decides to makes a bathroom run, walking slow like Little Steve past the light, he suddenly feels a creepy chill come over his body. Looking down the hall from the bathroom, Little Steve wakes reentering the hallway. "Look Chris, look here!" Chris half frozen In fear stumbles in the hall running for the boy's big bedroom. Joey, now awake from all the screaming, runs looking toward the hallway. Joey Yawns, "What's goin on?" walking down the hallway. Christopher pushes Joey's face, "Get out of the way! Run!"

Joey, now well down the hall, enters the bathroom. Preparing for his Return journey to the bedroom, Joey see's a movement in the hallway. Joey notices Little Steve peeking from the bedroom, Come-on, Steve! Go back in the room." Looking for a moment in the mirror, Joey hears a child's giggle from the sink. Joey opens the bathroom door then glances around toward the bedrooms. Joey shivering notices the hallway clear. Now frozen in panic, Joey drops the wash cloth and zooms for the bedroom! Upon reaching the bedroom, Joey scared realizes the door was locked. Joey then screams, "Open up, Chris, what's wrong with you?" Turning around glancing behind, looking down in the hallway. Suddenly a man's figure with a band strap on his head seems sitting in the open hallway. Too scared to stop shaking or ponder thoughts, Joey darts rushing past the figure to the master bedroom. Joey slams the bedroom door, floppy down in the big arm chair.

Michael, hearing the sounds, lifts his head glimpsing over from the bed towards the door then the chair totally unaware of Joey's presence. still half asleep. Michael slowly overwhelms with fear.

Yelling loudly, Helen jumps up in bed. "What's wrong?" Now staring at Michael, she shakes her head then notices Joe in the big chair. "What's wrong with YOU?"

Joey, in a whisper, "Mom, we have ghosts!"

Helen looks at her clock, "I think tonight, I'm sleeping on the couch," then looking to Joey, "if we do, they're not going anywhere; go back to your room and go to sleep."

Joe hesitated then moaned, "Chris won't unlock the door!"

Helen, leaving her warm bed, slowly throwing on her robe and walking down the long hall. Walking with a distinct stagger yells to Chris, "Open the door!" Joey glances behind her looking for the man who earlier was sitting in the hallway. No one present! Joey remains silent Chris opens the bedroom door with extreme caution, "I'm sorry!" Helen, who was upset by now frowns, "That's enough, go to bed!" Chris whispers, "We have ghosts!"

Helen, in a monotone, "I don't care, go to bed!"

In the meantime, Michael in the master bedroom returns to dreamland. The night returns to calm, with the morning quickly rolling in. Joe and Chris remained quiet at the breakfast table with Michael leaving shortly before sunrise. never kissed Helen for fear of waking her before leaving. The doorbell rings later with Jane bringing the morning coffee and little Sean. Jane, putting down her coffee cup found the living room more friendly. Glancing at Helen, she said, "What's wrong?"

Helen rolled her eyes and shook her head. "It's Sean and Michael" She glanced back to Jane, "They have the whole family acting crazy. Michael thinks I ought to run around the house at 2:30 a.m. playing some kind of ghost chaser!" Helen regroups, then smiles, "How was your night?"

Jane laughed, "Sean—he's looking for a priest!!"

Helen giggles, "What? Sean feeling guilty about something?"

Jane looks holding her cup up. "I wouldn't put it past him. No, it's still this ghost thing, Sean has sort of become preoccupied. We need a vacation, everything is getting to be too much of a hassle! His job wants him to work weekends, then they change their minds." She paused, "They holdup on his pay, then the bills go unpaid!"

Helen countered, "Michael makes good money, but he can't be home."

Jane, changing the subject, "So Helen, what's the latest on the conference night?"

Helen rubs her eye, "They're going to hold it at the other intermediate school."

Jane giggles, "O.K., run up their electric bill right?"

The phone rings almost on cue. Helen answers. "Yes, I'm mad. How are we suppose to survive without sleep?" Then glancing to Jane, "Hold on honey, I have a beep." Answering the incoming call, Helen returns to Michael, "It's the school, I'll call you back."

Moments later, the boys arrived with the usual clamor. Joey refraining from extended conversation with Chris, heads straight for the upstairs bedroom.

Helen, wanting the feud to stop, makes Chris tell the story.

Joe, upstairs, Chris blames Little Steve.

Helen, infuriated, called Joe down from upstairs. "What you going to do, hold a grudge for life?"

Joe looked over to Chris, who was obviously upset and sulking "Chris, you're forgiven!"

Jane listening quiet looks over to Helen, "I'm glad I don't have problems like this." Helen looks across," It's not over till I tell dad."

Sean, arriving after work knocks on the front door. Entering without fanfare he immediately recognizes Helen's distraught appearance. Sean, feeling guilty, sits in the living room. Helen walks in, "You and Michael just chill the ghost thing for awhile." looking back at Jane, "I'm not resting, we need to function around here." Sean looks up from the television, "I spoke to the priest he's going to call sometime this week."

Helen, short fused, angrily said, "Sean, when? Anything else?"

Sean without words looks beat up then glances to Jane, "I'll be over at the house if you need me." Sean glancing Helen politely excuses himself.

Helen looks frowning at Jane, "I'm really sorry!" Jane holding the pacifier with one hand while shaking her head, "I've been saying the same thing, Sean has been totally obsessed with this thing." The phone rings interrupting Jane's next remark. Helen grabs her pocketbook and prepares to get Little Steve, but instead answers the phone. "Father Fortune? What parish you with?" Helen was fighting to control her laughter. Then smiles, "How's tomorrow morning? Great! 9:00 a.m. We'll be here. Thank you, Father, Good-bye!" Jane starts packing up Little Shawn.

Helen frowns "Stay put! I'll only be ten minutes. If the phone rings, take a message." Just as Helen drives away the phone rings. Jane answers. "Sean, I don't know, she's just tired and uptight. Yes, I know, but gosh, you two are worse than the kids."

Sean glances his wristwatch, "Well, maybe all this will be over soon."

Jane picks up Little Sean, "By the way, the priest you recommended is stopping over tomorrow morning. Maybe we should leave them alone for awhile to let things simmer down." The next morning, Father Fortune calls.

Helen returns from preschool, greeting the priest. Helen looks across "Well, Father, what all did Sean mention?"

Father Fortune smiles, "I think everything." Father Fortune acting more on instincts looks around noticing the kitchen furniture "What's Your story?"

Helen scratches her neck, "You got three hours?"

Father smiles. "I'll start by blessing the house, then I'll take something to rinse down these heart pills.

Helen wanting to be helpful, "You like coffee? We don't have any luck with keeping Iced tea"

Father looks toward the steps "How many kids do you have?"

Helen rubs her swollen eyes, "Three, give or take, one grown up and one no one can see."

Father Fortune smirks, "Yea, Sean told me about the shaving crème. What exactly do these entities seem to want?"

Helen shrugs, "People to run around chasing after them at 3:00 a.m., when children should be resting for school."

Father Fortune returns moments later, "You shouldn't have any more problem I felt no resistance whatsoever. Coffee's great! I must go!"

On the following Friday, Michael got home early. Sean was ready from three weekends ago with one knee pad already on. Sean followed Michael in. Michael, interested in making the job easier, stood on one end while Sean rolled the other. Words were hard to find, for Sean was still half upset over Michael's wife. Finally he looked over at him and said, "You know, it's your fault I got blasted on by Helen."

Michael, half shocked, looked disorganized and drops the carpet. then looks over, This aint about you, it's me. I don't come to bed half the time, I don't seem interested in the kids, you all know the regular stuff. I don't unwind till 2:00 a.m. The kid's got more ideas than Santa Claus. Little Steve, he's right under your feet all the time. Sometimes all this takes it toll."

Sean added, "I still don't understand.

Michael reluctant, "If I printed money and got caught, I'd be terrible They'd say, Oh, he was such a loving father and a model citizen. Always helping In community affairs, helping people with money problems. Gosh! Shame he was a crook and a poor example to his kids. Yeah, let him rot in jail!"

Sean, using the staple gun asked, "How come you didn't put your name in over at Texto Company?"

Michael looks up, "I really don't like their products, I certainly don't want to get paid making them."

Sean said, "Well, that's it, we're done. Took some mean shaving crème, but I got my carpet."

Michael, not bothering to stick around looked restless and said, "Sean, I got to go. Come over when you get a chance, but I need some time home."

Back home, Michael walked in the door. Little Steve made his predictable attack.

Helen, talking to Jane, ends the phone call watching Michael close the front door in the living room. then making conversation, "Boy, that was quick!" Michael frowns walking around the kitchen, "It's just hard to find the energy or time." Helen curious, "How'd you and Shawn get along?"

Michael squints, "He's sort of angry, I think he tried to get me an interview at Texto."

Helen dropping ice in a glass, "I guess so, he went to school with the owner." Michael hugs Helen, "What's for dinner?" Joey, enters wanting to know about boxing, interrupts the quiet. Michael looks back around himself, "What Joey?" Joey smiles, "Welcome home dad, what's a TKO?" Michael looks back at Helen, "I think it's when the fight is stopped, one or both boxers are physically endangering themselves."

Chris then jumps in with, "Yea Dad, welcome home, Suppose they'll hold the fight again the next week?"

Michael laughs, "Who's going to pay to watch two "half beat up boxers" finish a fight?" Chris shouts "I would!" Michael laughs," It wouldn't be very good.". Helen interrupts, "Wash up! Dinner!" The boys head for the bathroom. Michael yawns, "Think I'll call dad after dinner." Helen thinks looking at Michael "He said he might drop over tonight." Michael smiles, "It's probably about the dog again." Helen, half puzzled, "Beam me up, Scotty."

"Oh, dad wants me to hold the dog while he gives it some vitamins or worm medicine," Michael. "Last time, I helped, Laddie almost bit me!" Helen watching her water boil sits down quickly with her apron on. Little Steve squirms next to dad's lap Helen not wanting to create more problems Looks over, "Michael, I think I saw something last night. It looked like a Little Steve." Michael frowns, "what?, That's just what we need, another Little Steve!" Michael remembering the last long weekend still at a loss for words drops his fork.

Suddenly the doorbell rings followed by a knock on the back door. Helen jumps up, "I'll get the kitchen!" Michael smiles answering the door to dad. Helen answered the door to thin air. As he watched the news, Grandpop was holding little Steve. Helen was telling the story about the Teacher's Conference. Grand pop said to Michael, "What's up with the priest's visit? I heard the news from my neighbor. He works at St. Peter's rectory."

Michael said, "Actually that idea came from somewhere else." Helen jumps at the turn to talk, "Our neighbors were trying to get rid of our 3:00 a.m. spooks!" Grand pop starts smiling, "Oh, spooks! That ought to be fun!!" Joey thinking fast, "Would you like to come spend a night?" Grand pop frowns, "I have a hard enough time sleeping now! No, Joey, you keep them over here!"

Michael laughs, "Thanks a lot!" Then Grand pop questioned, "Any more trouble?" Helen shakes her head "I can't really tell. When I do sleep, I try not to be Woken up." Glancing around at everyone at the seating arrangement, Michael Holding Little Steve, watches amused at grand pop with a palm computer game.

Once dinner was accomplished, Michael and Helen began discussing the plans with grand pop making excuse after excuse not to want to help. Helen gives in, "I'll come help, tell me what you need to do" Michael looks at Helen, taken by surprise starts feeling sudden guilt Grand pop smiles finishing his coffee, shakes his head Looking straight at Michael then calling it a night leaves for home. Helen looks at Michael, "Suppose the spirits aren't really gone? Michael watches Little Steve play with a game, "Let's think positive."

Joey and Chris leaving to play baseball, both exit through the living room. Helen reaching for Little Steve, yells, "Where you going? Little Steve starts Laughing. Helen frowns," Oh, no you're not!" Michael, surfing through the T.V. channels, looks out the living room windows. Joey and Chris start talking on the side, front lawn. the phone rings Helen answers it, holding tight to Little Steve. Helen smiles "Yea, here hold on, he's right in the living room." Helen walks reaching with the phone before making her way to the kitchen finishing dishes.

Michael takes the phone, "Father Fortune! How are you? No,— No problems so far. 'What can I do for you?, Helen thinks she might have seen something, but she's not sure." Michael lifts away, "Hold on, Father Fortune wants to come over for dinner some night." Helen looks up puzzled, "Sure, of course, anytime he's free." Michael laughs, "Father, any time you're free." Looking at Helen, "Next week?" Helen, "sure, when?" Michael thinks to himself, waiting for Father, "Sure! How's next Tuesday? O.K., that will be great!"

Helen leafs through the mail watching Joey and Chris enter the house. Chris yells, "Mom! Mom!"

"What?" Helen scolds, "You don't have to scream!" "Joey found a frog or something." "A frog!" Helen looks up at Michael, "I don't think so." Michael smirks, sitting down in a wooden kitchen chair. Helen starts laughing, "Does it have bumps all over it?" Joey ponders before answering, "Yes!"

Helen looks at Chris, "That's probably a toad! toads are usually on land, frogs like wet areas, like creeks, rivers, and swampy land." Chris interrupts, "What do they eat?" "Usually lots of flies and grasshoppers," Helen looks over at Michael. Chris and Joey exit in a hurry leaving Michael and Helen by themselves. Little Steve falls sound asleep by the couch. Helen puzzled, "Wonder what Father Fortune really wants?"

Michael reaches in the refrigerator "Don't worry till they hit you with it, no use trying to figure out the unknown." Moving around the refrigerator Michael stumbles on the chocolate milk, looking across at Helen he walks off to the living room.

Jane's curiosity, calling every hour. Helen looks quiet watching Michael's sudden departure. "Jane wants to know if they can come over?" Michael, still upset, remarks, "Sure, anytime." Helen, still on the phone glances back to Michael, "What about now?" Michael nods not making a sound. Still in agreement. only seconds later, the doorbell rings. Sean helping, holds the front door for Jane and Little Sean. Sean looks in the room anxious, then glances to Michael then nods at Helen, "We got to talk!"

Michael waits puzzled, "To the conference room!" Entering the front garage, Sean lets loose, "I think I solved the problem!" Michael closes the door, "What's problem?" Sean walks prancing "I don't know whether to believe in the another Dimension, or spiritual Plane, but help me here," Suppose years and years ago, hundreds of people were murdered around here, Suppose back in the beginning some of those souls were buried in unmarked sites. The victims many children had horrifying deaths of swords and rifles." Michael hearing all this, sets down on a grease can. Sean looks out across the lawn, "Suppose some two hundred years later, you and me are talking about it." Michael thinks quiet, scratching his neck, "Around here?" Sean again, "Within a hundred yards, or perhaps even closer? Just suppose there's some truth to their spirits walking in our time." Michael looks out the garage window, "How do we make peace with that?" Sean overwhelmed, "I don't think anyone can!"

Michael laughs, and shakes his head, "Don't let Helen know quite yet, I'll ask Father Fortune what he thinks next Tuesday night." Sean curiously looks back at Michael, "He's coming back?" Michael smiles "Yea, he liked Helen wants to meet the children, make sure thing's are all right." Sean looks back out the garage door.

Michael grabs Sean's arm," Did You mention any of this to Jane?" Sean looks back smiling, "No, I just walked in the door, Jane had called Helen Moments before we decided to come over" Michael points toward the kitchen Doorway," Maybe we'll get lucky and they won't know any thing. "Sean and Michael walk in from the outside garage through to the kitchen doorway. Jane and Helen sit smiling.

Michael smirks, "I was just talking about the truck job. What's up with you two?"

"Jane wants to know if we'll baby sit next week, They want to celebrate their anniversary,12 years and still together!" Michael grabs for a water glass, "Do I get to watch the sports on your Plasma?" Helen frowns, "Ah, no—Michael, actually Little Sean will be over here." Michael yanks open the refrigerator," Wow! Real fun, cool neighbors." Jane laughs uncontrollably, "You can watch it on Football and Baseball games." Michael squints "That's all the way next year, some time!" Michael b-lines Searching for the remote control, then surfing for the college season Schedule sits down. Sean, "Don't you think anyone else has problems?" Michael looks up frowning, "Sean, we'll deal with stuff the best we can!" Helen walks in feeling unusual tension, "I didn't think you two were going to start at each other!"

Michael and Sean look across at each other then quickly return silent. Helen walks out to the kitchen and restarts checking homework, she then calls on Joey for a missing assignment. Chris waiting his turn for homework review, uses the time to take his evening shower. Michael, confused over a work delivery throws down the remote grabbing a slip of tomorrow's work line-up. Then phones the base office to start leaving a message. Things begin to settle and unfold before returning to a normal evening.

Michael, hours later on his usual one man adventure, starts a channel surfing quest. Helen walks past on her last trip upstairs. Ten more times around late night T.V. Michael squints at tonight's episode, "Lost in Bermuda" losing television interest, he pushes the power off and darts for the upstairs. Helen yawns, already half asleep. Michael settles into the bed. Moments later Michael drifts in and out of sleep, Little Steve sneaks on mom's side of the bed Michael feeling subtle movements turns to his far side grabbing extra blankets Little Steve wakes screaming "Dad!" Michael's eye's open wide. Now aware of Little Steve's presence, Michael pulls the covers overtop Helen's body . . . Little Steve feels the blankets return and things settle down into sleep for with the Becker family finding their comfort zone.

Tuesday morning rolls in quick. Kids off to school, Michael speeds off to work before sunrise. Everyone leaves the house and goes where they're suppose to be. Little Steve leads the way out the door to preschool. Early afternoon the phone rings with Helen not quite in the door. Hurrying she makes it on the last ring. "Yes!" Helen, talking out of breath, "Around Seven o clock, Yea, we adults eat late do to Michael's schedule. O.K. See you tonight." Michael having traded schedules arrives later than expected. Father Fortune was already present and seated. Michael smiles excusing himself, and darts straight for the upstairs shower. Helen, making conversation, "What's life like at St. Peter's?" Father Fortune looks about curious, "How do you mean?" Helen laughs, "Well, is it a larger parish?"

Father Fortune looks across with a mouth full," Large for this area, I'm sort of the morning Mass Priest. Father John my assistant does the late mornings." Helen looks over at the coffee pot, "Yes! Michael knows Father John pretty well." Father Fortune curious holds chewing "Really?" Helen nods, "My father-in-law used to take them to old St. Peter's, then our new parish was built, Michael wanted to stay with St. Peter's." Then sitting down "There's something in the fine print that encourages families to attend where They live." Hearing Michaels loud voice yell down the stairs, Helen excuses herself to go investigate. "Take your time," Father Fortune forks another piece of salad. Hurrying her way back to the kitchen, Helen sits again thinking a little harder, "You don't mind me asking all these silly questions?" Father Fortune smiles, "No, anyway I can help answer questions." Helen's eye's light up, "O.K.! Do other residences in the area have any problems?"

Father Fortune frowns puzzled at her question then wipes his face, "You mean the strange sounds?" Helen, grasping at straws thinks to herself, "Yea that's a good way to put it." Father Fortune shakes his head, "I would have to check, I would imagine Somewhere something." with a half bothered look Father Fortune excuses himself for the hallway bathroom. Michael rushing down the steps, looks at Helen bewildered, "Where'd he go?" Helen smiles pointing to the hallway. Michael feeling foolish sits down serving himself a salad. Father Fortune walks out moments later, greets Michael then recites an evening table prayer. Michael smiles pouring salad dressing, "Tell me, Father Fortune, how big is your parish?" Helen bursts out in laughter, "Michael, I just asked him that!" Michael, looks across, "How was I suppose to know?"

Father Fortune thinks, before bringing up the million dollar question. "Does anyone here know the real story?" Helen cuts a piece of meat looking puzzled before glancing at Michael. Michael grabs at a piece of salary using his table knife. Remembering Sean's garage talk, "What real story?" Father Fortune spurts, "Several battles or military engagements involving Native Americans took place around here." Father Fortune lifts his arms up and puts his hands together," Someplace very close around here." Michael smirks at Helen with a gesture wanting a cup of coffee. Father Fortune squints over at a flowered kitchen clock, "Early Settlers and Native Americans left with what they thought were few options, attacked and killed one another." Native Americans, killed sometimes ended up in make shift cemeteries probably within a mile or so from here." Michael sips the cup in a loss for words, stares silent.

Helen wanting more information scratches her head, "How many do you think there were?" Father Fortune shrug's, "I would guess several hundred Maybe even more." Father Fortune stretches standing up. Helen looks across at Michael. Father Fortune shakes his head, "I must be going. "Helen gestures, "Father, what else? "Michael jumps up, "yea please tell us the rest." Father Fortune looks for his hat," When the Native Americans weren't interested in fighting any longer, they were sort of pushed out of the way." Helen pours more coffee. Father Fortune waves, "that's enough, right there." Helen stops pouring. Father Fortune frowns," Some drifted South, then later west others in broken tribes migrated where ever they could find refuge." Michael wanting closure, "Maybe they are wanting this area back." Father Fortune smiles looking weird, "I don't know. Helen pours herself more coffee, "Do you think that explains the shaving crème?"

Michael reaches for the creamer's, "We don't really know what they are or want, but they love to mess in shaving crème!" Father Fortune restless, "What was it about the children you said?" Helen suddenly remembers the locked bedroom, "There was one incident the other week which involved the kids running back and forth, "Oh, Succotash!, Michael, Father Fortune! Wait a minute." Helen shakes her head "The boys late last summer brought home an unusual rock. Michael, they're not sure, but they think it's an Indian something or another." Totally overcome by the Conversation Helen runs for the bedroom. Hidden In a box of old Christmas cards, with some unusual wrappings Helen snatches the stone. She then rushes back to the kitchen smiling," I found it." holding up the perfectly shaped almost crystal clear stone.

Father Fortune, Silent sits back down. without words, He takes the crystal holding it to the dinning room light. Michael, looking over puzzled at Father Fortune jokes," How would an Indian child the size of Little Steve get inside that?" Father Fortune smiles shaking his head at Helen, "This is the most unusual thing I've ever seen! Do you have any idea where they found it?" Helen silent at first, "I know they brought it in with them. It was so late that afternoon I wanted them to wash up for dinner." Joey, hearing the conversation, rushes to the rescue. "Chris and I found it in a pile of mud." Chris, attempting to stay upstairs, not fond of adult conversations hears Joey telling the story, then shouts, "Yea, it was almost dark!" Helen walks looking toward Chris, "Yea, but where?" Joey older, thinking hard looks at Michael, "Some construction site with a pile of junk." Joey looks back toward Chris "The ball rolled down a hill, landing in some old pile!" Joey glances back at Father Fortune then to Chris," Remember? The neighbor's dog got loose, we dropped the ball and started running for our lives."

Helen shakes her head, "Now I remember! You even asked permission and later took it to school." Joey views Father Fortune satchel, "Chris got in trouble for not being in class." Father Fortune hands it to Michael, "This might serve as a catalyst or Something, I'm not sure." Michael holds, "What do we do with it?" Father Fortune rubs his neck, "Keep it for now, put it back somewhere safe, let me know immediately if anything comes about strange." Father Fortune impatient for the door, excuses himself for another late evening visit.

Joey interrupts grabbing the crystal, then looks with his eyes close up next to the stone. "Hello, anybody home?" Chris grabs the stone then pushes Joey away. then screams, "I fond it! You gave up on everything, I'm the one who went down the last time looking for it."

Michael in awe, remarks, "Don't you boys know how to treat each other? Come on! Your brothers!" Chris frowns at Joey then walks away throwing the crystal across the table to dad. Michael upset shouts," Chris, go to your room!" Helen jumps reaching the stone Taking the crystal upstairs. Michael blasts, "If I tell grandpop, he'll be so angry You'll be graduating from high school before you're ever at the Monster Mash or a ballgame!" Joey sits watching in total silence. Helen passing Chris from upstairs, pauses looking back, "Let's see some of that homework!" Meanwhile downstairs the doorbell rings. This time it was Townsend's staring at Michael. Sean asks "What'd we miss?, the priest looks really played out!" Michael giggles, "Yes, I think we kept him occupied." Helen, taking over entertainment interrupts, "I think we got some questions answered."

Sean, waits watching Jane sit with Little Shawn. Mindful but angry listening to Jane, Sean shouts, "Is it my turn, yet?" Jane looks up annoyed at Sean outburst, "What?" Sean looks frowning with his arms out, "I never get to hold the baby!" Jane screams, "Yes, you do! More than I do!!" Helen opens the refrigerator, "I have a better idea." Sean looks up, "What's that? "Helen reaches for a ice tea pitcher, "We'll hold the baby!" Sean eyes light up, "Nice try, very predictable!"

Michael changes the subject, "How's the carpet look?" Sean sensitive about getting it laid looks up holding Little Sean, "It's actually very nice stuff, "I fell asleep on the roll by accident." Jane giggles, "I came home half an hour late from grand mom's."

Jane changes the subject," I want to know about the priest visit." Helen pours a glass of iced tea for Jane, "What, the shaving crème?" Michael empties his glass, Seems the boys found some Indian relic thing; it apparently was uncovered last summer during a construction site dig." Helen talking overtop Michael fumbles listening to Michael's storytelling. Helen stops, with a pitcher over Michaels glass, "Its made out of clear stone, like maybe a crystal." Michael looks up at Helen as she continues pouring, "It may have caused spirits or something to collect." Michael sips his overfull glass, "It's sure looks like a real Indian weapon, You know them tomahawks things, better than me. "Sean surprised, hands Little Sean back to Jane, Sean looks over collecting his thoughts," What makes you think, I know what a real tomahawk looks like?" Michael glances across at Helen," Some kind of weapon the Native Americans used!" Sean looks for the coffee cups, "If its real its probably worth a little money to collectors."

Helen laughs, "Yes! Finally my chance at new carpets!" Michael ignores, keeping serious, "Father Fortune couldn't explain everything, we thought it might be what was on our walls the other week." Helen sits down, "Maybe that's what it was all about." Jane rocks Little Sean on her arm, "That could explain why Judy couldn't get a reading." Sean sits with his coffee, "Where's it now?" Helen stares slamming her hand down, "Sean! I just put the darn thing away!" Michael jumps up, "I'll go get it!" Helen swallows putting down her coffee cup, "No! Spare our bedroom." Looking disappointed at Sean, Helen b-lines upstairs. Michael waits for the coast to clear, then adventures toward the ice cream in the freezer. Helen darts back then out of breath hands Jane the Crystal. Sean disappointed, "Gosh, they don't trust me with a rock!"

Michael watching notices Jane's excitement build then shakes his Head, "Helen, Who ever did this work was very, very talented!" Jane studies the stone passing it to Sean. Sean stares "Yea, you ain't kidding, there's not a mark on it." Sean looking closer, "It's perfect Crystal clear!!" Sean fascinated holds it up to the kitchen light, "It's so clear! I can almost see you Jane!" Sean walks out closer to a light in the dining room "It seems to magnify or even absorb the light rays."

Michael scratches his neck, "You'll get your carpet, Helen I just don't think it's fair to sell the boys out."

Helen snaps back, "The boys! Get real, the boys even forgot they found the darn thing." Michael makes a trip to the freezer, "Let's treat it like an heirloom." Helen looks watching Michael move to the refrigerator, "The kind that attracts spirits." Sean jokes, "Yea, that's cool!, We can charge admission make millions!" Helen opens a loaf of bread, "Then I can go and lay-away or order carpet for the whole house."

Joey and Chris enter the hallway. Chris apologizes, Little Steve pesters Helen for a cold drink from the refrigerator. Michael smirks, "I could watch the late night T.V." Helen rebuts, "Yes that's right! I can stay under all the covers!" Joey and Chris smile "Yea, we can quit school and play basketball!" Helen hands Little Steve a cup, "Little Steve can have all the toys in the world!" Getting back to reality, Helen takes the crystal, "I'll put this back upstairs" Michael takes one final look, shaking the stone, "Maybe it will bring some good luck." Sean wrestling with thoughts about the next long weekend, "Well, Michael don't forget it's your turn to help, next time your free!" Michael opens an ice cream sandwich smiling from the table, "I'm sure something will be crucial by then." Jane preparing Little Shawn notices Sean in the living room, "Sean, you about ready to leave?" Sean frowns looking out, "Yea, soon as you're done fooling around." Jane and Sean open the front door. Michael Walks them out, Watching Sean open the car door, "I'll keep you posted on the plant job." Michael jeers" If I get a chance I'll stop by and put my name in." Sean looks up walking around to his side, "Don't strain yourself!"

With the evening mostly over, Michael gets in the mood for late night channel surfing. Listening He hears a rinsing sound in the kitchen. Straining in the worse of ways, Michael forces himself to go see. Thinking to himself 'Helen uses the upstairs sink.' Reaching the kitchen, Michael makes an interesting discovery. Someone removed Barney from the fish aquarium and put him in the kitchen sink! The little blue fish was swimming around making a splashing sound. Michael carefully scoops the fish up and replaces it in the tank. Shouting out loud, "Helen, you still awake?" No response. Shaking his head, he returns to the television. Thinking to himself and yawning, 'If this stuff doesn't stop, I'm putting the stone in the trash!'

The morning springs forth like any other. Michael gone before 5:00 a.m., Helen wrestling with the mules. Steve not wanting to eat, Chris losing his homework assignment. Joe arguing about a lost sneaker. suddenly the phone rings. Helen looks at her sons, "Let the thing ring." slowly the answering service picks up, "Father Fortune calling, If you get this message before 5:00 p.m. please call our rectory."

Helen looks over to Joey, "Come on!" Helen waits joggling thoughts for a time, then sips down her warm coffee before darting out to start the car. Little Steve concentrating finishes drinking his fruit juice with one hand playing in Oatmeal. Helen grabs a washcloth wiping Little Steve's hand then exits with the trio. Little Steve Makes Preschool followed by the older boys, skip and jump to intermediate. Helen pacing herself to get the finish choirs, speeds back to a home in shambles! Thoughts racing along with emotions, Helen decides someone must have broken in! The kitchen resembles a scene straight out of a horror movie. Helen trembling removes her cell phone from a special pocket case. Jane keeping her mind on Little Sean at grand mom's returns from her morning exercise session. Jane listens to her phone ring still out of breath. Helen in an unusual voice asks, "You didn't notice anything unusual while I dropped the boys off for school?" Jane, removing a knot from a shoelace, looking around her own hallway "No, should I have?" Helen, walking around the rooms holding her cell phone whispers, "Someone's been in our house!" Jane rubs her toe feeling a large red lump, "Are you sure?"

Helen walks over to the back porch patio and stops, "Jane, you still there?" Jane pushes off her last sneaker," yea of course!" Helen whispers, "You got a minute get over here." Helen walks through each room, inspects for signs of an unusual entry. then makes her way to the outer garage. Looking carefully at the alarm system a second time she discovers a flaw. Helen shakes her head In amazement "The alarm things are off." still afraid of an intruder, Helen sneaks her way upstairs. Helen, Startled shouts, 'No!" All the boy's beds are in shambles! The bedroom drawers, the closets, even Little Steve's net of stuffed animals on the ceiling someway got pulled down. Holding her breath, Helen gambles for her safety to the master bedroom. The clothes and belongings everywhere! filled with overwhelming curiosity, Helen bends with her free hand for the loose shoebox under the bed. The box, Christmas cards, cellophane tape, The Tomahawk *now gone*!! Still thinking of an intruder, Helen tries to control her anxiety sneaking around every room in total panic. Pondering her thoughts, She thinks about the alarm system not set. Suspicion takes over!! Helen hearing the door alarm, rushes still in dismay opening to her neighbor. Jane frowns," You alright ?" using mother's Intuition, not waiting for Helen's reply, "It's something about the tomahawk." Helen tears up shaking her head, "Hey, it's gone, they got it." Jane walks around the kitchen curious, "Anything missing?"

Helen reaches for a coffee cup, "No!," then running water, "I better call the police." Jane stubbles with thoughts, "Did you make sure there's no one else still here?" Helen nods, "They left through the back door, Girl, I even checked for termites!"

Within moments, the police arrive,. Officer Startfirst walks straight into The kitchen. Helen smiles repeating the story sitting with Jane. Officer Startfirst darts around the bedrooms then makes his way downstairs to the Kitchen, "You couldn't have had your alarm system on." Helen shakes her head disappointed, "That's what I was thinking, myself our husbands were in and out every ten minutes." Officer Startfirst looks at Jane sitting with a cup, then looks back at Helen "Do you mind if we check the alarm." Then another policemen interrupts, "Where's Michael?" Helen looks up surprised, "You know Michael? The taller policemen smirks "Tell him officer James made a visit." Helen, reaching for Jane's empty coffee cup, walks over to the sink. "Did you go to school or something?" Officer James looks at Officer Startfirst, "No, Michael and I were in Scouts together." Helen roars, "Michael—a Boy Scout?" Officer James holding his composure, "He never told you he was in Scouts?" Helen rubs her tears looking puzzled, "No, I mean we never talked about it." Officer Startfirst responds to a call on the intercom. "We need to go, a police emergency." Jane laughs so hard she chokes, "Helen, you seem so surprised!" Officer Startfirst holds up at the front door, "Mrs. Becker, I checked everything, It seems like no force entry." Helen scratches her chin with a squint, "They just walked right in?" Officer Startfirst waits for his assistant, "Probably through the back. They heard you leave, then walked right in."

Sean in a field office tries phoning Jane on a land line. Busy signal. then tries his cell phone. Still no answer. Jane free after watching

Helen finish The police visit checks her cell phone messages. Aware of Sean's efforts, she phones back. Sean answers listening to Jane, "who else could of known about it?" Jane watches as Helen starts cleaning up the boy's room, "who else knew about it?" Helen grabs the net of stuffed animals, "I really don't think anyone." Sean, sensing the conversation between Helen and Jane, "Somebody knew!" Jane, watching Helen's struggle feels guilty," Sean, "I'll call you back, I want to help her put things back." Helen, upset shouts, "Who the— would make such a mess? Then, regaining her composure, "It has to be someone who knows us Someone who overheard us talking, someone that maybe watched the boys take it to school." Helen stops scratching her neck at Jane, catching her breath, "Did you or Sean mention this to anyone?"

Jane nods, "I told my mother!" Jane looks up, "My mother's stays with us a lot during the week, Sean—I don't think had much of a chance for anything." Helen throws down a checker board box, "I have to pickup Little Steve. "You want to watch the house for about ten minutes?" Jane looks around, "I hope whoever it was don't come back!" Helen jeers, "I don't think so, they got what they really wanted" Once Helen leaves, Jane takes a slow walk through the rooms. First the kitchen, then reluctant, she braves the back porch, Jane eye's widen aware the back door still open. Locking it, she feels a rush of fear, loosing her wits she runs full speed out through the kitchen.

A few moments later, Jane's curiosity returns which musters up her courage. She then starts walking upstairs, thinking of grand mom with Little Sean She looks in the bathroom mirror. Hearing sounds from the front downstairs living room Jane holds still quiet. She then hears a door shut, Jane yells from the bathroom. Helen hollers, "Where you at?"

Jane relaxes taking a deep breath, "I'm upstairs in the bathroom." Helen yells, "How come you didn't use the one down here?" Jane skips down the steps, "I thought I'd take a walk around and hunt for some clues." Helen smiles, washing her hands in the kitchen sink. One of the aquarium fish toys wiggles in the sink screener. Picking it out with a fork, she opens the water tank letting it drop in the water. Helen chuckles, "Jane! You didn't need anything out of Barney's tank?" Jane, looking from the kitchen table, "Wasn't me!" Helen jumps, "You just scared me half to death!" Just then the phone rings, Jane waves at the phone, "let the service take it." The phone recorder "This call is for the Becker's, would someone please return my call when they have a chance? This is Father Fortune from the St. Peter's rectory, Thank you." Jane sits calling grand mom to check on Little Shawn, "Helen, Why didn't you pick it up?" Helen squints "I want to wait to tell Michael about all this first, if I can ever reach him!, Father Fortune's on a different wave length right now, the whole world news will know and our families will still be in the dark." Jane watches, "I'd better check on Mom." Jane puts away her cell phone then gets up from the kitchen table. Helen grabs the portable phone then calls Michael's cell phone, she then surrenders finally leaving a request for Michael to call home with the truck Dispatcher. When the phone rings, Helen pauses taking a deep breath before explaining. Michael shouts upset, "How the heck did this thing happen?"

Helen shakes her head and looks at the fish tank, "Who was in the fish tank!" Michael glances his wristwatch, "No, honey, that was something else!" Helen curious, "Something else?"

Michael watches an expeditor approach, "Late last night something was doing it's haunt thing again. It had the water running in the sink. I got up out of the lazy boy and no one was in the kitchen but the faucet was left running! I Turned the water off, looked momentarily in the sink, well, I saw Barney swimming around all happy. I called for you, but no reply, so I kept it to myself; went back and watched the late night show." Helen frowns prancing in the living room, "Weren't you scared?" Michael laughs, "I was too tired to be scared, I just put the fish back and went quietly in the living room." Helen reenters the kitchen, then looks over to the front door. Jane enters overhearing in total amazement. Jane walks bouncing Little Sean looks up at Helen curious, "What?" Jane laughs then asks again, "What? Looking at the Helen's portable, Jane closes," Mom! I'll call you right back!" Jane grabs at Helen's portable then again asks impatient, "What?" Helen giggles shaking her head then summons Michael, "You want to tell her?" Jane takes the portable, "What?" Helen sits down dumbfounded.

Jane giggles at Helen then busts out laughing, "No! I don't believe it!" Jane, now in total awe, looks over at Barney. Jane smiles, "He looks o.k. to me!" Helen interrupts, "He just about lost his toy basketball a while ago."

Jane clues Michael in, "Helen found the basketball half down the screener." Jane looks serious at Helen, Michael claims, "It was late!" Then remembering Helen shakes her head, "No, It couldn't have been that late! I heard him climb in bed!" Just then the phone receives another beep, Helen closes; "Honey be careful, we'll see you later tonight." Now pushing for the call, Helen Hears Grand pop's voice, aware of the strange voice tones, Grand pop Becker asks "What's wrong? Helen stalls, "Somebody broke in our house, just walked right in and ransacked the place!" Grand pop staying calm asks, "Anything stolen?" Helen trying to maintain her composure, 'Yes sort of, thank goodness nothing serious, but the house is a disaster!" Grand pop, stumble's for words, "It's O.K. if I come over?" Helen looks over at Jane, "Yea, sure!." Jane jumps up, "Helen, I got to go check on mom, I'll be right back." Looking in thought "You want to watch Little Sean for a minute?." Helen smiles wiping the kitchen table, "This ought to be real fun!" It seems the door just shut when the doorbell rang. Opening the door, there stands grand pop!. He scans the living room, "When did all this happen?" He then heads straight upstairs looking in each bedroom walking carefully down the hall. Helen follows holding Little Sean," Somewhere between seven thirty and nine o clock" Grand pop thinking for a moment looks back, "You did call the police?"

Helen looks, "They just left a while ago, why?" Grand pop skips down the stairway, throwing his jacket on the couch, looking at Helen he walks toward the kitchen, "What's Michael say about all this?' Helen pours a fresh coffee, "He was really upset!, You don't know the half of it grand pal, we have spooks who not only like shaving crème but scare our family, take fish out of aquariums and put them in the sink, then on top of it, try to flush Barney down the sink by leaving the water running !" Grand pop smiles making a quick walking tour through the garage entrance. Helen, wrestling Little Sean stops talking when the door chimes start. Walking with Little Sean in her arms she peeks out the front curtain. Jane smiles closing the door aware the police sit across the street, "Did you see all that?' Helen hands the baby back then walks to the banister. "Grand pop!"

she looks back to Jane with big eyes, then shouts, "Grand pop!" Grand pop in a low voice, "Did you know we got cops all over the place?" Helen watches grand pop, "You scared me! I thought maybe something happened!" Grand pop walks back in from the kitchen then looks through the curtains at several more parked police cars. Helen watches, listening to Jane, "I wonder what it's about?" Helen looks for the card officer James gave her lifts out her the cell phone Just then she feels the cell phone shake and start to ring. Helen looks across at Jane with a weird smirk," Hello, Michael, yea, it's been really wild that Priest, Father Fortune keeps calling. I just don't feel up to talking."

Michael interrupts, "I got one more delivery, then I'm free for awhile, I'll call him from here! Yea, It's an easy number, I remember it from when I was a Kid." Helen stares at grand pop Becker leaning against the kitchen counter, "That's another thing!" Michael looks at his paycheck stub, "What that?" Helen smiles at Jane, "Do you know officer James? Were you ever in Scouts?" Michael, laughs, "yes. I'll think about it more later when I get down the road, there's another trucks trying to get loaded, I'm sort of holding up the parade. I'll call Father Fortune back, I better get off!" Helen looks at Jane, "What do you think I should tell the boys?" Grand pop interrupts, "Tell them the truth for goodness sake!" Helen looks around the kitchen, "Do you think that's a good idea?" Jane, sneaks back to the living room window, "yea, the cops left." Grand pop looks rocking Little Sean. Helen and Jane start walking the upstairs floors dividing the workload. Every few minutes, Jane's grabs at her cell phone. First, Sean, then Jane's grand mom, then Sean again. Finally with a large room in order, Helen and Jane race downstairs for the refrigerator. Drinking a bottle of cranberry juice, Helen looks watching the clock, "I best go get Little Steve, Grand pop, "You going to hold the fort down!" Grand pop looks up, "I'll try!, you know I have to leave pretty soon" Helen and Jane gather things up wave to grand pop before Jetting out the house. The front door closes, things return almost to quiet. the birds, cars, even a far off chain saw, Sounds to be coming from the front room. Grand pop, sitting in front of the T.V. notices the police running about. Waiting patiently, Grandpop looks at his newspaper. Thinking about Helen, he walks back through The main hallway. Retracing his theory, grand pop walks back in the living room. He hears the portable phone ring from the kitchen, listening he recognizes the voice, grand pop reaches picking up the phone," Michael?, "Grand pop glances the kitchen. Michael laughs, "No wonder I couldn't call you! Where's Helen?"

Grandpop rolled his eyes, "She went to pick up Steve."

Just then the boys start filing in from school. Joey, runs for the Refrigerator walking straight past grandpop.

Christopher shouts, "Grand pop!, How are you?"

Joey looks back puzzled and totally shocked, "Yea! Grandpop!"

Michael still listening, "Tell Helen to give me a call as soon as she gets back!" Grand pop, who by now watches the boys curious, "Anything wrong?"

Michael looks about the warehouse boxes, "Oh, you won't believe it! I called Father Fortune—seems he knows the inside scoop on things."

Helen opens the front door returning with Little Steve then gives a puzzled look. "Grand pop, who's that?"

Grand pop, waits cupping his hands while still listening, "Your husband!"

Helen drops her pocketbook reaching for the phone, "Yes, what's up?"

Michael jumps back in his truck, "It's a real long story. I'll wait till I get home. I just thought I'd tell you I talked to Father Fortune."

Helen said, "Come on, Michael,—Michael?" The phone now dead, Helen returns to her busy kitchen.

Helen shuffles into the living room staring, "Grand pop, do you think it's anything important?"

Grand pop stumbles for words, "It's probably something about what Father Fortune found out."

Joey ran down the steps, "Mom! Somebody's been in our rooms!'

Helen thinks about grand pops suggestion, "Get your brother, I've got something important to tell you two."

Christopher, runs down the steps walking past the bay windows slows noticing the police car parked in their driveway, "Mom! What's all the police about?" Helen thinks looking at Christopher then walks in the front room looking a second time, "I thought they left."

Helen, struggling for words, "This morning, when I took little Steve to preschool and you boys to school, someone ransacked our home." I called the police, they came right away. Helen takes a deep breath," Boys, who ever they were they took the Indian thing!"

Christopher becomes emotional letting way to tears.

Joey, not all that interested, reaches for the refrigerator handle.

Helen looks at Joey then back at Christopher, "Maybe it's a good thing it's gone!"

Helen looks across at grand pop preparing to leave, "Grand pop?" Grand pop wrestles with his jacket, "Boys, I'm taking you to see the baseball game." Christopher laughs wiping his face, "I want to go to the other place!." Grand pop thinks for a minute, "Would you rather do that?"

Joey and Chris grab at grand pop yelling in unison.

Grand pop," More than a baseball game?" Grand pop, looks at Helen smiling, "I better go check on getting the Tickets." Grand pop laughs waving at Helen before closing the door.

Helen working towards preparing dinner, clears out the freezer and glances back at the boys. Closing the freezer, Helen wanting to tell about Barney, she looses her train of thought thinks about something else.

The evening slips by. Little Steve plays with his toys. While dinner gets prepared, Joey looks across at Michael, "I'll watch for the spirits tonight."

Helen picks up Little Steve and brings him to the table, "I don't think we're going to have any problems."

The doorbell chimes ring just on the edge of her remark.

Helen shouts to Christopher, then walks back and answering the door. It was Officer James and some other policemen. Opening, she asks, "What's wrong?"

Officer James looks toward his partner, "Mrs. Becker, this is Officer George."

Helen face lights up in a warm smile, "Yes, sure come on in."

Sitting at the dining room Officer James drops down his notebook, he then looks up, "We've been around here all day, we just want to do a follow up."

Helen sits slowly moving a embroidered napkin to her side.

Officer George stares not blinking, "Did your husband or children know about the significance" Helen scratches her head irritated an uncomfortable then looks back feeling an emotional serge build then looks away with tears. Officer George notices Helen's body language then frowns focusing his eyes back at his notebook, "I'll come over some night when it's more convenient with you and your husband and when I have more time." Looking over to Officer James for support, Officer George smiles, "look, I know a little bit about it, it's a long story."

Helen not liking Officer George, "What—does it belong to the pentagon or something?"

Officer James interrupts, "Did the boys see anything?"

Helen shakes her head lifting herself from the table, "You mean back when it happened?"

Officer James looks back at Officer George, then back, "Anytime, especially around the time of the break in."

Helen assured walks looking out the kitchen sink window, then nods, "No, they were in school. I had left to take Little Steve to preschool."

Officer James glances across watching Officer George, helping himself to another coffee, "Yo! That's three to one! Give me a chance to catch up!" looking at his watch, Officer James smiles "Helen, mame, we must be going." Officer James lifts up from the table, "My partner doesn't know when he's overstayed his welcome!" Officer George smirks pushing the chair in, "But the coffee is *so* good!"

Walking back to the bedroom late that evening Michael pauses in the hall, then quickly slips down the stairs to check the refrigerator. Looking with a quick smile, Barney looks out swimming happily. Things tonight seem calm. Michael drinks down a glass of cold milk before returning to bed. Helens body lay fast asleep. Little Steve again on her side of the bed. Michael gently squirms reaching for blankets until he finds his comfort zone. Seems he just makes it to sleep when the alarm starts beeping. Another morning begins. Michael leaves the premises being the first one out of bed, keeping a special care of quiet he leaves the kitchen light burn. Helen, wearing a flowered wardrobe yawns preparing her usual coffee, Wrestling the cereal box she opens her breakfast flakes. Thinking about Michael having left, she reaches adjusting the refrigerator mix ups. Michael normally drinks the iced tea switching it in front of the milk. The phone starts to ring and Helen giggles reaching for the portable on the far counter. It was grandpop. Helen preparing Little Steve's breakfast sits him down at the table then starts toward the front room then upstairs.

Grand pop in a loud voice, "Tell the boys I got the tickets!"

Helen enters the upstairs hallway excited, "Yeah! Boys! Grandpop tot the tickets!!"

Grand pop listens, "Tell them I want to see some really good grades."

Christopher smiles listening to Helen repeat of grand pop's request. Christopher shouts, "I can see the "A's" now!!"

The phone again interrupts beeping. Grand pop listens then says good- bye.

Helen reaches for the door holding the portable. Jane and Little Sean make their way in to the living room.

Jane, out of breath, squints," Helen, Sean thinks he heard voices."

Helen, wasted in sub thoughts looks up, "Over at your house?"

Jane nods sitting down. Sean kept looking out the backdoor. Jane opens up her baby bag, "It sounded like a whole big crowd of noisy people."

Helen, prying, "Yea, go on."

Jane yawns, "Every time he'd go look—NOTHING!" Jane looks up, "I think I even heard some of it."

Helen jumps up from the table, "Why didn't you call or something?"

Jane holds a milk bottle to Little Sean's mouth, "Sean didn't start hearing anything till about 2:00 a.m. sure didn't want to start calling that late."

Helen pouring a cup of coffee, sets down the coffee pot, "Michael stayed up pretty late, I don't know if he heard anything or not."

Jane, holding the baby milk, "I think after all these things he would have said something."

Helen takes Little Steve from the chair, "Watch the house, I'll be right back."

Jane waits listening to the car leave, before making her own walk toward the back door. Looking around slow, she notices everything normal. Keeping alert, she walks back in then jumps when the phone beeps. "Honey, it's me, I'm on my first break, delivering a load of topsoil. What's going on? Call me."

Jane not interrupting returns to the living room stairs.

Helen walks in the front door, startling Jane. Helen hears the answering machine beeper. She frowns curious closing the inside door and then walks for the answering machine then looks back at

Jane. Helen looks around the kitchen Throwing down her pocketbook, "Who was it?"

Jane thinks preoccupied, "Your hubby!"

Helen drops down her keys, pushing the return call button.

Michael, reading a newspaper deep in thought waits patient looking up when his cell phone beeps. Smiling at a dispatcher he walks outside away from all the clamor. "Helen, What's up?"

Helen looks around the kitchen, "Everything's fine here. Jane and Sean think they heard voices out back so loud it kept them awake!"

Helen looks around at Jane walking through the living room, "Yea, their other neighbors, the Wagner's. Think they might of heard something" No, the same thing. They said it was really late sometime around 2:00 a.m. What about you, Do you remember hearing anything?' Helen walks back out in the kitchen still commanding the attention of Jane sitting quiet in a sprawled out position against the table.

Helen laughs at Jane thinking of her tired appearance than concentrates on some dirty dishes, balancing the phone on her shoulder she reaches, rinsing out a glass in the soapy sink, "Honey what's on the agenda for this weekend?" Helen keeps still not making noise, then adds "Well, Grandpop called happy about getting the tickets, Father Fortune called again and last but not least the upstairs sink needs unclogged. if you wait all day on it, it works O.K, otherwise, I use the down stairs sink."

Michael looks around at the dispatch office then thinking out loud, changes the subject. Michael opens the door bumping another trucker's coffee walking towards the parking lot." Helen you remember me mentioning something about the Indian?" Not waiting for her answer, Michael continues "Now that I think about it, I had the dream about one a few nights earlier, the one in the bedroom chair. Michael watches as a large box truck enters next to where He's standing "Yea, tell Father Fortune we can't wait! If he wants, tell him late Saturday afternoon."

Days pass. Saturday afternoon arrives with everyone waiting on Father Fortune, the door bell chimes loud noise mark a visitors arrival. Michael, looks up at Helen then pushes himself up from the kitchen table making his way through the living entrance to the door. Father Fortune laughs, handing Michael his black hat, "I smell something cooking." Michael looks out towards the kitchen, "Yea Father, must be the chicken dumplings!" Michael laughs taking Father Fortune's hat.

Father Fortune shouts out toward the kitchen, Hello!! Helen looks in waving with a half smile, opening a loaf of bread. Father Fortune starts in "Michael, we have a lot to discuss, How are things with the Becker's?"

Helen placing a table mat answers overtop Michael," Oh, just fine Father."

Michael listening still holding Father Fortune's hat, "How are things at St. Peter's?" Father Fortune nods excusing himself for the bathroom. Moments later he notices everyone seated. Father Fortune enters reciting a dinner prayer before sitting at the dinner table. Helen starts with the hard questions.

Father Fortune waits passing the potato salad, "When the settlers first arrived in what became our nation's capitol, that is, Philadelphia, (then taking a drink of iced tea) "the Native American population was—How should I say—up there pretty good!" Looking over at Joe and Chris, Father Fortune Holds up a cup for Little Steve, "Somehow some Indian brave found a rare mineral." Michael holds up his hand swallowing a large dumpling, "The mineral must have been very lucrative."

Father Fortune shakes his head not loosing his thoughts, "Once the Indian brave created a hunting weapon, he achieved some strange unusual success hunting game." Buttering his bread, Father Fortune looks over towards Helen, "The other warriors became very stand-offish, slowly worsening. Things started taking on greater and greater dynamic proportion." Father Fortune looks back at Michael, "After a while, the tribe started rumors claiming the Tomahawk possessed some kind of spiritual powers or enlightenment."

Michael yawns looking over at Helen then back at Father Fortune. "Enlightenment?"

Father Fortune slows down thinking, "It created a lot of trouble or muddy water, that's for sure. Both sides Settlers and Indians on a continuing basis became less trustful of each other. Slowly more and more hate and hostilities developed."

Father Fortune, holding Little Steve up in the air passes him to Michael. "Years later several tribes or groups came upon its whereabouts. Then it was put to rest with the original warriors, in an unmarked grave! The settlers or early inhabitants, searched forever, even a bounty was offered but never again was anyone able to find it."

Michael gets up from the table handing down a coffee cup from the cabinet then offers one to Father Fortune. Michael sits back down curious then looks over, "What's the big deal?" Father Fortune shrugs his shoulders, "It's said to possess a certain quality that causes people to grow obsessed over it."

Helen feels the urge to laugh, "Something like Gold fever?"

Father Fortune remains serious, "All I know, it's dangerous!" Reaching for the fresh coffee Helen just poured, "People start killing one another, seems they grow paranoid and all kinds of unfounded fear sets in." Father Fortune drinks down the coffee, blesses the house before preparing to leave.

Helen interrupts telling the story about the intrusion and the theft.

Father Fortune looks around amused at Little Steve, "It's probably a good thing, especially around kids." "Well, I need to get going, I promised I'd check in on someone on my way back to the parish." After Father Fortune closes the door, Michael and Helen sit discussing the bathroom sink. Helen asks, "How much do you think it would cost to fix that sink?" Michael drums his fingers on the table, "Oh!, About $45.00 per hour,"

Helen throws down the empty coffee cup, "How much?"

Sean passing Father Fortune laughs entering the living room then watches as Father Fortune opens his car door. "How did we end up on this topic?" Jane and Little Sean walk towards the kitchen.

Little Steve, wanting to be held, wrestles back down on the floor in front of Michael. Helen forces Little Steve up on her lap. Michael looks at Sean shaking his head, "I got to go check the sink upstairs, you know anything about plumbing?" Sean frowns," More than I want to admit, What did the priest say?"

Rich Jacks walks casually in his driveway and pulls open the back door. The kids off in school, the wife having left moments earlier. A perfect time to assess the spoils of thievery. Using the bedroom desk as a view pad, Rich uncovers the neckerchief wrap. Impressed with the appearance, he phones his close friend and confident. "Hello, yea, I'm back. No problem, soon as she went out the front. That's right." Rich continues staring, "It does have a weird way about it."

You can tell why the legend came about. This thing was worth the risk! I don't care if they called the cops or not. I do know one thing, This thing, IT'S PERFECT! When do you want to come over? No, Jackie doesn't need to know a thing." Then picking it up towards the desk lamp, thinking quiet, "I want small bills. You comin over later today or what?" Rich looks up rubbing his hair back in the wall mirror, "If they ask you how you found it, tell them you found It when you were walking."

Moments later the door bell starts beeping. Rich peeks through the curtains and opens the door keeping the chain across. One old gentleman Shouts, Come on! Then steps in the door sideways half out of breath. Looking at the stone, the old man frowns, "You know I don't want to be seen around here!"

Rich looks up humbled and impatient, "Pay old man, you can be on your way!' Walking in the kitchen, Rich throws his hands up, "Be quiet!" Rewrapping the stone, Rich listens for noise. the old man looks closer and whispers, "How soon is your family comin back?"

Rich irritated by the old man's lack of respect, "You just pay the money and be on your way!" The old man, half afraid, shaking wraps the stone, placed it in a large belt pocket, and opens his envelope of money, "Count it quick, small bills take forever!"

Rich, pausing in the count, stops again hearing a strange sound. Thinking for a moment, he looks to the old man, "I trust you, get out of here!"

The old man smirks, "I'll call you in a couple of weeks, I have another errand you can make." Then the old man leaves, laughing heartily.

The old man runs and jumps in the passenger side of a white van. A well built man, now speeds off. Looking over at his passenger, the driver asks, "What the hell took so long?"

The old man stammers, lighting a cigarette, "He don't trust anybody."

The driver looks out his rear mirror, "I don't understand why you use that weird guy anyway!"

The old man looks momentarily at the driver, taking a deep drag, "I see a lot of my own qualities in him, above all he delivers!"

Pulling into the driveway, the driver slams on the brakes. The old man unravels the stone with a pair of shaking hands from the pocket belt then from old neckerchief. The driver looks over then watches as a mailman delivers mail. He hands the old man five large $100. bills. The old man looks over stunned, "I thought I told you $400.

The driver frowns, "$100. to forget you know me."

The old man smiles still shaking with a nervous quiver, "You're well forgotten!"

The driver pulls out carefully around the mail truck at the mailbox then heads straight through town, veering off carefully at a fuel station. Remembering the neckerchief, he puts it in the glove box; locking it with his big thumb. He closes the van stretching his body heading for the cashier's window. Thinking about a girlfriend he walks zigzag over using a pay phone. Waiting for the phone to pick up, he looks out towards the van impatient and hang's up.

The driver starts up after refueling then drives several miles before leaving the bustling Community. The weather now changing. The driver closes His windows and turns on his wipers. There was a triple lane highway to cross, then a sharp turnoff. Reaching the night club, the driver parks out front. Making sure the coast was clear, he runs for the entrance way with the neckerchief in hand. Still raining out, the driver slows opening the heavy door Walking in out of breath, he approaches a bar cashier.

The cashier looks up with an inviting smile, "That will be $8.00. The cashier waits patiently, while a crowd starts forming.

The driver, realizing he left his wallet, In the van smiles checking all his side pockets, "Honey, this is business! I'm here to see John."

The cashier looks around irritated then phones, it seems to take forever with the line getting long. People upset behind the driver start to complain and Start becoming furious. Within moments, people started yelling, "We're getting wet! Come on!"

The cashier yells, "Be quiet! You'll never get in if I can't hear."

Moments later, the clearance is given, and the driver shouts, "Yeah!"

Strutting into the door, the driver turns around and facing a large crowd then gives them a dirty look! The crowded laughs shouting back rude gestures and is left suspended as the door springs closed. Continuing his strut through a front vestibule, the driver walks through to another inside office. A tall bouncer, stands at his side, the two wait patiently. John watching on a monitor screen shouts from the inside door, then opens extending his hand to shake. The driver overwhelmed returns the hand shake. Johns looks at the bouncer than back at the large driver, then bursting out in laughter, "You got my hammer?"

The driver looks over at the bouncer then walks in the office. The bouncer Forces his way between the driver and John looking out the venition blind. John Looks up, "Yo!, you can go, your slates clean. Try to stay out of trouble!"

The driver stands still thinking, then overwhelmed by joy looks over at the bouncer then leaves immediately.

John returned to his chair and remarked to the bouncer, "Do you know what this thing's worth to me? This thing is worth—Fort Knox!" Looking at a showgirl walking past the inside window, he remarked, "If I would have found this years ago, I could have had my way with everyone of them back to the model T's The bouncer laughed as John picked up the phone. John said, "Paul, it's here, yea, I can't believe the workmanship. Those tribes must of really known their shit." Then added, "There ain't a scratch on it! It's like it was forged!"

After John hung up the phone, the bands started tuning their instruments. The bouncer walked towards the cashier's station. John left by himself, continuously wraps and unwraps the handkerchief. Deep in thought, the phone rang. John smiles, "You're coming? Good! Hey Paul, I appreciate you calling me right back I'll pay yah for your time, I just want to know more about it."

The club now packed and the music loud, Paul arrives. John having a very active youth, hot spot. Paul carefully weaves through the crowds, the old retired history teacher slips on a step then finds John's outer office door.

The bouncer quipped, "You Paul? John's growing impatient waiting for you!" Paul squints, "You guys do something nice for an old patron a favor of sorts. Get my $8.00 back!"

The bouncer looked down walking in the lead down towards the main office, "You been here a hundred times, you never wanted your money back." Then the bouncer turns around rushing back up front to see the cashier.

Paul made his way through the busy offices finally reaches John's door. walking in, without a knock and catching John by surprise. A show girl, leans on the corner of the desk, walking swiftly out of the room.

John, at a loss for words yelled, "Yo! Next time knock!"

Within moments the two men settle down. John laughs unwrapping the find. Paul, holds the relic up to the light and pulls out a magnifying glass. Looking carefully at the object through the glass, he said, "You can see forever through this thing but not out the—. Suddenly Paul realized the office curtain's string on fire!

John laughs watching Skip and Paul struggle with the smoking window.

John, coughs thinks about Paul using the red neckerchief to block his face. John waits noticing Skip, hand Paul the $8.00 cover charge. John frowns curious keeping quiet then shouts, "I guess I found one thing I can use it for."

Paul, afraid to laugh, waits for clearance before sitting down on the couch. John walks around the desk grabbing Paul by the shoulder, "You want a drink or something to eat?"

Paul sits reviewing the stone on the leather arm, "O.K. How bout a cold beer?" John looks calling on the intercom, "One cold beer, one chicken meal; looking twice back at Paul, "Come on! Something else?"

Paul looks up shirking his shoulders in a blank stare.

Once things came back to the stone, Paul started telling his story. "It might be cursed!"

John looked puzzled and said, "Cursed?"

Paul nods, "According to a story, the Indians went crazy, the settlers started killing each other then it couldn't be found."

John looking curiously at Paul remains quiet. Paul looks irritated, "John, I never thought I would ever lay eyes on this thing, especially if this is really it.". Paul reaches at a cigarette offered by John," My grand pop told me about it, most of it just a legend." Looking out the window John holds up his hand, waving for silence, "Excuse me a minute." Leaving quickly, he called his bouncer. Seems two patrons were battling in front of the club. John exits leaving Paul eating and examining the stone. Paul finishes chewing looking around the office. Still no signs of John, or Skip. Paul reaches back at the neckerchief grasping at the stone.

John and Skip arrive later and look at Paul sitting quiet, "Two guys were out front fighting over something. Oh yea, this thing should be called the Missing treasure or "The Hope!"

Paul tired and sensitive looks up, "Maybe it *was* to the Indians!"

John, not appreciating Paul's input reaches for a cigarette, "I want more knowledge!" Paul looks away shaking his head, "I don't think anyone ever has it long enough to find out!"

John, looks over infuriated and increasing upset, "Look, Paul do me a favor, do some research! You can check all the websites or whatever! Paul, I'll even pay you, name the price!"

Paul jokingly said, "You can save me a cold draft!"

Leaving quickly, John looked to the bouncer, "What do you think of this guy?—Cursed?"

Skip, John's favorite bouncer, usually bought take-out dinner on his way to the club.

The following evening, John anxiously awaited his dinner. One hour later, no Skip. John called Skip's family and was informed of the bad news. Some time between 4:00 and 5:00 p.m., Skip showered and laid down for a quick nap. Seems Skip never regained from his rest.

John feeling strong remorse, continuously phones back to Skip's house. Skip's mother and ex-wife arrived late after spending time at a local store.

John hears Skip's ex wife Krista answer then asks, "Had he been drinking?"

Krista drowning in memories of the early years with Skip drifts Back to the present. she screams hysterically, "No!" Then quickly hangs up the phone.

John feeling a pain in his stomach, more aware he hadn't eaten. reaches in his office safe again pulling careful on the wrapped stone. In a reverence fit for kings, John slowly removes the red neckerchief. He glances up with a big smile at a new showgirl who just walked in. Thinking about an office meeting he had just a few hours ago John looks across, "Cursed! Then he takes a look holding it up peering through the crystal with the show girl standing with a blank stare, "I sure hope not!" The showgirl shot wired up from the band noise looks at the stone all the time not making a comment. Then she starts singing, "Maybe it's true."

John looks up annoyed in a sarcastic smile and said, "Yeah, right!"

The following morning, John decided to pay a social visit to the mother. But it seems Skip's mother refused to talk so John walked up with a bouquet of flowers and left them at the door only to hear the mother shout, "Drunk!" John, chocked with tears, "I'm under a lot of stress right now, I wasn't thinking."

Seeing the sorrow, in Skip's mother John pauses, "Look, I know he was heavily insured, send the funeral bill anyway. We'll get him an extra large stone."

The Skip's mother looks out with a smile through the front screen door with tears, "He loved working over at your place, you want to say something at the service?"

John looks in, Skip was my best ever, "Sure, I'd be honored!" Then he noticed the ex-wife pulling in. "I'll call you later." Lighting a cigarette, he walks minding his own business back down the lawn, jumping back in the car without talking he quickly speeds off."

After making it back to the club, John flops behind his desk reviewing his office messages. He quickly pushes review for each message. Call #2: "Hello, this is Paul, hope you got some cold beer." Just then John's favorite showgirl enters the room. Looking up at her he said, "That's all that guy thinks about, something to drink."

Just before the band started its first tune, John walked up to the band and grabbed the microphone commanding the floor. He began, "We lost one of our own; he was a wonderful, talented person. We usually have half off for ladies night, but tonight drinks are free. Make sure you sign the big card going round. Do old John a favor (he hesitated then he said), "make the funeral, he was a truly swell guy!" The audience clapped on.

Arriving at the office, John reached for the telephone. "Paul! That you? Yea, got your message, this better be good!"

Then Paul added, "Well, it is! When's a good time to come over?"

John replied, "How about sometime next week?"

Paul quipped, "Next week?"

John said, "Remember my bouncer? He just died in his sleep! I'm really out of sorts, emotionally burned out, tight on cash. How about around the middle of the week, you pick the time."

Paul picks up an old picture off his chest of drawers in his bedroom staring blank, "Wednesday sound alright around 1:00?"

John hears a noise watching a new showgirl pass then glances back to his computer, clicking with his mouse he accesses his calendar then reaches back to the phone, "Yeah, that will be fine!" Then scanning the office in thought, "We'll keep the Sam cold!"

The night went well, John contacted a security firm and placed an advertisement for a bouncer. A Liquor Control Board. visit showed no underage drinkers. John looked at his safe, felt the urge coming on. Slowly he spins the dial. Helping hold down the fort, John's brother Jim filled in for Skip's time slot. Walking in the office, John jumps back startled. "What do I need, Then breathes angry, What wrong, come on what do I need an etiquette reference guide?" Then, closing the safe John repeats, "Jim, what's wrong?"

Jim starts laughing, "What's that thing? John unfolds the neckerchief. Jim, stares motionless, "I know things get tough, but I usually don't need a tomahawk!"

John, frowns "Oh, you'd be surprised, never know about night clubs around here."

Jim still holding a cash drawer, "Where'd you come across that thing?"

John wraps the neckerchief, "Some guy used to work here got in trouble with a payroll officer and went to jail. I bailed him out and paid the fine. This was his retuned favor."

John's deeper thoughts resurface while logging off the computer. Jim holds the tomahawk. John looks back, "The funeral's tomorrow, I hate them things. The family's nice, the ex-wife; she's sort of tough"

Jim giggles not moving the neckerchief, "Being married to a bouncer, come on!" John watches as Jim talks not interested in the stone. Then adds

"I have a guy coming over the middle of next week," he used to be a History teacher."

Jim hands back the stone still wrapped, "You don't mean Paul?"

John grabs the neckerchief reaching for a cigarette, "You know him?"

Jim smiles watching a showgirl enter, "Yea, I had him in school." then looks back at John," Yea, Mr. Hayride."

John shakes his head, "I don't why I forget his name." Jim thinks quiet then repeats, "Hayride??"

Jim watches a showgirl excuse herself interrupting about a personal matter. Jim waits, "He's good!"

John waves the girl off nodding then furthers with, "Yea, anyway, he's been doing some research for me on this thing. It's suppose to go back in history or something."

Jim asked, "I'll see if I can get free, sounds pretty interesting."

John laughed, "Good! You can buy the Sam Adams. Your Mr. Hayride likes that over anything."

Leaving early, John gave Jim the closing procedures. "Whatever you do, try to keep it quiet. The police don't bother here much, and I want to keep it that way!"

Jim asked, "Do the bartenders count the drawers?"

John looked back and walked outside, "Yea, but we have one of the girls count them in the morning."

The night started out with a comedian show, then a magician named Ron, and last but not least, the band.

Jim, trying to relax, walked through the club several times. The show girls did their dance routine while the bartenders kept the fluids rolling. Jim first heard a buzzer and realized it was the office telephone. The bartender, standing over by the restrooms, signaled for Jim.

Reaching across the bar, Jim acted upset. Handing the phone to the bartender, Jim jogs for the office phone. Panting and out of breath, he pushed the door closed with his foot.

Jim quipped, "We're busy! Very busy! What's up?"

John, on the other end said, "Dam cops are here! I don't know, seems they're looking for something."

Jim said, "I guess today they don't even need probable cause or a search warrant."

John quipped to the police, "When you're done, I'm taking a video. I'm hiring an interior designer and I'll see who pays for it!"

John talking to Jim, "I never thought they would ever come here!" Then John looked at the Police Chief, "What—I didn't vote last election or some thing?"

Within moments, the police approached John. Waiting patiently, the police stopped their search.

John looked puzzled, "What you going to do, read me my rights?"

The officers smiled. John ending the call, "Jim! Tell Sam these guys are taking me in, I need a lawyer." The phone clunked down on John's end. Jim, puzzled by now, paced the office club floor.

Sam, a senior employee and part business opportunist, knocked at the office door. Jim still in a frenzy shouted, "Come in! Ooh, Sam! John called and wants you to call a lawyer."

Sam laughed, "A lawyer! What—he smack Joan?"

Jim added, "No, they ransacked the house, read him his rights."

Sam was seriously puzzled, "Give me the phone!"

Jim cleared the desk and walked to the door, "I'd better make sure things are all right."

Sam looked up, "Sure!'

Jim walked back out among the crowds. He could feel them getting louder and louder. One man was arguing with his wife, another a girlfriend. Two women were pulling at each other on the other side of the games. One complained about the chicken being burnt, another about the beer being flat. Jim watched his clock like a hawk. He returned to the office.

Sam, managing the office, called a part time bartender.

Jim, looked very tired and said, "How'd you make out?"

Sam looked irritated, "Everybody's booked but I knew this old dude when I was a kid, and he stinks as a lawyer!"

Jim said, "Let me call home."

Moments later the phone rang. Jim's mother answered. "Mom? It's Jim. I got a call, John's in jail. He needs a lawyer. I don't know who to call! Sam tried everybody!" Then he said, "He's right here, hold on."

Jim, looking at Sam, "She wants you!" Walking toward the door, Jim "I'm going to finish closing."

John returned 48 hours later finding things in shambles. His desk was filled with messages. John read a note from Sam. "Tell John if he wants to sell it, I got a good bidder." John, realizing the extent of his legal fee's dialed the number. He asked, "Paul, that you? Paul, I hate the idea of selling, Dam!"

Hesitantly Jim said, "Tell whoever, I'll consider."

The week passed quickly, soon it was Wednesday afternoon. What a tragic week! A lost employee, and charges that need a criminal lawyer. John paced the floor wondering what amount would cover his bail and a good lawyer. Finally Paul arrived with a guest. Offering to pay, the cashier waved him on. Paul knocked on the door, John shouted, "Wait a minute."

Moments later the door opened. John walked out smiling from ear to ear and said, "Let's talk over here."

Sam, the bartender, poured the group a drink. The guest introduced himself as Gerald.

Paul continued to talk.

John cut in with, "Excuse me, Paul." Looking over at a part time worker, he asked them to clear his office for him. John walked back across the bar to reacquaint himself with the invited guests. Now back at the he found them discussing the deal with Paul and Gerald.

Paul said, "Don't you want to hear the research?"

Gerald, totally startled, "I have to make sure it's the real deal."

John laughed, "Come on! I'll show you."

Paul, without words, walked behind Gerald and John. Once in the office, John yelled out, "Sam! Sam! Take my calls!" Opening the safe, John grabbed the neckerchief. As he opened it on the table, Gerald's eyes got big, "My God! It does exist!"

Paul, knowing the whole story, removed himself from the room.

John, realizing he upset the friend shouted, "Paul, Paul! I'll be right with you."

Gerald looked John straight in the eyes and said, "How on earth did you find it?"

John, growing very impatient quipped, "I'm waiting!'

Gerald, paused, then said, "I'm ready. How about $20,000?"

John looked straight at him, "You're a straight shooter, SOLD!"

Gerald handed over the entire envelope. John counted the thousands. It took only moments. Looking up, "You didn't rob anybody, did you?"

Gerald retorted, "No, it's all savings."

Excusing Gerald out the door, John looked for Paul. Yelling out to Gerald, "Did Paul ride with you?"

Gerald, at the bar yelled, "I'm over here!"

John walked quickly by and said, "Here, take this!"

Paul, hesitant at first, questioned Johns motives.

John said, "I needed the money, yesterday!" I got in some trouble. I needed the money fast!"

John looked at Sam, then glanced back at Paul and asked, "Will $500. cover it?"

Paul, now over his anger, said, "I got to go, that's plenty."

John quipped, "Stop in! I got plenty of free Sam Adams!"

Leaving in a hurry, Paul caught up with Gerald in the parking lot. Gerald said, "I really didn't want to spend that much, but it's perfect!"

Paul laughed, "Hope you have better luck than John did!"

Gerald stopped at the mail box when he reached Paul's driveway. Paul, with shaking hands, ran for the front door. Gerald euphoric, turned up the radio. Moments later, Gerald arrived at his parent's farm. Walking slowly up to his dad, Gerald opened the neckerchief. Gerald's dad looked with respect. Looking back at Gerald his dad said, "What on earth are you going to do with it?"

Gerald laughed "Hopefully become very rich!" Inside the house, Gerald headed straight for the bedroom. His kid sister begged to see it. Gerald said, "It's sort of cursed!"

Pam looked weird and asked, "What's that mean?"

Gerald added, "Hopefully we won't own it long enough to find out!"

Pam, still curious, "Is it real?"

Gerald replied, "Oh, it's real all right!"

Closing the door to the bedroom, Gerald takes it out of the wrap. Moments later, Gerald received a phone call.

Pam, outside the room said, "Gerald, it's your girlfriend."

Gerald, at a loss for words, quickly took the phone. Moments later, "You what?!"

Pam, looking upset, walked up the hall.

Then Gerald said, "I'll be right over!"

Walking past Pam, Gerald spun around and went back to the bedroom. Once there, he placed the tomahawk in a closet safe. Spinning the knob, he dashed for the living room.

Pam, still curious asked, "Did she say she's O.K.?"

Gerald looking upset said, "She said somebody hit her new car!"

Pam burst in emotion, "If you want. I'll come along?" Gerald's dad entered the house and said, "That was quick!"

Gerald rushed to the car and yelled to his dad, "Somebody messed up Joyce's car." Pam jumped in the passenger side and put on her seat belt.

Gerald said, "Did she tell you where the car was?"

Pam replied, "No! I handed the phone straight to you!"

Gerald called her back on the cell phone, "Honey, how bad was it?"

Joyce said, "I'm bruised up, the driver didn't even look!"

Gerald, now along the highway asked, "Where are you now?"

Joyce replied, "I'm right down the street at the towing station."

Gerald, in a sigh of relief said, "Least you're O.K.!" Driving into Fred's towing, the car was sitting off to the side of the garage. Gerald ran up to Joyce and give her a big hug.

Pam looked at the car and shook her head in sadness, "It's totally destroyed!"

As they were taking out the personal effects, the owner walked up. Fred quipped, "Watch it, I'm not suppose to let anyone around the car till the adjuster comes in an hour, new rule!"

Gerald retorted, "Does that include personal effects?"

Fred looked the other way.

Joyce screamed, "Come on, honey, we'll get the junk later!"

Gerald reached in the back seat for a favorite C.D.

Joyce angrily said, "God! You ever think I might want to get out of here?"

Gerald glanced over as he was pulling Joyce out.

Joyce said, "I've been standing there for almost four hours! Where have you been all that time?"

Gerald said, "I went to a business to buy an Indian relic."

Joyce, looking weird said, "Are you crazy!!"

Gerald glanced at Pam then to Joyce, "I all but got a buyer for it. Indian relics go for big bucks!"

Pam and Joyce looked at each other. Joyce was stunned, then looking back at Gerald she asked, "How much?"

Gerald, smirking, "A lot of paper."

Joyce, still needling, "How much?"

Gerald laughed, "Two dollars."

Joyce looked at Pam then glanced at Gerald, "How much???"

Gerald laughed, "O.K., four dollars."

Pam jumped in the fun and yelled, "NO WAY!"

Gerald pulled in the driveway and said, "I'll tell you when I collect my thoughts."

Joyce, totally upset by now, clamed up and shook her head. She looked over at Pam.

Once in the house, Joyce ran to the bedroom. She waited for Gerald's slow walk back, then said, "Where's it at?"

Gerald blasted, "Why don't you get a shower, something to eat and settle down!"

Dad was listening in the front kitchen. He walked back outside and headed for the outer garden. Pam ran out to talk to dad while Joyce finally headed to the shower.

Gerald, lying across the bed with hands over his head, waited to hear Joyce in the shower then he immediately bolted to the closet. Gerald opened the safe holding the neckerchief once more. Just then the bedroom door started to open. There was Joyce wrapped in a towel standing totally in awe. The two just stared at it in amazement. They both looked through the magnifying glass. "It's beautiful," said Joyce. They both stood staring at the tomahawk in total silence. Gerald held it up to a light and attempted to look through it. Grabbing the magnifying glass Joyce screamed, "Look out!" Unaware of the magnifying powers, the bedroom quilt caught fire!

Gerald glanced at Joyce, then threw the relic on the table. Looking back to Joyce, "Thanks, I didn't realize how powerful it was!"

They quickly put the flaming bedroom quilt out with a cup of water. Joyce held the relic and asked, "How much?" Gerald remained silent as he leaned on a chair.

Then Joyce said, "I bet it cost a fortune!" Noticing Gerald's irritation, Joyce refrained from prying further. Gerald took the stone back and looked at Joyce. "Do you know about this thing?" Joyce remained silent.

Gerald continued, "This stone has caused more trouble than the Boston Tea Party!"

Joyce, puzzled by now said, "How do you mean?"

Gerald added, "It saw battles, it caused a frenzy of distrust so great the Settlers and the Indians couldn't live next to each other." Gerald continued, "It got so bad, the Indians buried the stone with a warrior. The Indians claimed it contained spirits. Gerald looking closer at the tomahawk said, "Whoever had this thing sure knew what they were doing! Joyce, you check and make sure nothing's burning." Gerald, using both the magnifying glass and a magnifier on a head band looked even closer. "God! It's perfect!"

Joyce asked, "What do you mean?"

Gerald shaking his head, "I can almost see through it, yet there's not a mark on it!" He glanced again and said, "$20,000."

Joyce finally breaking her stare, "Are you crazy?"

Gerald laughed, "All business is crazy, it's all speculation." Then Gerald wrapped the tomahawk back up and said, "Supply and Demand, that's it. Gerald closed the safe. "It's no different than guns, jewelry or anything else. The only difference here is this has a story attached to it and a frantic search!"

Weeks passed and Gerald rested on his trophy. Joyce visiting her family mentioned the unusual relic. Joyce's dad looked puzzled and quipped, "You know, Joyce, I used to look for that thing."

Joyce asked, Dad! You know about it?"

Joyce's dad, "Everybody from the Revolutionary War soldiers to now have heard of it. Let's eat!"

As they were all sitting at the table, Joyce's brother quickly sat down and then asked, "How'd Gerald find it?"

Joyce watched her mother sit down and then said, "I had a hard time getting Gerald to tell me what he gave for it." Everyone at the table was dead quiet. Then Joyce's dad quipped, "Go on!"

Joyce reluctantly, "O.K. you really want to know?" Everyone became still then Joyce announced, $20,000!"

Joyce's dad, quiet for a moment, replied, "He's not planning on keeping it, is he?"

Joyce looked puzzled, "You believe in the curse?"

Joyce's dad, "Well, how long have you had your new car?"

Hesitant to say much, Joyce's mom finally said, "Honey, tell him to get rid of it!" Looking at Joyce her mother continued, "It belongs someplace else like—maybe a museum or something."

After returning to Gerald's home, everything seemed to be calm. Walking past Gerald's dad watching T.V., Joyce headed to the back bedroom. Gerald asleep awakens like a lion! He angrily said, "I bet you told them every thing!"

Joyce was silent as she gathered her thoughts, "What would you have done?"

Gerald, attacking, "They don't need to know! It didn't cost them anything anyway!"

Joyce, on the defense, "My mother said "Sell it to a museum!"

Gerald quipped, "Why sure, honey, I'll just walk in tomorrow and say, "Hey, Franklin Institute, want to buy my real cool tomahawk? I only paid $20,000, but I'll sell it to you for -$25.00!"

Joyce laughed, "That's about right!"

Gerald, now in a total rage said, "Look, when I want to sell it, you'll know!"

Joyce asked, "What about the curse?"

Gerald quipped, "I'll sell it soon as I get a serious bid."

Joyce, upset added, "I'll live back at home till that day comes. I want to live in a happy family, not turmoil!"

Gerald pranced through the hall following Joyce to the back porch. Then he shouted, "Joyce get back here!"

Joyce now at the car said, "You're obsessed with that thing!"

Gerald quipped, "I have to put it on the market! I had a buyer last week, a jewelry store wanted it. He collects."

Joyce, curious, "A jewelry store?"

Gerald said, "He called me back and cancelled."

Joyce said, "It's the curse."

Gerald, still looking upset said, "Joyce, trust me. I promise it shouldn't take more than a week or two."

Joyce looked at the rental car, "Honey, my family thought tit might have had something to do with my accident."

Gerald quipped, "How do you like the way this car runs?"

Joyce added, "It's actually nicer than the one you bought. Cheaper, too."

Walking back in the house, Gerald's father called them over. "Let's go outside." Gerald and Joyce looked startled.

Gerald's dad said, "There's some truth to the legend." He looked at Gerald, "Yesterday I thought you left the bedroom T.V. on. I went in your room to shut it off. NOTHING! Then I thought maybe you left your walkman on or some other gadget. NOTHING! I've owned this house all my life, I've never heard voices." Looking firmly at Gerald, "Take that thing somewhere else!"

Joyce was shaking with chills. She refused to enter the house.

Gerald glanced over at dad and remarked, "Thanks a lot!" He shrugged his shoulders and said, "I'll keep it at the bank."

Joyce watched Gerald's displeasure, "You still own it, I don't know if that will stop the bad luck."

Gerald looked over at Joyce, now in a bad mood. "That 's the best I can do, it will have to wait till morning."

Joyce remarked, "Gerald, if I hear one sound at 3:00, I'm out of here."

Gerald looked out the window, glanced back at dad, "Is that O.K. with you?"

Dad hesitated, "I'm having the priest over as soon as that thing's out of here."

Walking back towards the bedroom, Gerald turned back around and stepped accidentally on Joyce's foot. "Wait a minute." Walking back to the front room for dad, "What did the voices sound like?"

Dad paused as he rinsed out his cup, "All kinds of sound, animals, kids, noise."

Gerald, prying harder, "Could you make any of it out?"

Dad becoming irritated, "Water, like a waterfall or something; a small child."

Joyce remembering her dad's stories, said, "My father told us when we were small, he looked for it. It went all the way back to the Revolutionary War."

Dad looked at Gerald with a scared frown. "You put that thing back or get rid of it soon! All right?"

Gerald, by now was tired of the controversy, "I promise; soon as the bank opens."

The evening set in quickly. The family conversations shifted from news to sports to finally Joyce's car. Gerald shook his head and looked over to dad, "Joyce likes this much cheaper rental more than the car that got demolished."

Dad glanced across at Joyce, "You were lucky in that accident."

Later, while Gerald was taking a shower, he began thinking about the American Revolution.

Joyce walking down the hall approached Gerald who was heading for the washing machine. She asked, "What could have caused the curse?"

Thinking silently, Gerald replied, "It could have been the Native Americans wanted the thing left alone so they made up the story."

Joyce was trying to contain her composure, then burst out laughing.

Gerald looked over, "What's so funny?"

Joyce said, "They wouldn't have acted like that."

Gerald again irritated, "What—you an Indian major in college or something?"

Joyce furthered, "I don't think the history books say anything like that."

Gerald threw the last of his wet clothes in the hamper, "You really believe all that bull?"

Joyce turning red, "You probably flunked history." Joyce and Gerald closed the door and lay across the bed. Flicking on the T.V. Joyce said, "I have to get a shower. Just then Gerald's dad shouted from out front and asked Gerald to check channel 6. Gerald's dad was complaining about the change in weather—seemed the perfect cue for Joyce to get her shower. Like clockwork, Gerald spins the dial on the safe. Holding the neckerchief, Gerald noticed a change of hue! Gerald looked closer, the relic seemed to have changed colors! Looking even closer, he used his head band with the magnifier. Becoming upset, he shouted, "Shit!" Now putting his eyes almost right up against the relic, he noticed the pronounced chance in the color from bright crystal to pink! Struggling for an explanation, Gerald said out loud, "No one knows my combination! *No one's been here*!

Joyce, entered the bedroom and said, "Oooh! It changed colors!"

Gerald remained calm and said, "It *might* be the weather."

Joyce chuckled, "Or someone just used it." Irritated by Gerald's mild obsession she asked, "Will you put that thing away once and for all!"

Night setting, Gerald went to the front of the house to spend some time with dad. Joyce was talking to a girlfriend who was sleeping in the spare bedroom. Gerald finished a show and reached for the front room telephone. Holding the phone up to his ear, he heard Joyce and shouted in a calm voice, "Is it my turn to use the phone? You got your own phone!"

Joyce made a cell phone call in Gerald's room. Looking toward the closet door, Joyce saw a light flicker. Getting the spooks, she walked out in the hall and to her own room. Gerald finished his call to a friend then retired to the bedroom. Joyce coming in an hour later found Gerald fast asleep. Walking back up the hall into the front kitchen, Joyce helped herself to a cookie and a glass of milk. Joyce pondered her next move. Thinking about the accident, she yawned and headed for her own bedroom.

Hours later, Gerald peeked in Joyce's room. She was asleep. Gerald b-lines for the bathroom closet. He smelled something burning when he opened the door. Opening the safe quickly, Gerald was met with a terrible surprise. Gerald started screaming, waking up the house. "No! No!" Here under the tomahawk was the remainder of the $30.000. Some $10,000 had burnt up!! Throwing the tomahawk to the corner of his bedroom, Gerald scrabbled through the ashes. Joyce ran up the hall and watched Gerald reach time after time into the foot safe. Bringing out the valuable, charred box's remains. Opening the box with a key, Gerald slammed the box down in a fit. "No! No! No!"

Joyce asked, along with Gerald's dad now standing behind her, "What's wrong??"

Gerald screamed, "All my collectable baseball cards, my rare autographs, my old collectable money, even my baby pictures!"

Gerald's father said, "How'd a fire get in there?"

Looking puzzled, Gerald quipped, "I have no idea!"

Joyce ran for a broom, while Gerald's dad ran to the window. While he wrestled with the stuck window, Gerald kicked the tomahawk under the bed. He shook off charred old World War II newspapers, he looked over at Joyce. Grabbing the broom, he started sweeping out as much ash as he could see. As he ran the broom under the bed, the dusty red and white handkerchief appeared. Gerald bent down to look. He carefully used the broom handle to fish blindly in the dark for the stone. Joyce grabbed a flashlight from dad and handed it over to Gerald. Keeping her composure, she headed towards the front kitchen mop closet. Gerald's dad, moaning, reached down next to his son. Both were looking furiously. Where was it? They finally found the tomahawk in a far corner under the bed. Running for the bathroom sink, Gerald quickly inspected his prize possession. Joyce started mopping up, while dad took out the cardboard box filled with ashes. Very carefully, Gerald rinses off the treasure and wrapped it meticulously, carefully replacing it in the safe.

Chapter Two

FATHER FORTUNE

The following morning, Joyce lagged in the bathroom while dad made coffee. Gerald remained in the bedroom. Joyce, not hearing any noise rapped on his door. Gerald cracked open the door with one eye still closed. Stumbling around, he found his cell phone. Dad yelled from the kitchen, "Today Gerald, not someday!" Finding no sympathy, Gerald pushed the buttons slowly, "What time does your safety deposit box lobby open?"

The young woman put Gerald on hold, clicking back she replied, "We're open now."

Gerald glancing at his watch, "9:00 a.m.?" The teller excused herself putting Gerald back on hold.

Again opening the phone circuit, the teller said, "Sir, I'm sorry, I'm new here. We're open from 11:00 to 5:00 p.m., Monday thru Thursday."

Gerald, impatient said, "Thank you."

Gerald, falling back to sleep, heard someone knocking at the bedroom door. It was dad, "What the heck's wrong with you? It's almost 10:30. Your girl left two hours ago."

Gerald awakened abruptly screamed, "Dad!"

Gerald's dad walked back up the hall and Gerald yelled again, "Dad!"

Gerald's dad, "What?"

Gerald replied, "I'm going to take a shower, the deposit boxes at the bank don't open till 11:00 a.m."

After his shower, Gerald went down to the kitchen and reached for the refrigerator door.

Dad rocking in his rocker, came out to the kitchen. "You know your girl friend ain't too crazy about either one of us."

Gerald, pouring a cup of iced tea, glanced back smiling and said, "How do you mean?"

Dad glanced at the table and asked, "Mind if I take a look?"

Gerald with a frown said, "Go ahead, dad."

Removing the stone from one of Gerald's green socks, Gerald's dad quipped, "Let's just call it horse sense."

Gerald, now curious, "You heard something last night?"

Dad glanced back at Gerald with a big smile, "Might have." Then looking at the stone in the kitchen bay window, he said, "It's beautiful! I'm not crazy about women all the time, anyway. After your mom, I had too much fun minding my own business. But you're smart, young and mouthy. You might make it."

Gerald remained quiet as dad ended with, "Try to keep peace with the Indians." Looking back to Gerald with a big smile, still holding the stone, added, "I like Joyce, she's not lazy." Gerald finished lunch with a mouth full, "Was it last night when the trouble hit?" Gerald's dad remained quiet.

Gerald, reached for the green sock with the precious stone and remarked, "Any more advice?"

Gerald's dad frowned. "Get rid of this thing, keep Joyce."

Gerald, resenting the advice, held his hand out impatiently. Gerald's dad reached slowly with the stone in hand and gave it back. "Gerald quipped, "I got to get goin."

When Gerald arrived at the bank, the senior teller made him sign in. With business accomplished, Gerald headed back to his car. Driving past a branch newspaper office, Gerald turned back around. He decided to place an ad in the "for sale" column. On the way back home, he stopped for gas. As he passed the insurance agency where Joyce worked, he decided to drop in. He soon found that Joyce, not wanting to be interrupted, continued with a client. Gerald glanced around the office, read the wall bulletin board and made a discovery. On the bulletin board he saw: 'Wanted, unusual acquisitions! No item too big or small. Call anytime.' Gerald removed the business and asked permission to have it. The manager chuckled and said, "Sure."

Once back home, Gerald b-lined for his bedroom. His fingers nervously dialed the number. An answering machine kicks in. Leaving his number, Gerald walked out looking for his dad. Walking out to the back yard, Gerald found his dad sitting on the mower. Not wanting to startle his dad he waited till he started back towards the house. Waving frantically, he finally got his dad's attention. Gerald's dad shut off the mower, held up his hand and asked, "You put that thing in the bank?"

Gerald quipped, "Yes! I placed an ad, made a phone call to an investor. I'm putting It online."

Gerald's dad waved for him to stop talking, "Son whatever that stone attracts, has in it, lets out or whatever didn't leave when you did!"

Gerald listened silently while his dad continued, "I went in to call my neighbor to make sure he took his insulin. The bathroom door slammed shut. Thinking maybe you came back, I shouted down the hallway, 'Man, that was quick.' Not hearing anything, I thought you were still mad from this morning or maybe something else happened." Dad, now laughing, "I went down the hall to check on things, realizing you were in the bathroom. I waited patiently, but heard nothing. When I spoke to you, no one answered, so I tried to open the door." Gerald's eyes were now big. Dad continued, "When I went around to the outside and looked in, no one was in the bathroom! I went and got the metal steps, pried open the window, climbed inside the bathroom. Out of breath, I hesitated, then reached for the door, turned the knob, and like child's play—the door opened!" Gerald started to talk, but was waved off again by dad. Dad continued, "I checked the bathroom door, it wasn't locked! I walked across, went into your bedroom, and Nothing!" Gerald was thinking maybe the stone becomes a catalyst for souls or something. Gerald's dad, "I called the rectory; they're coming right out. Son, don't try to reason with anything demonic or spiritual unless your guided with help!"

Gerald, not knowing what to think asked, "Do you think we should just wait for the priest?"

Gerald's dad turned off the mower and said, "Good idea. Go get something to eat, fast food or something and we'll wait for the church."

After mowing the remainder of the yard, Gerald's dad brought the riding mower in. As they were both sitting on the back porch, a dark car pulled in the driveway. Walking up slowly, the priest introduced himself. "Hello, I'm Father Fortune. You called, I hope I can help you."

Dad quickly told the story then invited Father Fortune in the house. Father Fortune removed his black hat, scratched his head and sat at the kitchen table. Father glanced over to Gerald, "What is it?"

Gerald, remaining calm said, ""It's a native American weapon."

Glancing back at dad, Father Fortune laughed. "Is it a tomahawk?"

Gerald and his dad stopped and stared at each other.

Father Fortune quipped, "We must be having a run on them or something." Then with a big smile, "Two boys, not far from here, found one and brought it home."

Dad glanced over at Gerald, then to Father, "Is there any truth to the rumors of a curse?"

Father Fortune removed a leather shaped holster slowly and unveiled the holy water. Preparing his belongs, Father Fortune glanced at Gerald and his dad. "I'll be back in a couple minutes." Father Fortune returned with a big smile and asked, "Where's the thing at?"

Gerald, pondering his reply said, "It's in a safety deposit box pending transfer to a new owner."

Gerald's dad asked, "Excuse me, you're not leaving without at least a cup of coffee, are you?"

Father slowly retuned to the kitchen table and sat down. Gerald took the priest's hat and vest and walked toward the living room. Gerald's dad slipped Father a fifty dollar bill in an envelope. Father Fortune looked at Gerald's dad in amazement. "What's this?"

Gerald's dad replied, "I really appreciate you coming right out!" Gerald walked back toward the kitchen, shook his head and shrugged his shoulders. Gerald's dad said, "Since Gloria left, I don't put up with a whole lot of bologna!" Looking over to Gerald, Gerald's dad continued, "This guy's got everything going for him, don't appreciate nothing', nice girlfriend, good family, makes good money hustling."

Father Fortune sitting in the middle of all this looked embarrassed and said, "Gentlemen, I really have to go. I got a lot of other stops."

Both looked at Father Fortune and said, "Father, we're glad you came, so quick Thanks for your input!"

Father Fortune reached for his hat and walked to the kitchen door. "If you have any problems (he paused) you won't." Both followed him to the car.

Gerald followed dad slowly back into the house. Gerald called the acquisition office on his cell phone. The investment company transferred the call on to James Floyd at a field office. Gerald, using a business tone said, "I'm wondering if you know anyone that is interested in making an early American artifact acquisition? The phone remained silent, then finally came to life. Well the truth is, Gerald, I'm part of an investment group."

James Floyd, glanced at his vehicle, "Look, I might be interested, what price range are we talking?" James, being coy, "Oh, what did you say it was?"

Gerald quipped, "I didn't."

James paused, Gerald said, "It's a very historically sought after Native American tomahawk, a relic from the early American period.

James laughed, "Relic?"

Gerald, in a very serious voice, "Oh, yes; relic!"

James, scratching his head, "How so?"

Gerald looked around his bedroom, "It's crystal."

James paced in a circle and asked, "What price range?"

Gerald, sitting on the edge of his bed, said, $12,000, firm!"

James, using his mechanics of bargaining said, "I still don't see why so much?"

Gerald furthered, "You see it once, you'll change your mind, plus there's a local legend."

James looked around, "Yeah, that's it, I'll have to see it! How soon do you need to know?"

Gerald replied, "Soon."

James getting in his truck, loosened his shirt button, "O.K.; How's today?"

Gerald glanced at his watch, "One hour at 1st National. It's in a safety deposit box."

James, looked in his personal checking account from his glove box. You'll take a certified?"

Gerald, edgy, "What bank?"

James laughed, "Yours!"

Gerald, controlled his emotions and maintained a business tone of voice then said, "That will be good."

James, talking overtop, "One hour."

Now back in the house, Gerald waked out from the bedroom, approached dad in the kitchen and said, "I'm pretty sure I have a buyer."

Dad, sitting at the kitchen table laughed," Already?"

Gerald nodded, "I have to meet him in one hour at the bank."

Passing the insurance office, Gerald continued on. It had been two days, no phone call from Joyce. Thinking to himself, maybe 'not ever.' Pulling into the bank, Gerald spotted the James Floyd investment vehicle in the lot. Walking in the side entrance, Gerald approached a tall, thin man. Gerald asked, "Are you James?"

The man stood up from the waiting room, "You must be Gerald."

Approaching the counter, Gerald requested to have the box opened, plus use of a room. Within minutes, Gerald walked in the little side room. Like clock- work, Gerald unlocked the drawer. Slowly Gerald's hand nervously pulled out the stone.

James, immediately without a word, shook his head.

"Here, Gerald looked up and asked, you sure?" (now holding the envelope).

James laughed, "Absolutely!"

Walking back out front, the teller immediately made sure the drawer was returned properly with Gerald signing a form. The three headed toward the front counter. Gerald signed the check and remarked, "Would you please deposit this?"

James waited patiently and glanced around the bank. "I've been with this bank since I was in my teens."

Gerald smiled, "It was a pleasure doing business."

On the way home, Gerald grabbed a burger at a fast food restaurant, unwinding slowly before reaching the house. Immediately, Gerald headed for a quick shower, than an afternoon snooze. Gerald walked back slowly to the bedroom door. He heard, "Did you sell it?"

Gerald, half asleep, "Oh, yes, he wanted it right away."

Dad quipped, "She hasn't called."

Gerald looked up with one eye shut. "Good!"

James Floyd returned to his office late in the afternoon. His secretary was preparing to leave and asked, "Where on earth have you been?"

Looking curiously at the stone, James asked, "You want to see something like you've never seen before?" Both began staring; spellbound, next to a low beam table light.

James immediately asked, "Karen, will you bring me my magnifiers?"

Karen hurried for the secretary's office, found the glasses and ran back.

James, holding the stone up at the window shook his head. "It's almost transparent."

Karen watched smoke begin pouring out and shouted, "Look out!" Just then a beam omitted from the stone began burning the office curtain.

James glanced at Karen and remarked, "Wow! Bet I can't do that again!"

Karen, still in shock remarked, "It's absolutely beautiful!"

"Look, I have to go," said James. James, glancing at the clock on his desk, looked back to Karen, "I'm sorry, see you tomorrow."

James tucked the stone in his pocket, followed Karen out of the office and to the parking lot. Karen looked up, "Don' t get any crazy ideas with that thing."

James chuckled, "If I do, you'll be the first to know."

James, arriving home, checked on grandmom. The phone rang. James, looked startled and asked, "What? My God—anybody hurt?" James hurriedly got dressed. As he walked past his grandmom he said, "Something's come up, I have to check on the Forge." Looking back, "Tell Susan, she'll have to run Julie to practice." Leaving in a hurry, James forgets to lock up the stone in the safe. Running back in the house he passed grandmom for the second time. "What was that thing?" she asked.

James laughed, "I'll tell you when I get back. It's an investment I'm holding on to for someone." Then literally running out the door, James sped off quickly. He immediately approached the barricade.

Officer Startfirst walked to the car. James, emotionally drained, asked,

"How bad is it?"

Officer Startfirst replied, "Right now, the back side's the worst."

James immediately asked, 'Anybody hurt ?"

Officer Startfirst, "Bad smoke inhalation, so far no one serious."

Walking closer to the scene, James looked in horror, "We lost this one."

Officer Startfirst, "Think so?"

James called home. Grandmom answered the phone. "Susan took Julie to practice. Did something happen over the forge?"

James glanced back at the ruins and shook his head. "Word travels quick., Grand mom"

Grand mom laughed, "It's on all the news channels."

James glanced at his watch, "I'm on my way home." Having entered the kitchen buried in smoke and soot, James headed straight to the shower. Putting his pants and shirt in a brown grocery bag, he lowered them out the bathroom window.

Julie was returning from practice, "Dad, are you O.K.?"

James replied, "I'm O.K. Our Forge is gone!"

Julie remained calm, "What?" James looks up from the chair rolling on a pair of socks . . . Julie pries further, "Dad!, What about the workers?"

James looked for his wallet, "So far smoke inhalation." Walking toward the kitchen he remarked, "I think everyone got out all right. I'm waiting for my Manager from the hospital to call or at least the police. James grabs a glass of Water," Officer Start first I hope will get back with me."

Julie's girlfriend, Carol started giggling. "Officer who?"

James stared at Carol, "Officer Startfirst." Slowly James started smiling, "Hey, That's his name."

Julie looked across the living room, "Dad, can Carol stay for dinner?"

James looked edgy "You better ask your mom or the real boss." James looking at grand mom then he said, "I'm really sorry, I just don't want you upset or sick or something."

Grandmom, who was looking out the kitchen window said, "James! I would have to be blind to tell something was seriously wrong the way you were running around!"

Moments later, James received a phone call. Hearing the voice, James knew it was the police. James asked, "How bad was it?"

Officer Startfirst, "We suspect arson, you have a major loss. It was up in a flash! You have a lot of enemies?"

James continued, "I'm too busy for all that love, hate, stuff."

The policeman added, "The reason we suspect arson is the way it went up so fast."

James said, "Whatever papers you need signed, I'll drop by and sign or you're always welcome to come out here."

Officer Startfirst added, "We're having a fire investigator flown in from Harrisburg. He may want to talk to you, that'll be later in the week."

James asked, "How's my manager fare?"

Officer Startfirst, "They're still at the hospital, but no causalities."

James asked, "Are they here local?"

Officer Startfirst replied, hesitantly, "Ah, yes, they all are."

James said, "I'll go see them after dinner."

Officer Startfirst, "We'll be in touch."

Julie, worried for her dad asked, "Did anybody get seriously hurt?"

James answered, "Bad enough, smoke inhalation."

Susan looked at grandmom as she sat down to dinner, "Seems you always get left out of things."

Grandmom shrugged her shoulders, "I usually find out through a little work."

Susan glanced over to grandmom, "Did you ever find your tickets?"

Looking defeated grandmom replied, "I wish I could remember."

James looked at Susan, "One of those or more were for the state jackpot!" That would sure help right about now!"

Julie giggled at Carol, "What's so funny?"

Carol laughing said, "I'm still giggling about Officer Startfirst."

Susan took Carol home shortly after dinner and Julie helped dad dry the dishes. Grandmom watched the news which showed last minute scenes of the Forge.

James, standing next to the couch said, "I wonder what happened? Officer Startfirst thinks it was arson."

Grandmom looked serious and shook her head, "Arson! Who would want to destroy a Forge?"

James replied, "I have no clue. I honestly haven't been in there since we bought it. The employees are dedicated, I always let them handle the money. I think they'll find something else to be the culprit."

Susan walked in the door slowly. "James, I swung passed the Forge, the firemen are still fighting the fire! It makes you want to help fight the fire!"

James chuckling, "I came home for that reason!"

Susan, looking back at the sink, said, "Oh, my gosh!"

James added, "I didn't know what do with myself!"

Susan walked in the living room and sat down on the arm of the couch. Staring at the T.V. she asked, "Anything else on the news?"

Julie, who had a crush on a fireman, said, "I saw Timmie dragging a water hose."

James walked out back then back in again. Susan was still sitting on the arm of the couch. James said, "I have something I want to show you, I almost forgot!" Walking back to the spare bedroom, James spun the safe dial. He slowly removed the stone. Walking up through the hall, James slowly unwrapped the neckerchief. Flicking on the ceiling light at the end of the hall, James quipped, "Take a look at that!"

Susan unbelievingly looked, followed by grandmom, and then last, Julie.

Holding it in the light, Susan took the first real look. Susan peered spellbound, "It's so beautiful! What is it?"

James laughed, "A very expensive acquisition!"

Julie looked even closer, "I've seen this somewhere. Yea, this past spring, the two Becker boys brought it to Mr. Richard's class." Julie, looking to dad, "I don't know, but I think it's haunted or something!"

Susan frowned at Julie, "Julie! You know we don't believe In that stuff!"

James, curious, "You actually saw this before?"

Julie continued, "Yes, this is it!"

James looked puzzled and asked, "How can you be sure?"

Julie continued, "There ain't none like it known to man."

Suddenly grand mom moved closer. Grand mom looked through her bifocals. "James, your dad and some friends spent years looking for this!"

Susan said, "Wait a minute, my grandfather told us about looking for it."

James laughed, "I'm the only one being kept in the dark."

Julie added, "The boys were very upset. Someone last summer broke in and stole it. The Becker's were furious!"

Julie, prying further, "Dad, do you know about the curse?"

James retorted, "What?"

Julie answered, "The boys did some research, seems the settlers and Indians became totally untrusting of each other."

James was totally consumed in the history, "Go ahead please."

Julie looked at mother, "Go ahead."

Julie continued, "I wasn't thinking when I first saw it. It's cursed!"

Susan gasping for air, "Julie! What's wrong with YOU?"

Grandmom, thinking about the Forge quipped, "You bought that thing yesterday?"

James was quiet

Julie added, "All I know is it causes a lot of trouble."

James, looking for an angle, looked to grandmom.

Grandmom remembering, "I wish your grandpop was still around. There's a whole lot more, but I'm too old to remember."

Susan, looking to Julie, "You got your homework done? Let's get started. I want to see it."

James, now in the kitchen recants the story in the office. "We were looking at it through the magnifying glass; it caught the window shade on fire!"

Grandmom looked puzzled and said, "What on earth possessed you to want to own it?"

Susan looking weird, "It's all about business."

James looked up and quietly laughed.

Late into the night, James still sat there staring. First late night television and then late, late night television.

Susan, coming from the bathroom, glanced down the hallway to the kitchen light. Walking to the kitchen, she noticed James asleep in the kitchen chair. She stopped and turned off the T.V. Then she tapped James on the shoulder. "That's what man invented beds for, but God, honey, put that thing away!"

James was startled, "I'm sorry, honey, I must have dozed off."

Susan checked the refrigerator and noticed the door partially open.

Susan inquisitive, "Were you in the refrigerator?"

James, in control of his senses said, "No, must have been Julie." Walking down the hallway, James placed the stone in the wall safe in the spare bedroom. Once in bed, all became silent. The morning sun seemed to come up just as James fell asleep! Julie off to school, Susan prepared breakfast for grandmom and James. Susan said to James, "I have to work half a day today."

James, on his second cup of coffee, glanced at his watch, "I should call the police. I must go check on how the workers made out."

Grand mom was listening in and added, "Do me a big favor, take that thing in your wall safe with you."

James, totally overwhelmed said, "Where am I going to keep it? Oh, I'll do like the guy I bought it off of did, he kept it at the bank."

Susan glanced at grandmom, "That better grandmom?"

Grandmom said, "Yes dear, thank you."

James went and got the stone and showed it one last time. Then he wrapped it in a clean red silk cloth. James then left the premises Grand mom watched the news thinking her dream had come true. Slowly edging toward the kitchen, she found the heavy duty battery lantern. Flashing first under, then to the far side, Grandmom saw some papers lying in the back left side. Carefully using a broom handle, she swiped towards the corner. Like a lucky punter, grandmom, in a reverse swing pulled the papers out from behind. In her hand was a light colored group of lottery tickets. Running for her list of numbers, grandmom found the prize of her life!

Morning came too quickly for James, first the hospital then back for lunch.

Susan laughed and said, "You would have felt real good if I would have left you sitting there."

Looking over to grandmom in the living room, James asked, "How was your night?"

Grandmom said, "Something like yours but at least I went to bed."

Susan asked, "What's wrong mom?"

Grandmom continued, "I wasn't even asleep. Something kept talking to me about the refrigerator."

Susan giggled and looked at James.

Grandmom said, "Whatever it was, seemed it was pulling on my night gown sleeve."

James laughed, "What?"

Grandmom added, "In my dream it first showed me a big river."

Susan added dramatically, "A river?"

Grand mom continued, "This person was very upset. Then he pointed me to the refrigerator."

Susan joked interrupting, "When I finally got up, James was sound asleep in the kitchen chair. The refrigerator was cracked open."

Grandmom remembering more, said, "The person was trying to get some thing in the back of the refrigerator."

James, half asleep, "He or they were probably hungry."

Susan looked first to James then back to grandmom, "Do you remember anything else?"

Grandmom added," It was a whole lot of people running." Now completely overwhelmed by emotion, she looked down the hall. Then she said, "Thanks, whoever you are." Walking out to the kitchen she bumps her daughter. Susan, at a loss for words, then she said, "Come look what it was"

Susan, not understanding the emotion said, "What?"

Grand mom walks back to her living room chair, "You'll won't believe this!" The phone beeped while Susan wiped the kitchen table. Grand mom said, "Susan, you heard me, They can wait!" Susan throws down the washcloth walking from the kitchen, letting the phone ring, grand mom hands Susan the tickets. Reentering the kitchen, Susan overwhelmed in joy answers on the last ring.

It was Julie. "Everything all right?"

Grand mom follows Susan to the kitchen listening close, Then in a firm voice, "Come home, NOW!"

I going to be late at school."

Holding the tickets against the newspaper Susan said, "What about your cheerleading practice?"

Julie added, "Yes, I'm going straight from here with Carol."

Grand mom curious, "Is that O.K. with Carol's mom?"

Julie laughed, "Yes, but—(grandmom cut her off). "Come home now!" Then she quickly walked to her living room chair. Susan irritated by grand mom's outburst notices the phone go dead before hanging up.

Soon Julie arrives late by Carol's mom from cheerleading practice 1. She was singing when she came through the door then asked, "Where's mom?"

Grandmom, looking stern, said, "Sit down! Here, check this for me!"

Julie laid down her book pack, grabbed the tickets and newspaper. Within a few moments, Julie started jumping up and down. Julie checked a second time and was totally euphoric. Looking at grandmom, Julie said, How come you couldn't find them?"

Grandmom answered, "I had a dream which pointed me in the right direction."

When James finished in the bathroom he smiled at julie with the same euphoria. Looking at grand mom he said, "That's great, when we claim this prize, looking over at Susan returning from the basement," You would agree that we can sell and move somewhere else."

Julie was surprised and said, "I love school here, but I'd move in a minute!"

Susan's head still spinning looks across at Julie," You really hate it here that much?

Susan, at a loss for words, looks over at James, "I not so sure about all this."

Grand mom sits at the far end of the kitchen table, "We hit the big one!"

James looks around out the kitchen window, "$40 million!!!

Susan turns peering with a frown over to grand mom, looking puzzled back at Julie, "You Think this will really help? Then scratching her leg, "just cut and run."

Grand mom said, "Yes, I know a new school for Julie would help." and the peculiar thing was something in my dream kept trying to tell me they were behind the refrigerator!"

Julie looked at Susan and said, "Mom! Dad and I were taking one day going back about maybe something out west."

Susan said, "Honey, what about your friends, Carol for instance?"

James said, "When things settle down, maybe I'll sell my half of the investments."

Susan walked In the living room and sat down on the sofa arm and asked, "Grand mom, do you think these tickets are valid?"

Grandmom answered, "I know they are!"

James quickly called a lottery office. "I think we have a winner of the jackpot!" The manager said, "Congratulations! Bring your tickets by as soon as possible so we can validate them."

James excitedly said, "I'll be right over!"

Grandmom whispered, "I want to go along."

James waked out from the back room and said, "Keep your fingers crossed."

Susan retorted, "Grandmom wants to come!"

James looked bewildered and replied, "Grandmom, I'll call a limousine service if you want!"

Grandmom laughed, "No, I just want to know for sure!"

Getting in the car, the four of them could see the Forge. James looked down from the overpass and said, "I hope Sam forgives me."

Susan glanced down, "Was he hurt?"

James said, "No, he seemed to want to see me, but your mother had other plans."

When they arrived at the convenience store, all four went inside and waited in front of the lottery manager in suspense. The manager smiled and validated all the tickets. Grandmom jumped for joy! Julie, totally ecstatic yelled, "Mom, we're going to move!"

Susan was thinking about a better work vehicle, paused momentarily then said, "I suppose if grandmom and your daddy want!"

James said, "I might be able to drum up interest in selling the Forge grounds."

Susan looked amused, "Do you think that's a good idea?"

James, without fanfare, "Oh, yes, absolutely!"

Grandmom said, "When all this comes about, let's donate that stone to one of the area museums."

James, stunned said, "Now that's worth thinking twice about!"

Julie jumped in the conversation with, I'd rather see that than have more harm come to someone."

James looked odd, and said, "Maybe, I really don't want to sell it."

When they got back at the house, grandmom said to James, "I never ask much, "looking James straight in the eye!"

Susan lashed back at James, "Do grandmom her favor!"

James quietly said, "I'll do it under a strong peaceful protest!"

Juie, upset, "Your Forge burnt down the very day you brought that thing in the house!"

Susan, totally embarrassed by Julie's remark yelled, "Julie, watch your mouth!, will you?"

James called the hospital and said, "I'm going back over and check on Sam."

Susan was totally out of sorts and added, "What do you want me to do?"

James laughed, "I know it feels weird."

Grandmom added, "Don't bother getting my tickets." Everyone laughed.

Julie asked mom, "Do you think dad will stop and get my ice cream?"

James looked tired, "I'll stop on my way back from the hospital."

Once dad left, Julie walked out in the living room. Grandmom was drinking coffee. She looked towards the television then back to Julie and inquisitively asked, "Where would you like to move?"

Julie laughed, "Washington state."

Susan laughed, "We're not moving there!"

Grandmom quipped, "It doesn't matter too much, but some place a lot warmer with a nice town."

Susan added, "We already have that living here."

Grandmom added, "We could keep the house, just have a second place to change environments once in awhile."

Susan quipped, "James would never want to keep this place!"

Julie laughed, looking to Susan, "We talked about all that before about a month ago. I don't think he's even in reality yet."

Susan really mad, "Will you watch how you say things?"

Grandmom said, "She's right! He's so out of touch right now with the fire, the stone, and now $40 million!"

Susan looking surreal said, "I'm going to conduct my business as usual. I'm going to work and everything."

Grandmom added, "Julie, what about you?"

Julie shrugged her shoulders, "I guess that's the only way to maintain gravity, otherwise you float out in space."

When James reached the hospital, Sam was doing well. Calling home Susan commanded the evening with Julie doing homework, grandmom watching news, and Susan reviewing the budget. James mentioned about the Forge. "I'll call the realtor tomorrow and see about an appraiser."

Susan asked with caution, "What about Julie's ice cream?"

James said, "I'll stop on the way home."

Finding the ice cream was no problem, finding the Forge was. Seemed the whole Forge was totally destroyed. Using his cell phone,

James contacted the police headquarters. "May I leave a message for Officer Startfirst?" James, unaware of the total disaster asked to speak to a police officer.

"Hello, this is James Floyd from Floyd investments. Does anyone have a progress report or a file up on Floyd Forge?" Picking up the switch board telephone lines, a voice said, "Officer Keys, may I help you?" Again James repeated is question.

Officer Keys quipped, "Yes, Officer Startfirst will be in tomorrow and he's preparing the arson report."

James, relieved of the concerns, pulled into his home driveway.

Julie greets her father at the door. "Dad, how are you? Did you bring my ice cream?" Loudly laughing, James handed the bag to her. "Satisfied?"

Julie returned to her bedroom.

Susan, hours later looking beat, gazed with a yawn towards the kitchen and said, "I don't know about you, James but I'm bushed!"

James drops a calculator on the porcelain table then heads for the living room, Susan b-lined to turn in, wondering out loud, "Do I give my two week's notice?"

James, "Honey, anything you want." James lifts back up remembering a pet project in the basement.

Returning to the living room hours later James was thinking about the Forge. Who would want to burn a Forge? Flicking on the T.V. from the kitchen table, James stirred his cup of late night coffee.

Grand mom yawns making her way to the kitchen, "Oh, James! I didn't know you'd still be up." James waking from a daze, "So you're the one who left the refrigerator door open the other night?"

Grandmom retorted, "No, James sorry wasn't me. I never got up the other night."

Waving downward as he yawned, "Forget I even said anything."

Grandmom asked, "You're going to find a nice home for the stone?"

James returned, "Yes, grandmom, first thing tomorrow morning."

After taking another shower James decided to call it a night and drifted off To sleep in a big arm chair facing his bedroom suite. The chaotic days having just past were on his mind. First, the tomahawk, the Forge fire, now the big win. Unwinding slowly, James drifted into sleep land. Susan was snoring and the wind was blowing, but

James lifted out of the chair having a difficult rest. Later Susan woke up and headed to the bathroom. Several hours passed—finally James jumps in bed, things are dead silent.

*   *   *

Walking along a river, James sees a crowd of people. James realizes it's in a frontier time. Glancing at the excitement, James runs in for a closer look. Suddenly it dawns on him it's Native Americans. Still walking closer, James realizes the whole town was there. It seemed many were taking turns diving frantic in a deep river. Sitting on the river bank, James made a horrific discovery. A huge pile of clothes and weapons were lying by his right side. Glancing a second time, James sees the stone. Unaware of it's history, James wakes up shouting.

Susan, scared out of her wits, screamed, "What's wrong!!!"

James said, "I'm sorry, I just had a bad nightmare!"

James, very excited, tried to fall back to sleep. He knew the dream was only a dream so he desperately tried to revamp. Hoping for a little luck, he saw the sun coming up and heard Julie in the bathroom. Rolling over for one last try, he heard Susan say, "Honey, it's 8:00 a.m. Flipping the sheet covers back in anger, James headed for the wake up routine.

During breakfast James told Susan about his dream. Susan laughed. "Maybe you interconnected with something."

James said, "I saw the tomahawk, it was *so real*! There were a whole bunch of spears, arrows, and some kind of leather wrapping. The whole town was upset about something in the river. I glanced back at it; it was so shiny! I took a second glance for some reason, and then became overcome in fear."

Looking over to Susan walking past out the door for work she said, "Don't forget to file up with Officer Startfirst,"

James added, "Yes! I'll call today around here to the museums !"

James watches Susan leave for work then looks across the kitchen table at grand mom before calling long distance information on the phone. James writes down several local numbers and started calling in a continues wave. First the most famous, then the least famous. James left messages when the answering services kicked on. Then he called back at the police station. Once transferred to Officer Startfirst,

James said, "Hello, this is James Floyd, from Floyd investments. Is there anything that I can do to help with your reports?"

Officer Startfirst said, "That was one heck of a fire! Hope you had plenty of insurance."

James said, "Oh, yes, I have some on the business and the property, plus it's listed in an investment concern."

Officer Startfirst said, "It had to be arson the way the property went so fast up in flames."

James said, "I don't know much about old buildings and all, we would have stopped using the Forge years ago, but different business's kept begging us to take work."

Officer Startfirst, "You mean your not running it for profit?"

James continued, "NO! An investment council decided it would help augment some other investments that we have part ownership in."

Officer Startfirst, "Do you work there at all?"

James replied, "I've actually never been inside the whole place."

Officer Startfirst, "Well a little late now I suppose. You have time stop by and we'll finish this thing up."

James replied, "Yes, officer, I'll be in sometime today."

Officer Startfirst, "Yes, that will be fine. If for some reason I can't be here, Officer James, my assistant can expedite the form."

James quipped, "I'll see you then."

James called the museums again, this time he strikes pay dirt. The answering machine picked up—"Hello, I'm John Harold, how may I help you?"

James said, "I need to speak to a curator." John Harold replied, "Yes, speaking."

James added, "I own an investment company. I'm wondering what is required for me to fill out and what do I need to do to make a gift to your museum?"

John Harold, curious, "I'm sorry, a gift?"

James continued, "Yes, I came into an investment which has been sort of a local legend."

John Harold said, "Sounds interesting."

James went on, "I bought an Indian relic through private business dealings. It's from the early Revolutionary period. I want to donate it as a gift to the museum."

John Harold asked, "Do you have the Indian relic in your possession?"

Chapter Three

THE MUSEUM

James was getting impatient and asked, "When's a good time for me to stop by?"

John Harold, "I'll have to check; our Native American relic area is being worked on. Could I call you back later today?"

James said, "Yes, today would be fine."

John added, "O.K. Today."

James said, "Good! Hope to hear from you soon." James answered a beep from Susan, then proceeded to the bedroom.

Grandmom, walking out of her bedroom said, "Thank you, James."

James said, "It's not gone, yet. Just some hot prospects." John then called the hospital hoping to reach Sam's room. He got another beep. He answered the beep.

"Yes, this is John Harold calling."

"Hello, James speaking."

John Harold said, "James, anytime you want to stop by we'll be glad to have the gift. What did you say it was?"

James, "I didn't. It's a Crystal Tomahawk."

John retorted, "I never thought it existed. There was some kind of bounty for it. I wonder if that's the one."

James said, "I'll bring it down in about an hour."

John Harold said, "Yes, I'll be here, and thank you!"

James arrived at the bank around 3:00 p.m. just making the bank cut off. James drove to the museum in about 40 minutes. James notified security for his clearance. As he approached the main office with a box, a senior secretary greeted him upon arrival. "Hello, I'm, Mr. Harold's secretary, have a seat. He'll be right with you."

James sat in a red, velvet chair and reached for a famous newspaper. Mr. Harold walked out quickly. "Mr. Floyd, I'm John Harold. glad to meet you Come on in." James walked with the box to the main desk.

John Harold filled out a form and said, "What do you consider to be the estimated worth?"

James thinking quickly said, "Mr. Harold, it's around $12,000."

John looked peculiar and asked, "What makes it so high?"

James repeated the legend story. John Harold walked around the desk, and said, "Let's have a closer look."

James removed the stone covered with the red silk cloth from the box. John Harold, totally taken back by the beauty exclaimed, Oh! I see what you mean!" John, now holding the stone, "Let's take a closer look." Holding a pen light in one hand and a magnifying glass in the other, John slowly walked the pen light down the stone following with his eyes. Looking up he shook his head and said, "This thing is absolutely beautiful!! Talking, while holding the light and magnifier, James shouted, "Watch Out!!: John looking down suddenly realized the magnification power.

James quipped, "I had a mishap the day I had it in my office. It can create a fire very quickly!"

John said, "Some earlier owners probably used it for that while cooking. Then John passed the stone back to James and quipped, "I'll have my secretary fill out the essential gift form. If you're not in a hurry, come with me, we'll take it to the Native American exhibit area."

James, carried the box passed the general admissions area. Wearing a visitor's tag, James passed security back behind the window displays. He remarked, "Feels funny being the exhibit, rather than looking at one."

John continued walking with a smile. As they approached the last window, John said, "Right here we have the stone and hunting methods."

James looked around in a semi circle, "Wow! I never thought of so many ways to catch wild game."

John Harold added, "I'll have a rotating table brought in. We'll have it somewhere over there. You can come back next week, it should be on exhibit by then."

After shaking hands, James handed John the treasure. Walking back out through the glass windows, James peered at the different animals. Walking a few steps behind and said, "Yes, I know what you're thinking."

James shook his head, "It's so hard to believe all these creatures were around here."

John opened the door in the main front office. His secretary handed James the completed signed form. John turned to James, "Mr. Floyd, thank you so much for your gift to our museum."

James felt a loss of words, simply said, "My pleasure and well, thanks for the tour." He left for home and stopped at a local convenience store. Passing the lottery machine, he started to chuckle. He drove home past the Forge noticing the road was now clear. James reviewed his empty message board on his cell phone. James was still thinking about the museum when he walked in the door. Grand mom looked at him with curious eyes. James removed the gift paper and handed it to grand mom.

John Harold returned to his office and headed straight into the main office. Punching his beeper, John notified his curator assistant. "Chuck, I'm sorry, this is John; how about stopping over at the office before you leave." Within minutes, Chuck knocked on the heavy, oak door. "John, you wanted to see me?"

John, not knowing where to start, "I want to do a fresh Native American exhibit. I want one of your assistants to check on everything and anything on a Crystal Tomahawk."

Chuck looked puzzled and slowly said, "We have the Crystal Tomahawk?"

John quietly said, "Yea, Chuck, some guy with an investment firm acquired the stone and donated it to our trusted hands. We'll run the usual adds in the circular and let our members know in the mailings. We'll set up a special rotating table and have a voice history presentation."

Chuck, taking notes, asked, "What about a special silent alarm?"

John paused. 'Yea, maybe the works."

Chuck asked, "Where's it at?"

John laughed, "Never mind for now—it's in a safe. It's valued at $12,000!"

Chuck walked out past the secretary and waited for her attention. John followed Chuck out, "Yo, Chuck today!" Chuck not realizing John's present, looked up smiled and moved on."

John Harold quickly returned to his private safe Slowly turning the dial, he finally pulled the door open. Taking the box off the floor, he put the stone into the small metal box. He spun the dial, pulled on the door, realizing all was safe. Alone in the office, John Harold left the office corridor.

The following day started out hectic. Three other guests required John's time. In the afternoon, the insurance agency called back to let John know of the stones insurability. Checking on Chuck, he found special display exhibit nearly completed. John walked through the floor talking to Chuck on the cell phone. He was met with a gentle surprise. Chuck reached for the last of scenery and began shoring up the room. Chuck's presentation nears completion way ahead of the schedule. Still talking on the cell, John looked in and tapped the hall window. Chuck, startled, jumped and turned to the glass.

John said, "Yea, just open it up right here, I'll walk in and take a look."

Chuck laughed, "If you have time, I want to show you the information we're going to use on the presentation placard."

John, now interested, "You got the rough draft with you?"

Chuck quipped, "Yea, sure do!"

Walking almost in a run, John strutted the long hall. Accessing the back with a special key, John does a walk, than ran down past the same window on the inside now approaching Chuck.

John looked around the window display and said, "Very good, Chuck, Holy Cow, good job!! Where's the placard going to sit?" Chuck added, "We'll put the silent alarm lazar on the two edges of the table."

*   *   *

The Early Years

Legend is that settlers and Native Americans, in search of a peaceful coexistence, stumbled on an unusual find. Superstitions, harsh environment, forced food ration, and later a unusual distrust, led to increased brutal attacks. This stone became the focal point, or catalyst, for emotion. Native Americans and settlers searched franticly for it's possession. Generation after generation would find and lose the stone, sometimes under seemingly impossible circumstances.

The loss and frantic search seemed to fuel the legend inevitably leading to a belief in a curse.

A local investor donated the stone as a gift to our museum. Special thanks to James Floyd Investments.

*   *   *

A few days passed before John Harold removed the stone. Walking down the lobby seemed to immediately create a crowd. Still in the red silk cloth, John called to Chuck.

John said, "Since you and the work crew did all the work; Chuck, I'll give you the honors."

Walking back around, Chuck set down the stone, still wrapped on the rotating table. Chuck said, "I think I'll move it, ah, right there!" Glancing out at John Harold, now smiling at the spectators, Chuck began the unwrapping process. The crowd seemed drawn to the display even moments before the unveiling. As he unwrapped it, shimmers of light began radiating through the window display. Looking with awe, Chuck glanced back out to round at John Harold and the spectators. Positioning the lazars, Chuck's assistants began stepping back. Chuck quipped, My God, it's beautiful!!"

The crowd began swelling almost immediately. Tourist, three and four windows down, could see the refracted light show. John, now out front of the displays standing with quests quipped, "Chuck, that's good enough. You guys come out here—you're not going to believe this!"

Chuck and the work party assemble out in the inside museum. John Harold pushed out towards the middle and met Chuck and the work party standing in the lobby. Chuck quipped," I was going to hit you up for a raise, but, Holly Goodness!"

The crowd's now some sixty people, seemed totally lured.

John laughed," I can almost feel it's radiance."

Walking back to the main lobby, Chuck and the work party turned opposite directions. John walked quickly to the main office and called a special meeting. John's secretary led the group to the main meeting room.

John began, "This past month, I was reluctant to accept a gift from James Floyd Investments. The gift has caused such an immediate interest, I think it would be fitting to set up a special corridor display so that we can generate funds for our new roof."

John's secretary said, "I walked out shortly before this meeting began. The whole hall clear back was swarming with people!"

One senior advisor said, "There are museums in New York that would pay a fortune for this!"

John retorted, "Sell it! Absolutely not!"

John Harold said, "We could use a boost in the arm!"

John's secretary added, "I agree, people come here from all the world."

The senior advisor said, "You do what you want, I'm just saying there's nothing like a fast roof job."

John shook his head, "That's out of the question. Are you aware this stone was sought after, lost several times; looked for to no avail then suddenly thanks to a family who was generous; we simply lucked out!"

The senior advisor said, "Did you know they cut the budget twice in the last five years? Soon we'll be setting up a display on the advances of modern man and the quest for electric power."

John quipped, "I'll go to the board and see if I can't squeeze a nickel out of them."

Chuck, waiting back at the main office, was skimming through the magazines.

A beep comes across his radio. Chuck asks, "What's up men?"

The worker said, "Chuck, maybe you should come take a look."

Chuck said, "Save me the walk, I'm in the main office."

The worker retorts, "O.K. some woman is down on her hands and knees holding a crucifix, praying and bowing to the stone." The worker continued, "People are getting upset."

Chuck said, unaffected, "Did you ask her to get back up?"

The worker laughed, "Think I better hope you come down here quickly."

Chuck retorted, "O.K. I'll call security."

The worker replied, "Chuck, If you do that, it might make some waves in the press." He paused, noticing John and the secretary's voices approaching the office doors.

John, irritated said, "Chuck, there's a lot of windows to tear down."

Chuck interrupted, "One of my workers is distraught over some tourist in the lobby."

John said, "What kind of problem?"

Chuck quipped, "Maybe for once I'll let you take care of it."

John continued, "What kind of problem?"

Chuck reluctantly added, "Religious."

John looked first to Donna his secretary then to the open door that ran towards the display. Pushing through crowds, "John reached the final display and politely asked "May I help you mame?"

The crowds were huge by now and put John on the spot. The woman bowing with her cross was completely bent over and seemed to be totally in a trance! John again asked, "Mame, may I help you?" Then looking back at the jeering crowd, John called security. Seems security was tied up with separate a separate alert. John was growing impatient by now, "Lady, listen! I've called security. Get up now, save yourself unnecessary embarrassment and you can come visit some other time." Security approached the restless crowd. dispersing the crowd with a bullhorn, they approached John Harold. John said, "If I could have only gotten her to respond, I would have been able to let you guys take care of other problems."

Walking up slowly to the lady, the security officer respectfully said, "Lady, it's time to go home." The lady on her knees kept bowing and praying and never even looked up!

The security officer called in reinforcements. Within moments the room was full of help. The big muscular security officer carefully grabbed the crucifix. In a calm voice he said, "Come on, mane, time to go home."

Shouting from the top of her lungs, the woman yelled, "Be prepared!"

The security guard wrestled with the woman. The lady was kicking and squirming and looked at John and said, You! here me, Be prepared!"

The following morning the janitor cleans the window display. George Andrews noticed oil streaks from fingers were much more pronounced. Using a fresh bucket of cleaning solution and a squeezy he performed his usual routine. First, the push mop—a long, long walk, then the wet mop to take up the majority of footprints. Each corridor contained 8 showcase windows per annex.

Two hours earlier, George slowly brought the Monday morning heavy gear to the floor. Thinking about this past week, he reminisced about the house sale. He was a long time resident of the Philadelphia area and selling the family house was no picnic. Thinking about the years with his children, George remembered the picnics along the riverfront and the trips to the zoo on Girard. Selling the home came without fanfare. People are interested in this region of town. Parting with memories and toys the children used, was the hard part. Stripping a floor prior to a wax job seemed to take forever! George, wasting no time now stripped one—3 window display enclosure, then moved to the next. He applied the was 2 sections behind the area he had stripped. Once completed, George walked back across the fresh wax and started the windows. George began cleaning the windows adjacent to the newly acquired prize. Wiping down across the now heavily smeared glass, George reached for his eyeglasses. Watching the shimmering lights dancing off the stone, George thought back about his young children. Wiping the next glass then across to the other side. He remembers the lost son killed in Viet Nam. Museums and zoo's were some of their favorite places to go growing up. Walking back over towards the stone, George remembers feeding his lost son his first baby food. He remembered taking them to school, to sports practices, even to church. Reading the placard overtop of the display, George remembered the lost letters sent home were saved and placed in safe keeping. George looking at the display said, "You guys had it made!" George started moving his head around in a circle, becoming spellbound by the shimmering refracted light. It seemed to bounce back at the stone making a complete circle. George remained motionless and amused, thinking momentarily back at his lost son in Viet Nam. Coming to his senses he returned to the present. He felt a loneliness befall him. Looking back once more, George thought to himself, "If I could only find the letters and lost pictures.

*   *   *

School bus after school bus filled with children seemed to visit the museum spot making the morning crowds swell quickly.

John Harold announced each school party on the main office intercom. John said, "Don't forget our new exhibits, "Ear Rings from Ancient Egyptian Times." and the new Native American exhibit, "Find the Tomahawk." The people seemed excited and attracted. adults are as amused as the children. One young mother discussed her daughter's disappearance. Slowly the crowd build and build. Chuck ran into the main office knocking on the office door and quickly goes in.

"Now what, Chuck?" John remarked.

Chuck asked, "Do you have any idea how much weight our floors can withstand?"

John, looking out the window, "I haven't the faintest idea, besides what relevance has that got to do with setting up stuffed Tigers?"

Chuck added, "No, I'm serious! This place is getting an unusually high volume of traffic." John turned from the window and walked over to the Curator's office water cooler. "I can feel the floor rumbling two floors over and down."

John, drinking down the cool, spring water said, "I'll have somebody check on it this week."

Chuck replied, "I'm back to the Tigers."

John's secretary, using the computer, felt the vibration so pronounced she could barely type. Alarmed, she buzzed John in his office."

Donna said, "If you want the search on antelope, see If we can keep the building still enough so I can type the search in."

John irritated said, "Chuck just walked two floors to give the same advice."

George arrived home early afternoon and found the house empty. Reaching for the mail he remembered the busy morning on the tile floors. As he walked past a swing set in his backyard, he got a brainstorm. 'I know what I did with those letters. I gave them to Marsha. Marsha, his sister, lived several miles away. Running to the house he called Marsha.

"Marsha, next time you get some free time, will you look for those pictures and letters from Jerry? I thought about them at work, but I couldn't remember for weeks where I put them!"

Marsha said, "George, I'll bring them over as soon as you get settled in."

George added, "I even forgot who I gave them to."

Marsha responded, "Remember last Thanksgiving? We were sitting in the living room."

George said, "I don't know how I ever forgot that."

*　　*　　*

The first week of traffic seemed unending. Bus loads of children visited every day. Chuck, looking for anew avenue of interest, was hanging around the new display window. First a son stricken with polio viewed it with his mother's guiding help. A runaway daughter looked for a place to escape police detection. Day after day the crowds seemed to pass through.

John Harold, who was waiting for a supply truck peeked out the main curator's office door, "Chuck, come on in!"

John looked with a frown and said, "You're worse than those children. They're here for a class trip, you were here too, way back when you were a kid. Now it's your turn to sep up the displays."

Chuck, laughing, "I'm just like they are—drawn for some reason!"

Finding places to walk seemed to be getting harder and harder.

Chuck, working his way behind the window, walked up through the wooden canoes, through the bears; through the wild wolves and finally up at the end of the "Native American Village." One small boy giggled, "He doesn't look right in there."

Reaching carefully for the crystal stone, Chuck placed it next to the wooden tent peg. He removed the dusty, velvet linen from the rotating table. The children on the outside window looked in amazement. Chuck, smiling, wiped the wooden rotating table while replacing the new, clean, red table silk. Facing the crowd, Chuck noticed the homeroom mother's talking in a circle. Picking the stone up, Chuck sees the display of light rays bounce into a spectrum fountain-like appearance. Aware he was being watched, realizing he unconsciously had limited control over the rays of light. After sitting the stone back in position, Chuck aimed a beam of light directly at the homeroom mothers. Positioning the stone in its rotating orifice, he grabbed a bottle of window spray and began cleaning the inside window case. Watching his clock like a hawk, Chuck waited patiently for John Harold to leave for lunch. John usually eats from 11:00 on and usually runs on schedule most days of the week. Slowly walking back through the window casements, one by one, Chuck saw the tall figure make his daily journey. As he walked faster through each window display, Chuck stepped out onto the open tile floor just as John closed the double wooden doors. Walking fast, Chuck breaks for the main office entrance. Arriving just in the nick of tome, Chuck talked to John's secretary.

Seems John was invited to a neighboring museum. Chuck checked on his work party while Donna finished a letter to a Washington museum. She said, "You going to buy lunch?"

Chuck laughed, "Oh! It will be my pleasure. Will it be Turtle burgers, or pterodactyls?

Donna laughed, "I really want a tossed salad and some real coffee."

Chuck said, "Let me check on Joshua, he sometimes goes for some real coffee someplace. He owes me a big one anyway."

Donna laughed, "Why's that?"

Chuck added, "I found a dentist for his daughter at 3:00 a.m. last month."

The phone rang with Donna answering with, "Yes, John? Aha, no, he's not here." Rolling her eyes then laughing she said, "I'll tell him if I see him. No John, no phone calls. Enjoy your luncheon with the art people."

The museum hosted a lot of in house programs and seemed to have a speaker on just about everything. This month special speaker forum will include, Arnold Friends, the topic: "Strings! Do they exist?" Chuck, not interested walked with Donna to the museum luncheonette.

Joshua approached with the coffee and hands the cardboard carton directly to Donna. Joshua chuckled and said, "Just forget him, I'll never get out of debt to him anyway."

Chuck laughed, "That's right, back to work—now you get them stuffed tigers!" Chuck, sitting on a corner table, focused his attention on Donna alone.

Joshua, knowing the body language left immediately. Donna was talking about a television series, and was watching across through the large lunch room window at Arnold Friends.

Chuck, had his back turned. "I wonder if there are such things?" asked Donna.

Chuck, thinking about the television series asked, "What, the unfaithful relationships?"

Donna replied, "No, Chuck, the guy out there in the hall!"

Chuck glanced back and said, "Oh, him!" Then he added, "Who knows?"

Donna listening intently to Chuck as she continuously glanced out the large bay window. Watching the crowds begin to thicken, Donna said, "Excuse me, Chuck, I hate being rude, I want to go listen."

Chuck, again braking his train of thought said, What?" Turning around in the chair looking out the window, Chuck saw the mass of people. Looking back at Donna, who was by now half out the luncheonette, Chuck said, "Donna! Holy Cow, wait!" They pushed through the crowd so they could quickly get to the entrance, Chuck and Donna stood starring. Donna looked over, spotted Joshua from Chuck's work party. Pretending she didn't see anyone, Donna quickly glanced towards the guest speaker.

Chuck, impatiently said, "Look, I'll catch you after work later on."

Donna quickly said, "It will have to be around 7:30.

Chuck laughed, "Why so late?"

Donna added, "I have an old closet over at mom's that needs cleaned out. She's been after me to clean it since last summer."

Chuck joking, "I'll tag along if you like?"

Donna giggled, "I really don't think that would go over too good. I'm not legally divorced yet!"

Chuck, looking bewildered said, "7:30 will be fine!" Heading back out in the main lobby, Chuck used the service elevator to the fourth floor. Walking briskly through the window casements, Chuck found Joshua busy at work. Startled by Chuck's approach, Joshua quickly jumped to his feet. Chuck l laughed, "What you got a guilty conscience?"

Joshua added, "You seeing that woman or something?"

Chuck, puzzled, laughed, "Joshua, worry about something important!" Grabbing the dirty bucket of water, Chuck exited to the water faucet.

Joshua glanced across the other hall and said, "That Indian display case is always busy."

Chuck returned with the bucket and glanced over with out stopping. "Joshua, you ought to see downstairs in front where the forum room is."

Joshua played coy and asked, "Why's that?"

Chuck added, "It's packed! That Arnold Friends guy can really pack a crowd!"

Joshua peered back at the Indian display, "Funny how that one woman keeps standing there talking."

Chuck, looking amused, said, "I'll go check things out." Handing the sponge back to Joshua, Chuck started the long walk back out to the window displays. Walking right up to the young lady, Chuck became immersed, listening to her talk. Wondering her concern, Chuck listened carefully for an opportunity to butt in the conversation. Wilma, a long time resident in the suburbs of Philadelphia, conducts on the spot spiritual quests for her listeners. With her website, Wilma has used her psychic ability to help solve several crimes.

Breaking her continuous lines of unbroken sentences, Wilma glanced warmly over to Chuck, "Please don't let me intimidate you." Then Wilma asked, "You the guy they call Chuck?"

Chuck, looking totally overwhelmed, forgot his train of thought.

Wilma continued, "The spirits in this hall claim you are a fine man."

Chuck looking puzzled, "How can you tell such entities exist?"

Wilma said, "Oh, no doubt—they're here; as a matter of fact, one little boy wants to say hello." Wilma waiting for a rebuttal added, "You helped a lady with her son yesterday and another lady connected spiritually with her runaway daughter."

Chuck listened as he looked back at Joshua behind the adjacent window display. Chuck quipped, "I don't understand."

Wilma replied, "There's a guy downstairs who is discussing the exact same phenomenon."

Chuck paused, "Oh, you mean that Arnold Friends guy?"

Wilma added, "Yea, him."

Chuck continued, "He's hosting the "Existence of Strings Forum.""

Wilma reached for her business card, "I'll be moving on. You get a chance, call me!"

Chuck, still had questions. What about the little boy?

Wilma on the other side of the annex shouted, "Call me."

Joshua walked over to Chuck and laughed, "There's a fool born . . . ."

Chuck waves off Joshua's comment. Joshua looks back picking up an empty bucket, "What else is on you're rush list for today?"

Chuck shrugs his shoulders, "John wants someone to check on the roof repair guy."

Chuck, putting Wilma's business card in the front of his wallet said, "What's the rest of the workers doing?"

Joshua, irritated, said "I'm not in to that, you better go check." Chuck walked off shaking his head. Joshua returned from behind the window casements, and looked for George, the janitor.

George, who was in the basement, returned through the backroom service elevator. Dave shouted, "George! Where the heck you been?"

George, carrying a can of wax said, "I've been busy! I have supplies to bring up."

Joshua looked out the window, "George, you see the Indian display?"

George said, "I've been here several years now, I've never seen that kind of activity."

George said, "There's something to that rock!"

Joshua asked, "Do you think there's any truth to it?"

George looking at his watch, "Joshua, you're holding me up, you know I mentioned the other day that I wish I could find those letters from my son, the one that got killed in Nam. That night when I was bringing in things from my backyard, sure enough like a rock, it just hit me! I must have taken that house apart six times looking for them, and all the time my sister had them!"

Joshua asked, "What's that got to do with an Indian exhibit?"

George quipped, "In my opinion, a lot."

George walked past John Harold who was returning late. John asked, "Hey George! You want to see if that supply truck came in?"

George laughed, "About five hours ago, remember I'm on the midnight shift." Chuck walked towards George and said, "Joshua just told me, just now about the lost letters you found."

George answered, 'Yeah, but Chuck will save that story for tomorrow, I was suppose to be home two hours ago."

Joshua asked Chuck, "Did that Friends guy leave yet?"

Chuck said, "Yea, I don't understand why that guy has so much draw." As they were leaving together Joshua asked Chuck, "Think John made any progress at the meeting ?"

Chuck quipped, "John always has a good meeting. Those museums have nothing but the best people attending. Joshua, I'll call you when I get home. I want to find out some things, if it works out, maybe we'll trade schedules for a Week or two."

Joshua said, "Yeah, that means I get your pay scale, too!"

Chuck, waiting at the elevator, "I wonder what John's got in store for us tomorrow?"

Joshua looked at his watch, "You going over to the club tonight?"

Chuck said, "No, I got some small shit to do, then I'm going to try to catch up with Donna."

Joshua looked disappointed and replied, "Well, if you change your mind, I'll be over by one of the hot spots on the waterfront."

Chuck laughed, "Joshua, I'll let you know, I call you with my cell sometime around 8:00." Joshua walked off, "That will be good."

George, clocking out last asked, "How come I'm never invited?"

Chuck, spinning around, "George, you're always welcome."

Chuck retorted, "Anyway there isn't no-in—the way things work, today you just walk in!"

George getting in his car still quiet, "I'll try that sometime, if it doesn't work, I'll have you bail me out of jail."

Donna walked out the front entrance. Chuck laughed, "I want to go check on something, I'll catch you tomorrow. Waving, he darts over to Donna's car. Out of breath, Chuck asked, "You still going over to your mom's?"

Donna looked up after starting her car, "Yea, Chuck, I'll call you some time around 8:00 p.m."

The morning began with the usual routine. George waxed the far annex first; found himself ahead of schedule. Walking over towards the service elevator he noticed the crowds forming as soon as the museum opened. Today early by the Indian display. A woman was kneeling in total reverence, another waited patiently outside the main curator's office. Suddenly, without fanfare, John Harold stepped through the main double doors of the curator hallway.

George felt a squeeze on his shoulder. He turned slowly around. John Harold laughed, "Ahah! Got you! We're going to have a change of leadership"

George, surprised, "What do you mean?"

John stopping, "Oh, not among you guys. Up here with us. We're going to have a new curator."

George overwhelmed, "Where YOU going?"

John added, "We're having a luncheon at 11:00, I'll give the details then. Make sure to tell Chuck, Joshua and the rest of the work party."

George looked back over towards the crowd, then asked, "It's something to do with that over there, isn't it?"

John, unlocking the curator's main office door said, "Who knows. It's more money . . ." Just as the door latch activated, a tall, thin lady interrupted, "Excuse me."

John turned and asked, "Yes, how may I help you?"

Janet, a lady from a school bus trip said, "I have something important to discuss."

John flicked on the lights and said, "Yes, have a seat over there. Donna, my secretary, will be bringing a fresh pot of coffee up in about two minutes."

Janet seemed very impatient, walked slowly towards the leather couch where the magazines were lying on a heavy, oak end table.

John opened the interior office. He pushed the memory button on his answering service. Donna approached her desk and started conversing with the waiting visitor. John pushed the intercom and asked, "Donna, may I see you a minute?"

Joshua and Chuck opened up the big outside doors and entered the waiting room. They were both upset. Donna looked puzzled and realized something was wrong.

Chuck quipped, "Did he tell you?"

Donna said, "Tell me what?"

Chuck heard the intercoms shriek, "I guess you'll find out."

Within moments, Chuck recognized the woman on the couch. Chuck looked awkward, "You're not here because of me?"

Janet paused, "Well, sort of—in a good way."

Donna returned in tears and looked over to Chuck. Chuck didn't bother to look and remained completely interested and sustained with Janet. Donna, remaining mildly in control, exclaimed, "Chuck!" Donna, not gaining attention, talked louder, "Chuck!"

Chuck, irritated, looked towards Donna. "I know." Then back to Janet. Donna shook her head and talked out loud and said, "How come I'm always the last to know?"

John walked back out into the office waiting room, noticed Chuck in a hurdle. John said, "Chuck! This isn't 11:00." Then looking to the visitor, he added, "Come on in." John glanced over towards Donna, "Hold my calls, will you?"

Donna looked up, cleared her throat and said, "Sure."

John at his main desk pulled the chair out for the guest. Laughing, John said, "I usually offer cigars to the guys. What can I get you? Would you care for some coffee?"

Janet chuckled, 'Yes, coffee, two creams, please."

John summoned the request through the intercom. Then looking back at Janet, "What brings you to my office this early in the morning?"

Janet replied, "It's about the American Indian display."

John chuckled, Yes?"

Janet, seeing John gleam, said, "It helped me find my daughter."

John totally absorbed asked, "How's that?"

Janet continued, "Well, you know last year I lost my daughter. She was gone, no trace! We had all the regular searches going everywhere. I brought her class to the museum as a homeroom chaperone."

John, thinking about Donna, interrupted, "Donna, I'll take a refill." John smiled and said, "Thank you. Go on."

Janet said, "One of my employees, the one you chased out of the lobby-"

John laughed, "You mean Chuck?"

Janet smiled, "He was setting up the display with the stone."

John pointed to Donna handing Janet her coffee. Then added, "Yes, the new Tomahawk display." (John rolled his eyes).

Janet said, "Thanks, Ooh, it's hot! Well—your employee flashed the glare from that stone, trying to be funny, over towards us. We were a group of mothers."

John interrupted, "Thank you, Donna, that that will be all." Looking back to Janet, John looks at Donna exiting the room. Oh, Donna, do me a favor and stick around for awhile, I need a letter written."

Donna said, "I'm not going anywhere." John looked back a second time, "I'm really sorry. Please continue."

Janet went on, "The lady I was standing next to was also a homeroom mother. She was on her hands and knees in front of the display case."

John looked completely puzzled, "Why?"

Janet remarked, "I met her this morning in the parking lot. Her son is stricken with polio, he went for a treatment last week. The doctors thought he was getting a lot worse because of his complaint of pain."

John, totally overwhelmed was staring at Janet.

Janet, almost in tears, "He's having a full recovery!"

John loosened his shirt and rolled back in his chair. Spinning awkwardly in his chair he looked out the window, then back at his wristwatch. Shaking his head, he turned to face the visitor. Janet realized she hit a nerve, waited to continue. John looked to his guest, "It's not even 10:00 a.m. The driveway is full of busses and tourists!" He peered at his coffee cup, "Please continue."

Janet added, "We were joking, that is us girls. We were saying some thing to the effect, (chocked in emotion) 'wouldn't it be nice to have some medicine man help us or something.' That's when Chuck gleamed the reflection off the stone at us."

John remained somewhat skeptical thinking the stone was really the healing help.

Janet, now almost screaming continued, "That night I had a dream about my runaway daughter. She was walking in a desert." Janet was becoming even more emotional, "It wasn't along a road, I mean a *real* desert."

John looked weird and interrupted, "Excuse me, this will only take a minute." Looking out the waiting room into the open corridor, John suddenly panicked, "Donna, what the heck's all this?"

Donna paused, "It's something to do with the Indian display."

Shaking his head, John called for Chuck on the walkie talkie. Looking over to Donna, "Tell Chuck I want to see him." Walking back into the office, John noticed Janet peering out the glass window towards the parking lot. John chuckled, "Don't jump. I've had a lot of havoc this morning." John reached for the chair, "Please sit back down."

Janet, obeying promptly said, "Well, anyway, someone saw her and called the hospital. I saw all this in my dream that very night!"

Janet looked at Donna walking back in the office. John looked up. Donna quipped, "I'm sorry, looking over to Janet. "You got a whole lot of people here."

John looked upset and said, "Tell them I'll be out in ten minutes."

Janet ended with, "Well, I not only saw my daughter while all this was happening, I saw the medical crew, the ambulance, even the name of the hospital."

John said, "Please continue."

Janet looked bewildered, "I didn't have any dreams about anything till after the visit here."

John, unmoved, continued staring.

Janet lifted herself up from the chair and said, "The police, the whole intelligence community, no one had any idea!"

John, not knowing what to say by now simply said, "Well, how can we help you?" Janet looked directly at John and said, "Just one big thanks!"

After Janet left, John asked for Donna to return to the inner office. Donna, totally upset by John's decision to leave, sits in the same chair formerly occupied by Janet. "John, what prompted you to accept?"

John looking awkward, "You must be kidding? I'm closer to home, I have a better benefit package, I'm even more involved in science." John suddenly realizing the pain, "Hey, come on, thanks for the feelings, they're truly appreciated."

Donna looked straight at John, "You don't get it. This museum came to life when you were here."

John looked back out the office window and said, "I don't think there's a problem with life around here. Did Chuck answer the page?"

Donna hesitated, "Yes, he's out in the front annex."

Looking back to Janet, John quipped, "Janet, sincerely thanks!"

Janet smiled, "No, thank you!"

Donna, handing John the walkie talkie, "What on earth was all that about?"

John looking smothered said, "You really don't want to know." Then looking at his watch, "Call them in for the meeting, I'm going for a "squeezing" walk in the annex. We'll treat them to lunch with pizza and chicken"

John pushed through the packed room. When he made it to the window casements, he quickly walked by the moose, the bear and the wolverines. Then he stumbled on to Joshua. John looking upset said, "Don't anybody relay messages around here? We're having lunch in the main visitor dining room."

Joshua said, "I think Chuck's going to quit."

John, overwhelmed, "Why on earth would he want to do that?"

Joshua shrugged his shoulders.

John added, "I'll have a talk with him." He glanced out the adjacent window and noticed a lady praying on her knees. John looked back to Joshua, "What's all this about?"

Joshua hesitated, "She claims her son has had a miraculous recovery from polio."

John, banging on the glass said, "I got to get someone to make her leave."

Joshua chuckled, "I already have enough assignment to last two days."

John walked back through the wolverines, the bear, then the moose. Waiting for the elevator to open, he realized it was empty. Shaking his head, he quickly squeezed through the crowd back to his office. When he got back to the office, he yelled, "What's all this about?"

Donna said, "I told you before you took your stroll, you had visitors."

John forced his office door open and remarked, "Donna, send them all in." Reaching for his now cold cup of coffee, he summoned for Donna on the intercom, "Donna, any luck rounding up the crews? Where the heck's Chuck?"

Chuck finally entered the outside office with Donna. Donna excitedly said, "John's really upset and on the war path! Where you been all morning?"

Chuck said, "I've had an endless succession of emergencies since I walked in the museum door!"

Donna pointed to the curator's office door. John returned to his swivel chair and weeded through the crowds requests. He said, "Museum Gazette" wants to ask you question in about twenty minutes downstairs."

John, looking straight through the crowd saw Chuck. "Chuck! Where the hell you been?"

Chuck totally fuming said, "John, (shaking his head) it's been one upside down morning."

John laughed, "Join the club!" Then looking back at the irritated news media said, "People—relax! We have a very distinguished curator coming on board. She'll do a lot more for this museum than what I've been able to do." Looking over to one lady reaching up with her hand, John asked, "Yes?"

The lady said, "I'm with the "Tribune," will the museum have a funding implement for expansion this spring as the board promised?"

John answered, "No, I don't think so. We're having a budget problem connected to the present exhibits." Looking around John paused, "I'll be here shortly after 1:30 for the rest of you." Then John looked towards Donna, "Please no more questions."

After returning from lunch back at his office, John pointed to the main curator hall door and more news people, "People, thank you all very much for your support these last couple years."

After the meeting, Joshua retuned to window casements to lock up supplies. He noticed the display room annex was filled with tourists. People were amazed by the stone. They were standing and staring. Betty, another lady in deep prayer, finally returned to her feet. Chuck, Donna and most of the employees were now in the main meeting room. George walks through the elevator pauses with a quick glance of the floor, yawns finding Joshua in a trance, several windows down George tapped him on the shoulder. George said, "Come on! We're going to be late!"

Joshua, returned to reality and remarked, "You didn't see that?"

George asked, "See what?"

Joshua shook his head, "That kid."

George looked around quickly, "What kid?"

Joshua furthered with, "Some little kid walked up here somewhere and disappeared."

George laughed, "I got just the solution. How bout some fresh coffee and late lunch on John! Then added, "Plus, I still want to work here, how bout you?"

Joshua, emotionally upset, walked out through each casement with George. First the wolverines, then the bears, and finally the moose. Turning the key to the service elevator, George realized the elevator was right at their very floor. George looked back, still noticing Joshua staring out behind towards the Indian Display. George laughs, "Can't beat that for service."

John, entering the dinner hall, excused himself. He said, with a big smirk, "If I can't talk Chuck into staying on, one of you two are next up for the team l leader position." Then John began his speech, "Ladies and Gentlemen, I hope you enjoy your meal. It's our last one together. I'm leaving first of the month for my new position in New York." Looking over to Chuck, "If we can't solve Chuck's ambitions to leave, well, I guess Chuck ; you're going to!"

Chuck, a little embarrassed smiled while talking to Donna.

George asked, "Who's the new guy?"

John looked awkward and replied, "We sort of got a switch deal."

George asked, "What?" The room suddenly became quiet.

John added, "I'm leaving for New York, closer to home. I'd like to introduce your new curator. He'll start in two weeks. I want to thank him for making a special trip from New York to meet all of you. By the way, he's a she!" John said laughing. A tall, thin lady slowly approached the podium. John said, "May I please have a round of applause for Miss Pauline Johnson!"

"Hello, everyone, my name is Pauline Johnson. I've met most of you, sometime ago. The rest of you, I'm looking forward to meeting. Can we go around the table and sort of introduce ourselves?"

Looking at her left, Donna was first. Donna quipped, "Hello, my name is Donna, I'm the secretary to the curator." Chuck looking up said, "Hello, my name is Chuck. I'm the display room project coordinator. I've been here 6 years now but I may be leaving for another job. And—oh yes, I'm the team leader!"

The group was made up of both sexes and several cultures. Ending with George, he said, "Hello, everyone, my name is George. I work mostly as a janitor. I've been here since this place was a parking lot! I want to say, I'll surely miss John, who has helped me with scheduling and a lot of other things, too,"

Chuck, thinking carefully, said, "Ah, Pauline, what's your background with museums?"

Pauline, not expecting a challenge paused. "Well, I'm an undergraduate of World Cultures University, I've been employed the last 3 years with the museum that John's going to. I have done several field archeology studies."

George, looked leery and raised his hand. "You think you can run a big place like this?"

Pauline, grasping for thoughts, "I hope not to be alone. I'll have the regular budget people, the regular management staff and most important—all of you."

George said, "I don't want to be rude, but did you say regular budget people?"

Pauline said, "I'm sorry, I forgot to mention, the rest of the team, even junior understudies coming along."

John, unaware of the total picture remained quiet.

Chuck looked over to John, "How come you didn't mention any of this?"

John, fiddling with his pen, "Chuck, I haven't had time to call home."

George looked over to Donna, "What's your view of all this? Who's going to pay the salaries?"

Pauline quickly said, "Most of them are paid through grants. The budget comes under the state funding."

John, holding his tongue, breath, and emotions remained quiet.

Chuck looked upset and shook his head. "Now you see why museums have a hard time attracting new help?"

John Harold looking hurt, "Chuck, I agree with what you're talking about."

Donna, kicked John's leg and glanced down at her wristwatch.

John, glanced down and said, "Oh, I'm sorry people, we have to close our meeting. If anyone is having qualms, we'll try to settle them before my departure. If that doesn't work, we'll hold another afternoon meal like this one!"

Pauline, still standing next to the speaker, "It's my sincere pleasure to be here. Thanks for coming!"

Chuck signaled to a group of workers to help clean up.

Donna exited and quickly shook Pauline's hand. John Harold signaled for Chuck and said, "Donna, I'm sure things will be fine, they're a fine bunch of people." Then looked to Chuck who said, 'Can't we discuss this some other time?" He looked at George then said, "George has questions; I'm sort of under the gun to."

John threw his hand up and then put them on his hips and said, "I think you're just a little shocked."

George quickly said, "You going to come back if she can't run this place?"

John, turning red, "Absolutely not! George! You know that I'm not like that!"

George said, "Yea, but all them hot shots are the same. I sure hope you're right!! George cut John off and headed towards the open main entrance. Looking towards Joshua, George glanced back. "Excuse me, John." Then he ran to catch up with Joshua. Joshua talking to a worker, glanced over towards George. Joshua grabbed a newspaper and started to wait in line. George rushed up and grabbed Joshua by the shoulders. "Wait up!" George, rushing to clock out, walked back and grabbed a newspaper, too. "That was some chicken and pizza!"

Joshua looked behind at George and said, "I don't know why they just don't condemn this place and build another sports stadium."

George rub his eye then laughed, "I'm going to leave that alone."

Joshua furthered with, "That woman doesn't know a thing!" Joshua looked at the female behind the counter and said, "No, honey, we're talking about some one else." He then paid for the newspaper.

Chuck reached the two in time and looked back to see if Donna was coming.

George annoyed quipped, "She's probably catching flack off John,"

Chuck smiled, "No, I think John's quiet as a mouse."

Joshua and Chuck both started laughing. Joshua said, "John didn't know about all this stuff."

George added, "He thinks anyone can just walk in and do this stuff." George walked down the steps land looked over to Chuck, "Bet you're glad you're leaving!"

Chuck smiled and looked over to Joshua, "George, you're a troublemaker!"

Joshua walked towards his truck—glanced over to the other museum. George and Chuck were still waiting for Donna. Joshua asked, "Wonder if those people over there have the same problems?"

George shouted back overtop Joshua's loud truck engine, "I doubt it!"

Joshua, spinning his truck tires, headed out onto the busy highway.

Chuck looked the other way with his arms hanging over his own driver's door. He said, "I know it's going to be a tough transition."

George laughed, "Chuck, I got to be going." Chuck smiled.

George tapped the horn and pointed over to Donna for Chuck to notice. George ran over to the car. "We'll get some of this stuff ironed out before Joshua takes over."

Chuck looked startled, "Joshua or you, takes over?"

George furthered with, "You don't think I'm gong to run around like some kid checking on everybody."

Chuck looked puzzled, 'Yes, we'll get some of this stuff ironed out tomorrow."

George looked up and noticed Donna. "Hey Chuck, have a good night." Donna waved to George and said, 'Chuck, I don't expect you to wait on me. I guess Joshua already left." Donna looked back towards the building and said, "Gosh, the whole parking lot's empty! I couldn't get free. That Pauline talks and talks. John, I thought he was going to sprout wings and jump out the office bay window!"

Chuck silent glanced at Donna, "You gong to call me?"

Donna looked back towards the road with all the traffic and laughed, "Yea. what time?"

Chuck added, "I got to catch up with Joshua and grab something to eat. How's seafood?"

Donna giggled, "You're not bringing Him?"

Chuck burst out laughing, "Are you bringing Pauline?" Kissing her on the cheek, he said, 'I'll call you around 7:00 p.m." Chuck revved the sports car and sped towards the highway.

Donna rolled up the car's window and started her ascent from the hill to the highway. Glancing at her clock, she was stuck in traffic! She grabbed her cell phone, "Mom, I'm really sorry, a late afternoon meeting about change in command ran real late! I'll see you in about twenty minutes. I have to stop for gas."

The next two weeks flew by. Chuck decided to stay till well after John's transfer. Joshua, uneasy about the new curator warned Chuck to make an extra space for him in case things didn't work out. Finally, John Harold's last day arrived. George didn't arrived around 3:00 a.m. and began his usual cleaning job.

When Donna visited the main curator's office she said, "John, when you leave, who's going to make coffee for you?"

John chuckled, "My wife! I won't be leaving the house for an extra 40 minutes. That's long enough for a whole lot of things!"

Donna laughed, "We're going to miss you.

John chuckled, "Funny now that I'm leaving, Chucks' leaving, too!"

Donna said, "Same reason sort of, he wants to attend school this fall."

John looked out the window, "Wonder what makes this place so interesting?"

Donna entered the office slowly and walked towards the large window. "It won't be now that you're going."

John glanced back, "You'll give her a chance, won't you?"

Donna laughed, then hesitated before she said, "I think that's the kind of question you should be asking her."

Chuck knocked on the office door. He was told to enter.

John looked around the room and noticed the cigar case. Reaching for the box, Chuck laughed and said, "I need something stronger than those things!"

John chuckled, "Well, here, we'll smoke two at a time."

Donna said, 'Let me get out of her first" As she walked towards the door, Joshua grabbed the knob. "Come on in, Joshua, I was just getting ready to leave.:"

Joshua, a bit anxious said, "Chuck, where's the long ladder at?"

"It's in the basement behind the large oil tank," said Chuck.

Joshua asked, "What about the reachers? You know, the things we use to pull the chandelier's closer."

Chuck laughed, "I got work to do, I'll call you late tonight, Good luck, John."

John peered out towards the parking lot through the big picture window, "Donna, tell George I want to see him." Walking with his large cigar still in his chops, John threw his suite jacket over the swivel chair. As he walked towards the fish tank, he heard someone knock on the door. "If that's you, come on in."

Pauline walked in and said, "John, I hope you showed me all I need to know."

John laughed, "That's why they call it a museum. We come here to learn."

Pauline asked, "This place is really something. I love the panoramic view. What's over there?"

John turned from the fish tank and said, "Wait a minute." Again a knock on the door. "If that's you, George, come on in!" John opened the door. Then he said angrily, Come on in!"

George hesitated at first, then started through the door.

John looked out the window and rolled his eyes, "That's Independence Hall," he said, looking at Pauline. He then looked back to George.

"Pauline, would you excuse us for a minute?"

Pauline, turning red, "Yes, of course."

Closing the door, John reached for the cigar box. "Here, take one home with you."

George waved the box with his hand. "What's up with the changing of the displays?"

John asked, "What do you mean?"

George said, "She wants the animals downstairs. Says there's not enough room."

John looked shaken, "Play the game, George."

George said, "That's a lot of work." John grabbed another cigar, "I told her to lay each room out on the computer software, if she wants the animals downstairs."

George interrupted, "You better get me some help," and stormed out of the office.

John threw his lit cigar in the trash and called for the temporary services. Pauline came out of the secretary's lobby and knocked on the door. John returned to the intercom, "Donna, tell Pauline to come on in." John answering the other end of the telephone waved for Pauline to have a seat. She heard him say, "That will be good, first thing tomorrow. O.K. Thank you." He looked at Pauline. "We have plenty of help." He pulled his pen through his fingers and moved sideways. "Pauline, Pauline. Did you bring enough people with you to run the whole museum?" He paused, "I sure hope so."

Pauline remarked, "There are five other work parties in this building. They can't be used?""

John laughed, "That place you come from has nearly five times as many work parties. Do they get used?" John waited for an answer.

She said, "Only when all other means have been expended."

John added, "I want a peaceful transition, not a disaster! You're a fine, young lady with a good background." He jumped to his feet and circled the desk. "This place is very upbeat. The town hosts a whole lot of events here and we want to keep good public relations." Pauline looked off to the side and said, "John, do you think I should apologize?"

John said, "The whole point is, most of these employees are old timers. He walked over to Pauline and held her shoulder, then he glanced out the window. "We need fresh blood and you're it!" Then someone knocked on the door. "Come in!" He said." Then, "Pauline most of these employees spend free hours on special projects. The younger ones even have families and second jobs." John looked at Donna, "Who's out there?"

Donna said, "The Mayor."

John looked back out the window, "Give them a chance to get use to you," he said talking to Pauline. He reached for the intercom. 'Donna, don't keep city hall waiting, tell him to come in."

Pauline greeted the Mayor, "Hello, I'm Pauline Johnson, the new curator. It' a pleasure to meet you."

John, reaching for the cigar box, noticed it was empty. Laughing, John shook his head and said, "I'm sorry, Mr. Mayor, we sort of over did the cigars. Would you like some fresh coffee?"

The mayor grabbed John around the shoulders looked over to Pauline, "This guy was great! Filling his shoes will be tough for anyone."

Pauline nodded, 'I hope I can."

The mayor added, "Any help you need that we can provide, please ask. We owe it to John!"

The Mayor, walking back out towards the secretary, was greeted with an autograph request. Stopping to look back at John Harold, the Mayor asked, "Where's that new exhibit with the tomahawk?"

The secretary and John answered in unison, "Around to your left, straight down the hall."

Exiting, as if on cue, John breathed a sigh of relief. Walking towards Donna, John looked back at Pauline, now behind his old desk. John remarked, "Donna, it's been my pleasure, I'm out of here!" Grabbing his package of peanuts and laughing he said, "I better eat them before I get help." Walking out to the main elevator, he glanced toward the main floor of the museum.

Peering down by the end, John noticed the Mayor, along with a group of people. Looking up, the Mayor said, "Take care John."

John waved before boarding the elevator. Moments later, he walked the main corridor towards the front lobby. Pauline, using the intercom shouts, "Please say good-bye and wish our friend luck." Moments later news media and reporters flocked him as he walked towards the main entrance. John humbled, said, "It's been my privilege." Walking out front, one lady from a local newspaper stopped John in his tracks. "John, do you think the Mayor enjoyed his visit?"

John laughed, "Well, if he didn't he's a good actor!"

Pauline watched from the office window. Returning to her desk, she summoned Donna immediately. Donna walked in within moments and found Pauline feeding the fish. Pauline turned, startled, "Oh, excuse me, I didn't think you'd come in that quick."

Donna chuckled, "I want you to feel right at home."

Pauline said, "I sort of started off on the wrong foot." Replacing the lid on the aquarium, she continued, "I came on too strong." Walking back to her desk, "I really have my own agenda, that's all."

Donna, reached for the empty coffee cup. Pauline said, "That was good coffee. I want to use the entire east third floor for the native American displays. Maybe special emphasis on the stone.

Donna, wanting to leave, kept stopping in her walk out. Pauline looked back out the window. "See those crowds? 40% of them are here for no other reason than the stone."

Donna said, "Miss Johnson, I'll get Joshua, Chuck, or George if he hasn't left yet."

Pauline looked puzzled, "Left yet?"

Donna replied, "Oh, he's usually in around 4:30 a.m. so the floors get stripped and waxed."

Pauline again, "Everyday?"

Donna replied, "Well, I think so. The traffic does a number on them."

Pauline paused, "Yes, Donna I'll start with George."

Donna returned to her desk and summoned Chuck on the short wave to check on George. Moments later, Donna let Pauline know of George's presence. Donna making light, "Go ahead, you're first."

George quipped, "That's just great." Laughing as he walked towards the now open door. Entering, Pauline looked over to a book lying over on her desk. Peering up, she stood leaning across the desk, not breaking her stare at the book. She extended her hand for a warm welcome. "I'm sorry, we started out on the wrong foot."

George refused to shake and remained seated.

Pauline drew her hand back quickly and said, "When it's all said and done, we leave here."

George asked, "What? Pauline, I want a good working relationship and a lot of input."

Pauline said, "It's about getting a lot of work done. It's about hiring a lot of temporary help, having them try a few schemes and maybe if I can create enough interest a new roof!"

George, sitting quietly looked at his watch, "I can only help on the things you let us. We tried right off the bat to help, but you had your own ideas."

Pauline paged Donna and said, "Hold my calls, will you?" Waiting for a reply, "Yes, thank you." Pauline looked across at George, "I hear you do an excellent job with the floors."

George said, "What's that got to do with this?"

Pauline started in, "George, here's the plan—I'll run it past you. John called the temporary help. Under all the changes, all animals will be in storage or on some other floor. The ancient Egypt collection goes with different displays where the Native American displays are now. The Native American displays will go on the other side where the floors are better and there's more room."

George shook his head, "The Egyptian cascades are so heavy and cumbersome! You'll have the Egyptian Mummies in with the Native Americans."

Pauline said, "No, George, you don't have to bring everything up from downstairs, just the main theme stuff. People like going on a treasure hunt. I'm going to convince Joshua. I want a unique "see through" display for the tomahawk."

George looked up towards the ceiling, "Will that be all?"

Pauline extended her hand, "Yes, that will be all, George."

Looking back down from the ceiling, George shook her hand warmly and said, "Enjoy your stay here."

Pauline reached for the door. "George, tell Donna to find Chuck."

George looked at his wristwatch and then looked back at Pauline. He said, "Chuck had a dentist appointment. I'll check when I go back out."

Pauline said, "Thank you." Then she pushed the button on the intercom. She heard, "I'm sorry, Pauline, Chuck left early today for a dentist appointment." Pauline looked uneasy and walked out in the hall. "I'm going for a go down stairs. Take any calls, Donna." Taking the service elevator, Pauline visited the museum roof. Walking along the narrow cement walkway, Pauline walked the several blocks of storm damage. Startled by a rush of pigeons and a distant fire siren, she reached the end. Using her fingernail she gently lifted a piece of the loose roof. Rubbing her face with the back of her hand, she started down the other side. Reaching a sunroof, she looked puzzled then stopped to examine it. Taking notes on a paper, she slowly reached the front main roof entrance.

Moved by the many buses of tourists many stories below, Pauline got a second idea. Running back to the service elevator, she returned to the office fourth floor. Walking down towards the crowded floor annex, she veered and Opens the door to her office.

The following morning, Pauline arrived extra early. She smiled as she passed George in the main lobby. Walking across the floor, she turned and remarked, "Good job on the floors!"

George looked up from his work and said, "Awful early this morning—Miss Johnson."

Pauline, holding her office keys replied, "That's right, George, couldn't sleep." Looking closer she said, "Gosh George, You've already done the whole other side?"

George laughed, "The sooner I get started, the sooner I get to finish up." Pausing he noticed Pauline still standing there. "Oh, that is, Miss Johnson, before the traffic gets bad."

Pauline glanced the main lobby, "What time does the rest of the crews get here?"

George looked around. "It all depends on the day's activities. We get supplies on certain days."

Chuck walked in next and rolled his eyes behind Pauline's back. Chuck quipped, "Excuse me, Good morning, Miss Johnson. George, the sirens need turned off."

Pauline jumped, "Chuck, you're early, too."

Chuck smiled, "I want to leave this place looking good."

George said, "This is Chuck's last week."

Pauline said, "I guess that puts Joshua in charge of the work crews?"

Chuck laughed, "He'll do a fine job, very energetic."

George, returning to work, slowly walked past Chuck and Pauline.

Opening the door, Pauline threw her pocket book down and reached for the light switch. She opened the interior office door using a memorized code. Turning the light on, Pauline opened the showcase window. Getting the desk light on, the stereo playing and the thermostat set, she slowly walked back out to Donna's office. She stopped momentarily then headed out the Curator's office door straight for the Indian display. Taking long, slender strides, she reached the display within moments. Peering in the window case almost in a trance, Pauline read the history placard. Stepping back, George walked up from behind. Pauline glanced over and said, "I wonder if any of this is true?"

George, wiping dust away, said, "Oh, yes, Miss Johnson, more than I ever thought."

Pauline puzzled, asked, "How do you mean?"

George laughed, "Promise you won't make fun."

Pauline looked with a smirk and crossed her heart, "Promise."

George continued, "When it first arrived, I was skeptical, too. It helped me remember my lost son's letters from Nam and some pictures! It wasn't even twenty four hours later that I remembered where I had put them!"

Pauline, not breaking her stare, George added, "I was preparing to sell my property. I was afraid I'd leave them someplace before I sold. I was walking in from the back yard and it hit me like a rock!" George, not bothering to finish started cleaning again.

Pauline, still interested, "Go on George, finish your story."

George looked up, "Oh, I'm sorry, my sister had them, I had given them to her several Thanksgiving seasons back."

Pauline looked around at George frowning, "You think the stone really had anything to do with that?"

George chuckled, "It sounds far fetched, but I made a visit here one night shortly before selling my property. I said to the stone, "If you have any powers help me find my son's letters""

Pauline shook her head, "So the next day you remembered?"

George, finishing the semicircle of window casements said, "It's like I looked for several years the same spots over and over! Here the whole time, my sister had them!"

Pauline looked back into the glass, "Do you know how we got so lucky?"

George laughed, "That's right, luck, that's all."

Pauline walked quickly back towards the end of the hall to her office. George headed downstairs for the break room.

Chuck, cutting her off at the main door asked, "You want to talk about something?"

Pauline replied, "Yeah, Chuck, good timing!" She opened the secretary's office door and walked over an opened the main curator's office door next. Pauline noticed Donna's belongings, looked at Chuck and said, "She might be bringing up coffee."

Chuck looked at Pauline curiously and headed straight to the fish tank.

Pauline noticed the messages mounting, and looked over at Chuck. "Gosh, I have two messages and it's not even 8:30 a.m. yet."

Chuck walking over to the chair in front of Pauline's desk, flopped down. Pauline returned to her desk, pushed down the intercom. "Donna, are you there?"

Moments later there was a knock, Pauline yelled, "Come on in!"

Donna, pushing a wheel cart brought in hot coffee and fresh donuts from the kitchen. Donna yelled, "Surprise!"

Chuck, smiling, "Wow, Miss Johnson, first week on the job."

Donna remarked, "Compliments of the luncheonette downstairs on your first week."

Pauline, felt welcome. "Thank them for me, better yet, I'll pay them a visit. Thanks Donna."

Donna waved, closing the main office door.

Chuck, impatient to get started, asked Pauline, "What's on your mind?"

Pauline, chocking on the thought "Give me a chance to get some blood flowing." Rushing over to the sink near the fish aquarium, Pauline grabbed paper towels and ran to her swivel chair. Looking over at Chuck she said, "I'm ready." She started, 'I want to bring about some changes in the actual displays."

Chuck sipping his coffee, walked over to the tray for more.

Pauline said, "It's going to require an enormous amount of manpower, but thanks to John (before me left), I have a whole army of temp. people."

Chuck listening remained quiet.

Pauline walked over to the large bay window, "I want to make more room for certain things which attract the most people."

Chuck laughed, "How on earth you going to do that?"

Pauline looked back from the window and walked over to the chair. "Earlier this week I spoke to George about it."

Chuck cut her off. "Where you going to put the animals?"

Pauline said, "The basement for a start."

Chuck quipped, "What I would do is rent storage some place till you're sure what you're going to use."

Pauline excitedly said, "That's a good idea."

Chuck said, "I certainly wouldn't even think about moving the Egyptian mummies."

Pauline jumped up, ran around and started pouring another cup of coffee. "Hold that thought," she said.

Pauline walked out and asked Donna, "Would you check on places in the area that have rental storage?"

Donna looked up, "Rental storage?"

Pauline added, "Yeah, we're going to see if we can't put some of the things in a temporary storage until some major changes take place. About 25,000 sq, feet to start."

Donna looking carefully said, "Sure thing!"

Returning to her desk, Pauline asked, "Where were we?" Then added, giggling, "The mummies."

Chuck interrupted, "There aint enough room for even half of the Egyptian displays."

Pauline paused, "Maybe we don't want to promote that theme anymore."

Chuck looked lost and stared across at Pauline. He yawned and said, "What do you mean?"

Pauline added, "Here, I'll show you."

Chuck walked around the desk, saw a computer layout of each museum floor.

Pauline said, "Here's the room I want for the Indian displays."

Chuck looked without a clue, "Where in the east room?"

Pauline giggled, "You're a quick study." She then brought in a side view up that showed the reinforced flooring. "See Chuck, this floor was build to have a little extra weight." Chuck paused as Pauline added, "If we put the stone on the east side, that leaves the whole west room for the Egyptian displays."

Chuck looked at Pauline in a frown, "But the Egyptian displays are way too heavy!"

Interrupted by a knock on the door, Pauline opened it as she said "Come in!"

Joshua walked in and asked, "Chuck, you busy?"

Chuck looked to Joshua, "No, what's up?"

Joshua said, "George wants to know if he can leave?"

Chuck looked around for a clock, "Why, of course. How are things out there?"

Joshua replied, 'Very busy."

Pauline looked at Chuck, and said, "Do you think he needs help?"

Chuck looking upside down at Joshua's wristwatch replied, "No, they should be going to break about now, plus George should be going home."

Chuck looked at Joshua, "I'm going to be awhile, you going to be O.K.?"

Joshua looked anxious and said, "Yeah, Chuck, take whatever you need."

Chuck looked at Joshua, "Say good-bye, Joshua."

Joshua laughed, "Good-bye."

Chuck looked back at Pauline and said, "The Egyptian displays will be way too heavy, and especially in the west room annex. Chuck, we're not bringing up the heavy stuff, just the main theme items.

Chuck said, "What's the point of all this change?"

Pauline said, "We're improving our image and enhancing our displays to create the most spectacular exhibits anywhere and hopefully create the enticement to get a new roof East!"

Chuck laughed, "Money."

Pauline snapped, "No! A new roof!"

Walking back to his chair, Chuck asked, "Is there anything else?"

Pauline added, "I know you're leaving for good this Friday, if you get a chance without falling off, go check the roof."

Chuck shook his head and waved his hands, "I'll take your word for it."

Pauline paged Donna through the intercom, "Donna, how's the storage coming?" Pauline looked over to Chuck, threw up her index finger and said, "Wait! One more thing. My interest is in making the Native American display a special area. We'll get our roof in no time."

Chuck looked towards the office door and said, "yea, right!"

Pauline added, "After lunch, would you send Joshua up?"

Chuck laughed, "He should be finishing up break."

Pauline added, "Yeah well, whenever he can get free, before 2:00."

Donna bumped into Chuck as she opened the door. "Excuse me, Chuck, I didn't know you were there."

Chuck held the door and said, "She's all yours!"

Pauline, in a burst of emotion quipped, "Thank you, Chuck."

Donna brought in a list of local storage companies. Donna pointed to one and remarked, "This new guy is closer, cheaper and much safer."

Pauline asked, "Is he available immediately?"

Donna replied, "He's got more than 25,000 sq. ft., too."

Pauline smiled and said, "Thank you, will you page Joshua?"

Donna nodded and walked towards the door. Pauline looked at the dirty cups in the sink and began rinsing them while waiting for the storage company to answer. As soon as the phone rang, she heard, "Yes, we were calling you back about the storage."

Pauline said, "Would you have someone meet us sometime this week? That's great! Thank you!" Turning around to her left, Pauline noticed Joshua standing at the door. Pauline quipped, "Please Joshua, have a seat." Joshua walked in and sat in the red, velvet chair. Pauline joked, "When John left he took the cigars with him. We'll be working closely for a couple months to rearrange a few displays."

Joshua jumped up. "Wow!" Do you want what's being done now?"

Pauline answered, "Yes, as a matter of fact. I'm bringing in a whole army of temporary help for the main changes; the bull work." She looked straight over at Joshua. "I need people to make the transition run smoothly."

Joshua looked annoyed, "Why so many changes so quickly?"

Pauline glanced back across the desk, ""Joshua, we're running out of time on a few things. I spoke to George and Chuck. It should go pretty smooth except for the part where I bring in the carpenters."

Joshua quipped, "I haven't the slightest idea what you're talking about."

Pauline continued, "I would have let you know first what changes would have been forthcoming, but I was afraid you'd hear it through the rumor mill."

Joshua smiled, "Rumor mill?"

Pauline glanced at the secretary's door, "Hold up a minute. Looking at Joshua she said, "What the heck is all that? I can actually feel the floor and walls moving."

Joshua smiled, "That's the excitement that Indian thing creates."

Pauline said, "Anyhow, I have a software program and I'll show you on here."

Joshua walked around the desk, moments later Donna walked in the door and said, "Pauline, I'm leaving early today, if that's O.K. Something weird on the home front."

Pauline looked across at her, "Yeah, that will be fine, Donna." Looking back to Chuck walking over by the fish tank, she added, "Joshua! I already ran this past everyone except the town mouse."

Chuck looked back at her, "Though I'm out of here Friday, I'm for whatever is best interest of the museum."

Pauline continued, "Do me the honors and come here a minute."

Chuck walked slowly from the fish tank, glanced at the office artifacts on her desk and remarked, "Is that real amber?"

Pauline quipped, "Yes, it is! There's suppose to be a caterpillar in there."

Chuck continued his walk and tripped over the plastic overlay under Pauline's swivel chair. Pauline pointed to her computer as Joshua almost collided into her desk.

Pauline laughed, "Pick up your feet!"

Chuck chuckled, "I do! Looking at the computer Joshua asked, "So that's the west room?"

Pauline added, "Yes, here's the side view of the room from a structural standpoint."

Joshua looked closer, then added, "Wow! Much stronger!"

Pauline quipped, "Precisely. I want to use the west room for all the Native American displays. I can bring up a good percentage of the Egyptian things for the east room."

Joshua retorted, "How on earth—? George has a bad back!"

Pauline interrupted, "No! We ordered three squads of temporary help."

Joshua looked puzzled, "What's the big push for the Native American stuff?"

Pauline looked back from the computer, "Well, thanks to John's promotional idea, the stone has become sort of a national treasure!" Joshua was silent; Pauline added, "The west wing annex is much better equipped for a larger display and with more up to date wiring. If we generate enough interest, we can go to the state and other donations for help." Changing the computer screen to the roof picture, Pauline asked, "Have you been on the roof lately?"

Chuck shrugged his shoulders. Pauline quipped, "It's so bad the pigeons don't sit up there."

Chuck smiled as Pauline said, "We're going to be forced to fix the roof or move."

Joshua picked up the amber, "Why can't we fix part of the roof, maybe in sections?"

Pauline was silent, then she said, "Whatever works, Joshua"

Joshua walked over to the aquarium, rinsed his hands off in the sink then said, "Wonder if I can talk George into staying over or maybe working daylight for a couple months?"

Pauline, looking out the window, "Joshua, whatever makes things Happen. Too many people can be as bad as not enough."

Joshua, looking renewed, "Am I dismissed?"

Pauline laughed, "Of course, thank you." Pauline walked out behind Chuck and realized Donna's early departure. Walking slowly out into the museum's west annex, Pauline began visualizing the new exhibit. Jotting notes In her head, she envisioned the new lighting and the elevated walk-up display with the magnifying invisible mirrors. She envisioned listening to a prerecorded message of Native American folk lure with the drums beating in the background and finally introduction to the stone.

Chuck and Joshua were conversing in the hall behind the window on the east room side. In agreement, they headed first to the curator's office. No one present, so they walked back around the main floor. Joshua quipped, "I'll check the west annex." Chuck, helping a tourist, waved and nodded his head.

Joshua returning added, "'Yeah, Chuck, she's in the west room." Both ran towards the entrance. When they reached her, Joshua tapped her on the shoulder, "Miss Johnson, anything else for today?"

Pauline looked around and said, "Any luck?"

Joshua, all smiles, "Yes, Chuck's going to have a talk with him in the mornings."

Pauline turned around and said, "Thanks Joshua, I really appreciate the extra support."

All three walked back towards the main curator when Chuck said, "People, I have to go. I have to check on my register for classes this afternoon."

Pauline, now curious, "What did you say your were studying?"

Chuck returned, "I'm eventually going for a major in archaeology."

Pauline laughed, "Good field."

Chuck asked, "What's that place like you came from?"

Pauline signaled, "Come in, you got a minute?"

Chuck and Joshua both followed her through Donna's now vacant office. Pauline turned on Donna's secretary light, "It's different—there the sky's the limit, but you'll seem never a real part of a team. Here it's the other way around."

Chuck laughed, "You lost me on that one."

Pauline sat down in Donna's chair. "It's so big you could feel like a tourist and be working on some project for ten years. There's not much interrelations."

Chuck curious, "You mean, there's a lot of colleges and undergraduate work doing their own thing?"

Pauline chuckled, "Yeah, exactly. I'd hoped for something more subtle."

Chuck laughed, "More boring?"

Pauline looked over and said, "More controlled. We really never get to know anyone."

Chuck looked around and come back with, "Yeah, that's great for people like us. This place just doesn't draw the big name sponsors."

Pauline added, "That might change in the not too distance future."

Chuck looked at his wristwatch and remarked, "I must be going, Miss Johnson." He looked at Joshua, "You got everything wrapped up?"

Joshua, returning from a daydream said, "Yes, yea, I do."

Leaving quickly, Pauline waked into her main office and checked her messages. She quickly returned to Donna's office and locked her curator's office door. Glimpsing at the wall, she noticed an old picture of John holding a large mounted Marlin. Shaking her head, she walked out in the hall. Exiting through the service elevator, she walked straight to her car. Chuck hurriedly waited by his vehicle. Joshua stopped downstairs to clock out and buy a paper. The cashier said, "How's your new boss?"

Joshua hesitant at first, "It's really way too early to tell,"

The other cashier laughed and said, "I thought she was with the clean up crews."

Joshua looked over as he paid for his newspaper. "How's that?"

The girl again, "She was in here before I was. I thought she was a burglar or maybe one of us."

Joshua waved with his free hand and walked out the glass revolving door.

The following week, things began to take on a different dimension. Pauline received a phone call informing her of the temporary help. Donna received notice after notice of letters from people wishing John well. Chuck arrived for the morning work and was greeted by a manager from the temporary service. George, aware of the moving, refrained from waxing the floors. Joshua was getting use to his new appointment as supervisor, but overwhelmed by the large crowd of temporary workers. Carpenters arrived around 8:00 and were lead to the west annex to begin clearing the old glass displays and measuring for the new showcase. Pauline greeted the manager of the temp. people and walked Pete to the west annex. Pete walked casually, but stopped at the west room's door. "These door are awfully small!"

Pauline noticed his quick study and asked," what do you think would help?" Pete shrugs, "If it will be any help, I'll have the carpenters remove the whole entrance wall,"

Joshua glanced back at Pete, who nodded his head, "Yeah, that would help a lot!" Pete ran through the room and summoned the carpenters. Joshua scratched his head and directed the temporary help to start with the middle showcase. Pete taped off the floors and summoned George to find a sign for the stair way. Joshua reset the tourist elevator to bypass the 4th floor. Slowly the project started to get underway. It resembled an ant hill with dollies and cardboard boxes assembling everywhere. Within what seemed moments, George patted Joshua on the shoulders, "See you tomorrow."

Joshua looked up startled, "Gosh, it's 11:00 already!"

George said, as he looked across the now vacant eastside center hall, "Tomorrow starts the real fun."

Joshua said, "Do you have any idea how the plate glass windows come out?"

George laughed, "Son, I know you know better, the whole partition swings out. We'll get into that tomorrow morning. We still don't have any idea which stuff to send to storage."

Pauline walked up from behind, "Yeah, we do. I'm going to put a piece of red tape on the stuff which goes."

George smiled, "I got to go, I've got to get some rest,"

Joshua looked at Pauline and asked curiously, "Miss Johnson, what about the animals?"

Pauline watch George leave and said, "We'll probably leave only the small animals here."

Joshua watched as an older worker wrestled a painting, "I better give him a hand." Some of the temporary workers walked past him to Pauline.

The one man, speaking in broken English quipped, "When this is all over, what's the big picture look like?"

Pauline laughed, "Well, actually there's more than one." She excused herself and walked towards the carpenters removing the west annex wall and doors. She said, "You guys are really quick!" Not saying a word, the three men lowered the painting down gently.

Pete, returning from the stairs said, "You have a lot of disappointed tourists downstairs."

Pauline, realizing her shortfall said, "Yes, and it's all my fault!" Running down the stairs, she greeted the people from the school buses. "Hello, everyone, *I'm really sorry*! I forgot to have my secretary call the schools on the roster to advise you of our work improvement." Reaching for a hand phone on the wall, Pauline phoned Donna from the front lobby. Her eyes scanned the sheets that were filled out as she patiently waited for Donna to answer. "Donna, we really messed up! We need to let the schools know that we're closed for the next couple of weeks." Turning around and seeing bus after bus form in the front lobby, she faced the crowds of people and said, "How many of you are anxiously awaiting to see the Indian exhibit?" The small children, comprising the largest group, raised their hands and started cheering. Pauline looking sad, said, "We're very sorry," then looking over to the homeroom mothers, she added, "We were so bogged down by a change of command."

One of the mothers cut in, "John's not here anymore?"

Pauline continued, "No, I'm the new curator." She put her hand out to shake. "John requested a transfer closer to home some years back. Finally his dream was realized. All the museum floors are free, you can have lunch on us in the museum basement luncheonette." Walking away she remembered, "Oh, excuse me, (smiling at one of the cashiers), "make sure you redeem all tickets for children with the school." Pushing the intercom for Joshua, Pauline waited for what seemed to take forever! "Joshua would you send someone down to the main lobby?" Joshua said, "Anybody?"

Pauline said, "Yeah, one of ours?"

Joshua replied, "O.K. Anything else?"

Pauline said, "No, things are going fine." Returning to Donna's line she waited patiently, Finally making contact she asked, "Donna, how's the log list coming?"

Donna laughed, "Horrible! I sent an e-mail to all the schools on the schedule. I got three back out of about 17 total. That's just today's schedule."

As she glanced at the endless procession of buses, Pauline remarked, I'll stay down here for the rest of the day and meet the buses as they disembark. I'm going to give out free admission for lunches for today and tomorrow's arrivals. We'll see that they get free tickets for later this year."

Donna laughed, "That's a *good* idea!"

Joshua asked, "You doing O.K.? What's the problem?"

"We forgot to cancel the school buses!" Pauline said. Joshua's eyes widened as he looked at the log book. "Ah, no Joshua, I got this. You go back upstairs."

Donna paged Pauline to the wall phone, "Pauline?

Pauline, "Yes?"

Donna said, "The e-mail responses are coming in. If you get a chance, call me back."

Pauline, curious, "What's up?"

Donna said, "You don't want to know."

Pauline laughed, "Oh, come on—try me!"

Donna whispered, "One of the temporary helpers beat the heck out of the manager."

Pauline replied, "What? You mean Pete?"

Donna continued, "Pete became irritated over something. One of the carpenters and Pete had it out!"

Pauline asked, "None of our people got involved?"

Donna laughed, "No, not a chance. They're way too busy!"

Pauline said, "I saw the ambulance come through. Here they come now with a stretcher!" Looking quickly, Pauline returned to the phone. "Donna, you still there?"

Donna said, "Yea."

Pauline continued, "He's on oxygen!" Looking at one of the helpers approaching her she said, "I'll call you back!" She asked the helper, "What happened?"

The temp said, "The boss was upset because one of his workers kept rushing the work crew. Pete just told him to take his time. The helper started yelling, something about taking the wall down wasn't part of the contract. Pete pushed him saying, 'Hey, if I say it's your job—well, the worker hit him. The two exchanged blows, but the younger guy was faster."

Chapter Four

THE GIANT ANGELFISH

The weeks passed quickly. The west annex was taking shape slowly. Pauline invited local civic leaders for the main event. With Chuck now gone, Joshua felt his new role forming. George was happy to be back at his normal routine and things quickly returned to normal. Within weeks, the crowds began forming. Children from all the schools on the eastern seaboard began the new journey. Donna, happy for Pauline, greeted her with coffee bright and early Monday morning. Pauline, busy with phone calls, greeted Donna in the usual way.

The west annex was now taking on a special appeal. First walking through a main Internal hallway, the visitors approached with the sound of drum beats which seemed to get louder and louder. Once inside, the visitors saw the Native Americans fish, dried meats and finally warriors preparing for battle. In a room lit with a blue overcast, a bright array of light was seen shooting from the base high into the sky or open roof. A water fountain display with the aid of a light display which flashed and turned was seen next. Children were delighted when a button was pushed and a recorded voice explained the process. An automated male warrior reached over and grabbed the crystal tomahawk clearly in view and painstakingly acted out a cutting, chopping ritual! Tourists walked uphill as they approached each display through a dark tunnel. Each exhibit displayed artifacts and Native American life on the eastern seaboard. A final bend in the tunnel prohibited newcomers from witnessing the robotic warrior reaching for the tomahawk. Children and adults could be heard screaming just prior to reaching the climatic scene! Once the tourist completed the inclined walk, they made a turn and exited from almost pitch darkness into the well lit exterior displays still in the west annex. Once the tourists adjusted to the bright light, they walked around the well lit glass display cases which displayed spear heads, arrowheads, and other routine field gear used by the local inhabitants. Staying within the purple rope perimeters the tourists continued on out to the main fourth floor entrance. Walking into the east annex, all the tourists are greeted with new displays of mummies from Ancient Egypt! As they walked past open displays, screams could still be heard clear over on the east side. Mummies, salvaged from vandals and violent weather are displayed. Some of them almost in perfect condition! As they children push buttons which activate voice recordings, a tour guide helps keep space between buses of upcoming groups. Al the visitors are treated with a continuous display of Ancient Egyptian personal effects. Ear rings, head braids, copper and gold laced coverings. Early figurines of Gods and royalties are also displayed. Walking further, children can touch a real burial tomb enclosure and exit back out into the main floor. The fifth floor region is exclusively for smaller children. Examples of Goldfish, and a salt water display that showed different brightly colored tiny fish. Yellow and blue ultraviolet lights help illuminate the different display cases. Even farther up, a giant Moray Eel and a live octopus can be observed. Trunk fish and even Star fish can be seen. Skeletal remains of long gone species and fossils can be observed.

Slowly the children return to the main elevator and stairways. Several gift shops and other areas permit children the opportunity to buy postcards and souvenirs. Clowns greet children in the lunch rooms while tour guides greet and separate tourist for different exhibits on timetables. Announcements of special exhibits are usually advertised through brochures and intercom communications. This museum had taken on a new life!

Pauline returned to the outer office and asked, Donna to bring a pencil. As she reached for a refill from the coffee pot, Pauline said, "I never knew the coffee could taste so good!"

Donna laughed, "No, I think you're just a little ecstatic over how well things are going."

George walked in around 10:00 a.m. looking bushed from all the excitement. He peered at the wall then back at the vacant desk, the he walked out and went home. Joshua, with his work crew, was preparing his 10:00 break.

In the main office, Donna prepared for her office dictations. Pauline glanced out the large office window and shook her head in amazement at the improvement in tourism. Looking over the desk to Donna, she began, "Dear Mr. Mayor . . . " Then another one for her home state museum. To John Harold. Finally a brief rest before the buzzer sounded. Yelling loudly in Donna's ear, Pauline summoned the guest through the main office. Watching with impatience, the door began to open. Pauline and Donna, in unison shouted, "Chuck!!"

Chuck, with a bouquet of flowers handed the flowers across the desk to Pauline. "Congratulations! Good job!"

Pauline smiled ear to ear, "Do you really like it?"

Chuck looked at Donna then glanced back up to Pauline, "It's great!! That last display really catches your eye!!"

Chuck giggled, "I wasn't interrupting anything, was I?

Donna said, as she jumped to her feet, "Here, sit down a minute!"

Pauline volunteered, "We were just preparing a letter to you old boss.:

Chuck said, "Don't forget to tell him Chuck says hello."

Donna replied, "Well, it's not that kind of letter. It's one of those, 'hit you up for some money' letters."

Pauline, turning red, "Donna! I'm embarrassed."

Chuck said, "Hey, that's for the museum stuff." Then looking at Pauline he added, "When you took archeology, was Ancient Syria in your studies?"

Pauline answered, "I really don't think so."

Donna walked out to the desk and asked, "Chuck, care for some coffee?"

Chuck glanced at his wristwatch, "O.K. I'm pretty well caught up on all the small stuff."

Pauline glanced at the fish bowl and noticed a fish floating on the surface. She said emotionally, "Donna, I think Charlie, the fish died!"

Donna and Chuck ran to view the fish. Chuck tapped the floating fish with his ink pen. "No, poor Charlie's gone!"

Donna said, "He lasted a lot longer than his friends."

Chuck reached in with a paper towel and grabbed the remains and headed for the bathroom.

Donna remarked, "Chuck, never mind, we ought to change the filter and water anyway."

Weeks passed and the crowds never seemed to slow down. Monies raised by special tickets more than covered restoration and set up costs.

Pauline watching from her office window, walked to her memo pad. Noticing a reminder of her day calendar, she pushed the intercom button, "Donna, what's this memo on my day calendar?"

Donna paused, "I think that's the one from two weeks ago."

Pauline furthered, "I wonder if they're still having it?"

Donna replied, "Oh, yeah, they'd have said something otherwise."

Pauline looked puzzled, "Try to find out what it's about."

Donna looked on the computer, "It's about the budget."

Pauline looked at the calendar and said, "This early?"

George walked in and took a seat. Donna finished her phone call and looked straight at George, "What's up, big George?"

George walked toward the desk, is Miss Johnson busy?"

Donna, looking puzzled said, "Here, I'll page her."

Pauline on the other end quipped, "George, please come in."

George walked to the red chair and looked out the window. "I've never seen buses all the way from here!"

Pauline smiled ear to ear, "Yes, George, together we made that a reality!"

George looked straight at Pauline and said, "I want to tell you about something."

Pauline curiously said, "Yeah, George?"

George paused, "I really don't know where to begin."

Pauline glanced around the room, "Just spit it out."

George said, "A few months ago, a lady was here who told some weird stories. One about a child being helped with polio."

Pauline giggled, "George!"

George started towards the window, "Do you think this is all about flashing lights and drum beats?"

Pauline, acting coy, said, "I can't act like it's anything else. If people, especially in high positions, start showing superstition, we're in trouble!"

George glanced back from the outside, "Have you been upstairs lately?"

Pauline looked puzzled, "What's upstairs?"

George said, "The upstairs right over the stone, on the next floor."

Maintaining composure, she clicked on the computer video scan for the west fifth floor. She said, "O.K. George, I'm there."

Bending over the desk on her side, George said, "Can you zoom in on the Angelfish?"

Turning the lights on remotely, Pauline spins the photo lens towards the fish tanks. Laughing hysterically she said, "I think he's out growing the tank! Zooming the rest of the tanks Pauline looked back at George, "Anything else?"

George emotionally stumbling for thoughts, "It's just this gut feeling."

Pauline laughed, "Who doesn't get them! Come on, George!"

George furthered with, "No it's a lot more than that!"

Pauline looked out at Donna, "Donna, you got a minute?"

Donna walked in and reached for the empty coffee cup. "Yes, Pauline?"

Pauline said, "Just stick a round a minute." Looking back at George she said, "What else George?"

A silence, then, "Miss Johnson, I know you think I'm crazy, but I feel it in my bones."

Pauline laughed, "Go ahead, George."

He said, "When I come in early morning, I feel like I'm being stalked. I don't mean watched, I mean stalked! Joshua sometimes thinks he sees things, too. Then when you reach around the stone to clean—"

Pauline giggled. "Emotion?"

George continued, "I feel emotion! I mean, power, invincibility, rage. That kind of emotion."

Donna finally said, "Maybe there's some truth to it all."

Pauline reached for her car keys, "Donna, I got to run over to the stationery store. Keep an eye on George, will you Donna?" George back from his daydream, "I'm sorry, Miss Johnson, It's time to go home anyway."

Pauline reached the outer office, "Tell everyone I'll be at the budget meeting."

Entering the hall, Pauline heard the usual screams from the display. Walking out the front main lobby, Joshua followed through the glass rotating doors, "Miss Johnson."

Pauline said, "Yes, Joshua? It's not about what George was in my office for, is it?"

Joshua laughed, Yea, but this is something different."

Pauline said, "How about tomorrow morning? We have an early year budget meeting today."

Joshua looked disappointed, "Yeah, sure."

Pauline asked, "How's being team leader?"

Joshua answered, "A lot more work!"

Walking off, Pauline turned the outside corner. Joshua returned to the building. He noticed the crowds becoming extremely thick. Pushing through to the elevator, he made his way towards the west annex. When he reached the middle corridor, a lady dressed in dark clothing walked up to Joshua and asked. "You the new supervisor?"

Joshua was startled by the straight forward approach and said, "Yeah, that's me!"

The lady paused and then looked Joshua straight in the eyes, "Hello, my name is Wilma." Then touching his elbow, "When you have a chance, may I have a minute of your time?"

Joshua giggled, "Well, how's right now?"

Looking over towards the far east corner she pointed and asked, "How about over there where it's not so crowded?"

Joshua looked curious and said, "All right."

Wilma looked where the stone use to sit, "Do you remember me?"

Joshua looked baffled, "No, mame, can't say I do, You must have me confused with Chuck or George."

Wilma said, "I came back because I think you ought to know a few things."

Joshua held his chin propped up with his arm on a loose push broom.

Wilma said, "I'm a psychic."

Joshua said, "A psychic?"

Wilma, "It's about the stone." She watched Joshua's body language. "You don't believe in us?"

Joshua said, "It's just that I've personally been experiencing some weird stuff. I don't know too much about all this."

Wilma added, "The stone is from a mineral which is very, very rare.

Joshua, now interested, "Yes?"

Wilma continued, "It seems to be a bridge to the other side. I mean *everything* on the other side!"

Joshua was getting hungry. "Can I call or meet you after work? It's our lunch break, I have some information to pass on to our people."

Wilma quipped, "Sure Joshua. Call me anytime at this number." She quickly handed him a business card.

Walking back through the cases, Joshua arrived at the middle elevator area quickly. Crossing through the thick traffic, Joshua hurried to the curator's office. Walking inside, he noticed everyone had gone to lunch.

Back at the service elevator, Joshua reached the first floor cafeteria. Keeping his head up, Joshua walked past the lines and walked straight to his subordinates. Looking across at the main lobby, Joshua remarked to his workers, "I don't think this place ever slows down." One worker named Jeff, handed Joshua a message. "This is from Donna. It's something about staying close to her office while the meetings taking place."

Joshua said, "That means you guys have to feed the fish."

Jeff said, "I thought George did that."

Joshua laughed, "Yes, that's right, he's scared to go in there." Sitting down to eat, Joshua looked over to the first floor podium and said, "Wonder who this week's guest speaker is?"

Jeff chuckled, "Some guy talking about frogs."

Pauline waked in, scanned the room and walked straight to Joshua. Grabbing his arm, she remarked, "Josh, do me a favor?"

Joshua turned and jumped with surprise, "Yes, sure."

Pauline continued, "Do you want to make sure all the trash and tables are clean, floors and everything for that meeting tomorrow?"

Joshua asked, "Jeff wants to know if he can have George feed the tropical fish?"

Pauline giggled, "I don't call those shots, you do."

Jeff giggled, "I guess that means "yes."

Joshua looked back to Jeff, "No, that means you do!"

Pauline walked backwards towards the luncheonette door, "Thanks, Josh."

Returning upstairs, Joshua checked on the fifth floor. As he approached the tropical fish he backed up suddenly, "Holy Cow!" The Angel fish was now the size of the tank! Joshua paged downstairs.

Hearing the page, Donna stood dumbfounded. "I'll tell her right away!"

Buzzing the inside door, Pauline answered immediately. "What??"

She clicked on the computer scan, "Donna! Wow! Donna, come here."

Donna, holding her composure began laughing and shaking her head, "I wonder what George has been feeding them?"

Both ran for the elevators. Pauline grabbed Joshua's arm, "Do we have a larger aquarium?" Donna looked puzzled, "I don't know what happened, but this isn't normal. We're going to have to call someone to take it."

Jeff and the crew returned down the downstairs luncheonette and curiously asked, "What the heck caused it to get so big?" Jeff walked quickly in a circle around the room. Everything else seems normal."

Pauline looked closer, "There's a whole or crack under the aquarium." Walking together to the elevator, Pauline remarked, "I have a friend up Boston, I'll see if they will take it."

Donna looked at Joshua's, "You see George, tell him we want some of that fish food."

Joshua asked, "Where in Boston?"

Pauline glanced at Donna, "Oh, I'm sorry, it's a big aquarium."

Joshua breathed easier, "I thought it was some museum or something."

Jeff walked out of the elevator, "You want the windows done on the west third floor?"

Joshua remarked, "Yeah, Jeff, I'll be down there in a minute." Jeff turned to his right and left the elevator.

Donna noticed the crowd all the way out the main lobby.

Pauline was busy on the cell phone. She received a nudge from Donna. Joshua looked towards Donna and remarked, "I hope the budget committee see some of this."

Pauline, making contact, "Yes, is there a Willie Smithson there?" Pauline smiled as Donna walked off. Joshua was worrying about his break and looked toward Donna.

Pauline remarked, "Willie! Yes, got a question. Can you use a giant Angelfish?" Silence followed as Pauline looked back at Joshua. "Can we take it up to them?"

Donna added, "We'd have to get a special tank."

Pauline asked, "How about if we supply the driver? Do you have anything we can use, Willie?" Then she said, "No, you don't understand—it's gigantic!"

Donna opened the office curator's door and held it open. Pauline looked out the window and said, "I can get back with you. That will be good, thanks, Willie." Pauline washed her hands at the sink. Joshua frowned at Donna and looked at his watch.

Donna quipped, "Go ahead, Joshua."

Looking over to Pauline, Joshua remarked, "I'll be back in about forty minutes. I have to go check on my workers."

Pauline said as she wiped off her hands, "Donna, we're going to have to take it to them. They'll lend us their truck."

Donna, turning from the window said, "I don't think we're insured for out of state."

Pauline walked back towards the window, "I'll check with the budget committee this afternoon." Closing the closet door she remarked, "I don't know what they would want to discuss, this early in the year."

Donna said, "Maybe I'll let you tough that one out by yourself. I'll stay here with the phones." She looked at the Angelfish. "I wonder if he's being fed enough!" She walked around the desk.

"Oh, I'm sure George takes care of that. He volunteered for the fish," said Pauline. Pauline, "He told Josh he didn't like going up there. It was something about getting the spooks."

Donna shook her head, "That's news to me. Who's been doing it?"

"Actually, I think they've been taking turns," said Pauline. Just then a knock on the door.

Recognizing the knock, Donna said, "Come on in, Josh."

Pauline looked up, "Who feeds the fish on the fifth floor?"

Joshua hesitantly replied, "Well, sometimes George, Jeff or one of us."

Donna laughed, "You mean George is scared?"

Joshua answered, "I think the old man's slowly losing it."

Pauline smiled, "I don't know, he can probably run circles around your whole crew!"

A strange thought crossed Joshua's mind as he returned home. Walking out to the mailbox, he reached in his wallet, suddenly remembering Wilma from several days ago. Sorting the mail, he returned to the living room, pushed the remote control with one hand then dialed the telephone with the other. Wilma answered. Joshua said, "Hello, this is Joshua from the museum. You wanted me to call."

Wilma, surprised said, "Yes, Josh how are you?"

"When do you have open?" he asked.

Wilma replied, "How about right now?"

Joshua asked, "How much?"

Wilma said, "Josh! I asked you over."

Joshua, looking at his watch, "How long is all this going to take?"

Wilma replied, "I wanted to talk to you about the stone."

Joshua paused, then asked, "What about it?"

Wilma laughed, "I live about three blocks down from you. I'll see you when you get here."

Joshua grabbed a piece of cold chicken," How do you know where I live?" Wilma laughed," I live, right down from you on east Chestnut." Joshua takes another bite, "I'll be there with my mouth full."

Wilma quipped, "Yes, I have that red and blue sign on the corner." Joshua arrived moments later. He read the sign as he knocked on the door. He slowly turned the knob, out of breath.

Wilma opened the door and greeted Joshua with a hug. "Come in, please."

Joshua, removing his sunglasses, walked through the kitchen to a small parlor. Wilma turned on the lights and said, "Josh, over here." Approaching a big, brown, leather chair, he flopped down.

Wilma got right to the point. "I first visited your museum about three months ago. I agreed to help with a field trip."

Josh glanced across at Wilma. She continued with, "I've been doing readings a long time. I never saw or heard of miracles."

Josh laughed, "You believe that stuff?"

Wilma answered, "You want me to prove it to you?"

Joshua squirmed in his chair, "Go on."

Wilma added, "One lady found her run-away daughter."

Joshua looked back unmoved as Wilma said, "I knew something was odd, different, the moment I got off the elevator."

Joshua rapping his fingers on the chair, "I know, I feel it sometimes, too."

Wilma said, "It has it's own aura."

Joshua asked, "What do you want with me?"

Wilma continued, "I belong to a mixed group of friends. I meet with them once every couple weeks. For someone outside, they'd be called devil worshippers."

Joshua reached for his soda, "Devil worshippers?"

Wilma laughed, "Well, anyone with a different scope of religion."

Joshua asked, "Different scope?"

Wilma continued, "We believe that some things are a medium to the supernatural."

Joshua paused in thought, "The stone?"

Wilma continued on, "Why else the feeling? The story's going back several hundred years."

Joshua remarked, "So what does all this mean?"

Wilma laughed, "If things go right, a whole library of things."

Joshua watched his clock, "How can I help? You don't expect me to steal the thing? Do ya?"

Wilma looked away silent, then she looked Joshua straight in the eye and slowly said, "*How about the other way around*? Suppose you could arrange to have us in after hours."

Joshua giggled, "Oh, you mean get me fired?"

Wilma looked serious, "No, I mean you act like you don't know."

Joshua walked towards the kitchen, I'd have to think hard about that one." He walked towards the door and asked, "How many of you?"

Wilma said, "Seven in our group, figure three including myself!"

Joshua, closing the door, "Once in awhile, people get locked in."

Wilma surprised, "It will only be for about an hour."

Joshua looked at his watch again, "I'm suppose to have a date."

Wilma shouted back, "Thank you."

Walking back to his truck, undecided, he walked back up the walk towards the house. Thinking twice, he turned and went back to his vehicle.

Wilma, watching through a window, ran out to his truck. Walking around to the driver's side, she said, "You wanted to know something?"

Joshua, curious, asked, "What exactly do you want to accomplish?"

Wilma looking around the truck said quickly, "I want to establish a spiritual medium. I hope I can."

Joshua looking puzzled, "Tell you friends Thursdays are the best, I'll call."

Wilma giggled, "Why Thursdays?"

Joshua replied, "It's the usual the least wired day of the week thing."

Wilma smirked, "Keep in touch, promise you'll let me know."

Joshua spinning wheels, pulled out into the fast moving traffic. Moments later, Joshua noticed Chuck's vehicle in front of his driveway. He blew his horn and opened the window. Chuck walking out to greet Joshua said, "Hey, Josh, what's up, dude?"

Josh laughed, "Hey, you're the man! What, you forgot where you live?"

Chuck laughed, "No, I was wondering if you wanted to go shoot some Billiards instead."

Joshua laughed, "Let me make a phone call."

Chuck asked, "What—you got a date?"

Joshua replied, "Yea, sort of."

Chuck laughed, "Good ol stand them up Josh—some things never change!"

Joshua smiled as he walked in the driveway. Chuck followed Joshua and waited at the back door. "Come on in, Chuck."

Chuck said, "I thought maybe—"

Joshua interrupted with, "No, heck no." Not being able to find his cell phone, Joshua reached for the portable. Then Joshua laughed, "We're off to play pool." Reaching for a cookie, Joshua headed out the back door.

Chuck laughed, "You're going to have to show me how you do that."

Joshua said, "Oh, girls never even know you're there half the Time, anyway." Jumping in the passenger side of Chuck's sports car, Joshua added, "You talk to anyone whose been married a long time. They don't know you're there."

Chuck drove past the museum and asked Joshua, "You doing O.K. over there?"

Joshua added, "Yeah, they got some big unexpected budget meeting planned for late today."

Chuck stopped at the traffic light. "Budget? This early?"

Joshua continued, "Well, Pauline had us workers do an extra good job on the floors and tables. We were aloud to leave early, I think they have some important people coming."

Chuck laughed, "Maybe it's a good time to hit them up for a raise?"

Joshua looked at a street fight, "No, I think we're scheduled for one here soon."

Chuck, looking straight ahead, "How's Donna?"

Joshua looked over to Chuck, "I don't know, that's your old flame."

Chuck laughed, "We're good friends! I'm busy starting school, I have no clue how that other place is doing, now I'm not there."

Joshua watched a pedestrian and said, "No."

Chuck looked over, "No?"

Joshua replied, "Yes, that's right, we can't fit one more tourist in that place. they literally stand out front."

Joshua pulled up to the pool hall, "They're still coming for that display?"

Joshua said, "You don't know the half of it!"

Walking into the bar, Chuck's greeted by friends. Joshua walks over and through to the billiard tables and starts to sets up. Chuck, talking continuously, becomes more and more detained.

Joshua interrupts, "You should break the balls." Chuck was talking and talking. Chuck said, "Josh!"

Both walked over to the table and Chuck started the game then said, "Feel better? So what am I missing?"

Joshua in control of the table called out the pocket. He looked up to Chuck, "When John left, then you left things got crazy. Pauline is wonderful, but it's like opening a flood gate."

Chuck made his next move. "I know the Native American room boosts business. What else?"

Joshua made two completed shots then said, "Chuck, it's like things just keep getting busier and more chaotic."

Joshua, winning the match, returned to the bar, "I've been there almost as long as you, Chuck, I've never seen them wait outside in line!"

Chuck looked straight at Joshua, "What's ol George think of all this?"

Reaching for his beer, Joshua looked over to the crowded rock banc, "George is becoming hard to work with."

Chuck looked peculiar and said, "George?"

Joshua, shrugged his shoulders refraining from comment, "How's school?"

Chuck gulped down a draft and said, "It's not what I thought it would be. In fact, I might transfer somewhere else." He looked back at the table, "Well, we lost that one." Looking back at the bartender, "Archeology is a big under taking. I just don't like the college approach."

Joshua giggled, "How's the new job?"

Chuck rolled his eyes and said, "How's you find out, You got about three hours?"

Joshua walked up to the end of the bar and noticed his former date at the end of the bar. He said, "Chuck, excuse me a minute." He walked reluctantly to her side. Joshua shrugged his shoulders, "I let the phone ring and ring. No response. He walked back around, "She acts like she's not interested in talking.

Joshua looks back at Chuck, "You still like Donna?"

Chuck answered, "Yeah, I still like Donna. But Donna talks too much about the same thing. Her whole life is that museum."

Joshua looked surprised, "It has a way of getting in your blood— you know!"

Chuck, cutting him off, said, "Yeah, If you let it!"

Shortly the band started playing. Chuck looked at his watch, "Joshua, I got to go. Tell George to get the lead out." Walking towards the door, Chuck looked back at Joshua, "Maybe you should try to make up with her?"

"And spoil my reputation, not a chance!"

Just as Chuck pulled out from his parking space, an ambulance flew by with the siren shrieking. Stunned for a moment, Chuck slowly left the pub parking lot.

Joshua reached his home around 10:30. As he walked through the back door, he heard the answering service beeper. Pushing the button, he waited for the message. It's Donna, if you have a chance, give me a call, this is urgent." He pushed the auto redial. He heard the phone ring. She answered, "Hello, Donna."

"What's up?" Joshua asked. Donna replied, "You want to cover for George in the morning?"

Joshua asked, "What happened?"

Donna hesitated, "George had a heart attack or something. We called his family and they're still in there with him."

Shocked, Joshua said, "Yea, sure. God hope he's O.K.! I'll call Jeff and let him fill my spot"

Chapter Five

THE BUDGET MEETING

Pauline arrived very early to check on things. She noticed the floors were already done. She walked into the board room. The tables were clean, trash removed, and windows cleaned. She walked into the office she found Joshua half asleep in the outer office. "What? Did you come in last night?" she asked.

Joshua jumped up looking at his wristwatch, "Well, as a matter of fact, I almost had to, the problem with George and all."

Everything went as planned the rest of the day. Later that evening, Pauline said to Donna, "You go on home, Jeff can handle the fish."

Joshua looked at Pauline, "Maybe I'll check on George this afternoon."

Pauline quipped, "He'll probably be in intensive care for a few days."

Joshua curious, "What was he doing?

Pauline continued, "He was doing the dishes when he started feeling faint." She opened the shades over her large picture window then walked to to her answering machine. Donna walked in and saw Joshua still sitting in the waiting room.

Joshua, seeing the coffee, said, "I'll take some of that." He shook his head and yawned. "I think you're right on cue."

Donna walked to the main desk and asked, "Pauline, you want me to check on the meeting?"

Pauline said, "Call the budget office." She looked out toward the outer office and said, "Joshua, come get your coffee. We're sorry about all this."

Joshua jumped up and walked in slowly. "This place is haunted or some thing!"

Donna giggled, "Haunted?"

Joshua said, "When I came in last night, I swear I saw some kid running around."

Pauline said, "I'm sorry, Josh, we're just sort of edgy over these meetings."

Joshua replied, "I'll wait till next week sometime."

The phone rang. Donna said, "Pauline, it's the hospital."

Pauline picked up and said, "Hello, this is Pauline." Looking over to Joshua she shook her head, remaining silent. Then she smiled and gave the 'thumbs up.' Great! I'm very happy to know he's hanging on." Walking over to the window, she said, "Tell George we're all praying for him. Yes, we'll be over as soon as we're free. Great! Thank you *very* much!!"

Breathing a sigh of relief, Pauline walked from the window to the outer office and said, "Make sure, no dumb phone calls this morning!"

Donna added, "You want me there? I'd rather be here."

Pauline looked towards her office, "Maybe that's a good idea. **If** I need anything, you'll get a page."

Joshua laughed, "With your permission, I'm gong home."

As Joshua, walked towards the outer door of the office he said, "Good luck!"

Donna looked up and remained quiet. Pauline pretended not to hear, shuffled papers and spins in her chair to turn on the computer. Suddenly, laughing out loud—"Frogs?? Donna did you see this?"

Donna knowing the main screen, "Yeah, I saw it."

Pauline moved through menus, "Yeah, the meetings still scheduled."

Donna walked in for the empty coffee cups and said, "Some guy from Washington and New York are the special guests."

Pauline looked at the names, "I don't recognize the names, it's been too long since I helped at the New York place."

Suddenly Jeff walked in and said, "Miss Johnson?"

Donna waked out from the inner office, "Can I help you?"

Jeff asked, "Heard anything about George's condition?"

Donna remarked, "We just had a phone call, so far things are going pretty well. You doing O.K. with the new shoes?"

Jeff laughed, "I haven't stopped dancing since I walked in the door."

Pauline walked out and asked, "You're Jeff, right?" She reached out her hand and said, "Thanks for helping Josh. You going to have time to do the fish?"

He said, "Oh, yeah the fish, one of my subordinates already did."

Donna looked at Pauline, "Wow, these guys not only do a good job, they learn the vocabulary quickly."

Pauline looked back out the window, "Stay with your crews today, we have a lot of big wigs looking around."

Donna watching the clock, "Pauline, it's 8:30."

As Pauline washed her hands in the small sink, she peeked in at the fish in her office aquarium, Donna gave her a salute as she walked out toward the office. Pauline giggled.

Later, Pauline noticed Jeff talking to a tourist. Approaching the elevator, Pauline looked back down at the floors. As she walked into the conference hall, she saw the room beginning to fill. Shaking hands with her friends from New York she made her way to the front table. Forty minutes later, the meeting began. A chief spokesman for the museums in the area began the introductions.

Each member stood while everyone else applauded their respective positions.

The chief spokesman slowly began about the upcoming changes and the new budget for 2004. The chief asked Pauline to remark about the capitol improvements and the new display.

After Pauline adjusted the microphone, she began, I've been at the museum about three months. I thought things through before deciding to change the display rooms or go for a new theme. It's made a monumental improvement in tourism."

One gentleman cut her off, "Excuse me, suppose I were to make or suggest an idea?"

Pauline looked at the man in the corner. "Yes, be my guest."

The older man was from a New York museum. "I have a group heading a world tour, they also have a twenty three city two year tour." He looked at his associates and said, "Suppose I could get the money for a new roof. How would everyone feel about a two year national tour of the Native American displays?"

Pauline said, "I'm sure that's the goal in the long run. Looking over at a guest from the budget committee, she asked, "How much are the estimates for?"

A man with a scratchy voice said, "$355,000." An older man from New York said, "I'll have the people from our budget get back with you."

Pauline looked towards the spokesman, "Well, I yield back to Mr. Harkins."

Within a half hour the meeting came to a close. Pauline first to exit, headed straight to the main office.

Donna looked up when the door opened, "How'd thing$ go?"

Walking straight to her desk, Pauline said, "Well, it wasn't what I expected. I thought we were running in the red, or something, Looking at the aquarium, "They want to put the Native American display on a twenty three city tour."

Donna said, "How are we ever going to get a new roof?"

Pauline said, "Some guy from New York has a committee which will fund the total repair."

Donna, skeptical, "That's $355,000!"

Pauline furthered, "He didn't even bat an eye!"

Donna added, "Well, if that's true, then that's a pretty good deal!"

Pauline walked to the window, "Do you have any idea how dead this place will be?"

Donna laughed, "1 don't think it will be as bad as you think."

Pauline looked back, "How you figure that?"

Donna, "The Native American display put us on the map. There's a heck a lot of other things just as interesting."

Pauline walked back to her desk, "Wonder how Jeff's doing?"

Donna giggled, "Jeff likes the job too much."

Walking out to Donna's office, Pauline visited the wall of famous pictures. glancing back to Donna, she said, "I'm going to check on things, I'll be back." Walking out past the elevators, Pauline pushed to go up. Using her cell phone, she asked, "Donna, you want to check some more on the deal with the Angel fish?" Walking past the tank with her cell phone, she turned to take another look. "Yeah, Donna, I swear this thing is still growing!" Looking around the room from tank to tank, she noticed all the other creatures were normal. Walking first past the Tropical Blue fish, then an octopus, she pushed the button. A mechanical apparatus extended down into the eels habitat. Within moments, a large voltage registered on the voltage meter. Turning back on the far side, Pauline checked the last of the tanks. Aware of their feeding menu's she noticed that all the tanks had been serviced. Glancing back at the Angel fish, she shook her head before exiting. Approaching the dinosaurs, she began thinking about new ideas. As she looked through the inventory, the ideas began to formulate. As she walked back toward the elevators, she thought of the other large inventories. Egyptian display, insects, dinosaurs, and maybe a new annex floor of unusual nature. Reaching the main floor in front of the museum, she journeyed towards the work crews, "Where's Jeff?"

The worker looked over in surprise, "Jeff went up to the main office."

Pauline called again on the cell phone, "Donna, have you seen Jeff?"

Donna said, "Yeah, he's right here. He just walked in.

Pauline gathered her thoughts, "Ask him if he wants to drive up to Boston and bring back their special van?"

Jeff asked, "Pauline, sure, when do I leave?"

Pauline said, "You'll need some help taking the fish back."

Jeff handed the phone back. Smiling he said, "I get overtime pay and room allowance, right?" Donna shook her head. "Pauline, anything else?"

Pauline looked around, "Have Jeff meet me first thing in the morning."

Donna said, "She wants you up here first thing before you start work."

Glancing at his watch, Jeff bowed out.

Pauline walked towards her office and glanced out at the late afternoon tourists. As she approached the elevators, she stopped and looked at the pigeons flying towards the roof top. She got off the elevator and walked toward the Indian display. Watching the crowds walk through the displays, Pauline had another brainstorm. Returning to her office, she called Donna to her desk.

"Donna, I think I have another idea."

Donna asked, "What?"

Pauline, pulling a pencil through her fingers, said, "Suppose we have an exhibit of Egyptian mummies with the same theme."

Donna laughed, "What you want—the whole museum on world tour?"

Pauline began giggling, "We can have Egyptian mummies on a display case walkway."

Donna looked at her watch, "Sounds good to me."

Pauline glanced at the wall clock, "Oh, I'm sorry, Donna let's go home!"

Closing the inside door, both quickly left for the elevator. Pauline pushed the buttons, "I have another big day tomorrow."

Donna looked curious, "Tomorrow?"

Pauline watched the floor light indicator change, "I have to figure out how to get that fish safely to Boston." Walking out the main lobby, the two women noticed the clean windows. With the building still crowded,. Pauline and Donna left the building.

Joshua reported to work on George's old schedule. The usual routine started to unfold. Dragging the water bucket up from the basement, he filled the wax can from the large tank reservoir and swept the rooms one by one. In touch with Wilma, Joshua began his usual routine. Sneaking the four guests in through the service elevator, then behind the main casements, Joshua said, "You wait here, it's going to be about two hours."

Returning to his usual routine, Joshua swept each floor with a push broom. Slowly completing each floor, Joshua began stripping the floors. Watching his clock, Joshua paused and peered towards the casement window with the hiding guests. Hours seemed to slip by like minutes. Taking a careful walk around the perimeter of the floors, Joshua walked up to the guest. "Try and keep the noise and talking down." As he exited the floor and came into the hall of displays, Joshua and his guests slowly made the pilgrimage. getting to the top of the displays, Chuck said, "Hold up!"

Walking with his pass key behind the displays, Joshua approached the crystal stone. Raising it out of it's holder, Joshua carefully slide past the robotic Indian. Opening the service door at the base of the display, Joshua rejoined his guests. As he handed the tomahawk directly to Wilma, Joshua said, "I trust you, no tricks! I'll be doing the floors." The group sat down on the inside of the elevated walkway in the new display room. They were out of sight, should any one pass by. Wilma slowly began the séance.

Joshua finished the main lobby and went to take a peek. Joshua completed the second floor then immediately headed for the west fourth floor. the second trip, Joshua realized the group was deep in a religious ritual. Walking back down slowly, Joshua glanced at his wristwatch feeling nervous. It was 4:30 a.m. He headed back to the fourth floor. Joshua said to Wilma, "I might be able to have you in again if you like." Wilma looked up, "What time is it?"

Joshua chuckled, "The security turns that camera facing here and starts walking around 5:00 a.m."

Wilma nudged her acquaintances and shook her head in compliance. Slowly the tomahawk is kissed ad passed down to Wilma. Joshua reached for the stone and quickly reentered the service door. The crowd remained quiet. Joshua returned slowly to the main entrance of fifth floor and back around the backside. As they slowly made their way to the elevator, Joshua listened for security. Then remarked, "Stay her till a little past 8:00, then walk one person every 15 minutes through the crowds into the main lobby. Returning to his job Joshua turned the lights on in the main lobby. After he finished the fourth floor, Joshua hurried to the fifth. Keeping track of time, he kept pace with the usual routine of chores and finished for the morning.

As he greeted Jeff on the way out, Joshua quipped, "How's things on your end?"

Jeff smiled, "Great! Today, Pauline's going to try to find a way to ship the fish."

Walking through the lobby, Joshua stopped and turned, "What fish?"

Jeff laughed, "You didn't know?"

Joshua shrugged his shoulders, "The Angelfish on the fifth floor is gigantic!" said Jeff.

Joshua said, "You mean the yellow stripped one?"

Jeff continued, "Yeah, it grew three times its normal size."

Joshua walked to the door, "I must of forgotten, I'll check on it after lunch." Joshua b-lined for a quick lunch at home. Passing the pub then George's house, here Joshua casually entered his back door. Joshua pushed the answering service. He then started his noon double time ritual. Turning the water on to rinse a cup out, Joshua heard the first recording. "Hello, it's Wilma. Thanks for sticking your neck out. Everyone got out safe. Again, thanks very much!!" Then Joshua returned to his favorite spot on the couch and pushed the button for a dial tone. Thinking of the museum He pushed return call for Wilma's number.

Wilma quickly picked up the phone. "Hello, this is Joshua."

Wilma stretched, yawning still half asleep, "Joshua, Is that you? thanks a million. We found out all kinds of things. I'll have you over some night you're free."

Joshua said, "Great!" dropping the phone down returning to the kitchen, Joshua heard the phone ring.

The answering machine slowly picked up. "Pauline calling. You know anything about a big net anywhere? If you not too busy, give me a call." Joshua closed the cabinet door and washed the last of his dishes in his sink. Later, as he watched the news in bed, that late afternoon. He dozed off moments later. Joshua started remembering the past night. Reaching behind the display, watching the scenes, sneaking the people back out. Slowly, deeper in sleep, he heard the door bell ringing, then a series of knocks. "Hello, Joshua, Can you hear me?" Joshua threw the sheets back and staggered down the stairs. He wrapped a towel around himself and managed to get only one slipper on. Joshua yelled, "I'm coming!" Opening the door, he is greeted by Donna. "I've been trying to reach you."

Joshua looked bewildered, "Donna! Come on in" Showing her a seat, he returned in proper attire. Yawning, Joshua said, "How may I help you?"

Donna said, "Pauline doesn't have any idea how to send a giant Angel fish to Boston."

Joshua laughed, "Couldn't this wait till tomorrow?" Donna watched Joshua rub his eyes, "Jeff said he'll work tonight for you.' Donna pleaded, "Will you stop over and show Jeff how to load this thing?" Joshua laughed looking at his wristwatch, "Donna, Its past 4:00P.M!" Joshua jumps up half upset, "Donna, how's he going to get it to Boston?"

Donna said, "Oh, Pauline made arrangements to have one of ours borrow one of their trucks."

Joshua shakes his head, today, I mean tonight!" "What about all that insurance stuff?"

Donna replied, "Pauline is looking into it."

Joshua shook his head, "Giant Angelfish?"

Donna remained quiet. Joshua said, "We'll net the fish quickly with a rope, slide it down the wall five stories. We'll have a Styrofoam container to put it in. They're not ready with the truck?"

Donna laughed, "No, Pauline wanted to do a dry run."

Joshua burst out laughing, "I'm not sure that's going to work. I'll call her from here."

Donna looked in her purse, "I'll save you the trouble."

Joshua sat back down, "Hello, Pauline? This is Donna. I have him right here." Handing the phone to Joshua, she walked around the kitchen.

"Hello, Donna, this is Josh."

Pauline burst into one long continuous sentence, "How am I suppose to get this fish moved?"

Joshua was thinking while she continued, "Probably one of the easiest ways is build some kind of box that holds water until we can get it in the truck."

Pauline settles down, "I guess I have a couple days yet. Do you want to have Jeff or one of the other workers fill in for you?"

Joshua said, "Yeah, that means I'm off tonight, right?"

Pauline giggled. "I already have it arranged, See you, Monday."

Joshua looked over to Donna and said, "Next week, there's going to be a luau. Donna, I don't mean to be rude, or change the subject."

Donna looked around, "George is in the hospital." Joshua looked back grabbing at his cup, "What?' Donna looks straight back," I don't know how serious." Donna jumps up looking out the front window, "You want to help check on him tomorrow?" Then walking towards the door, she said, "Pauline didn't want to mention it, so I did." Donna lifts around a coffee table, "Its something to do with his heart or chest pains." Donna looks back at Joshua opening the kitchen door, "I called several times, Pauline did too, he's out of intensive care.' That evening after resting, Joshua returned to the kitchen. Joshua was thinking about Wilma again. Walking to the telephone, he grabbed the remote with one hand, the telephone with the other.

Returning to the kitchen counter Joshua pushed the remote while making a chicken sandwich. Completing the meal preparation, he slowly pushed the auto dial on the phone. Wilma's answering service took the call. Joshua said, "Wilma, this is Joshua. Let me know when I can schedule an appointment." Putting the phone down, he walked back upstairs. Joshua began preparing for his pub night.

Joshua decided to call the hospital. George was in a private room. The operator connected them. "George, this is Joshua."

George talked in a broken voice, "Josh."

Joshua said, "George, when you allowed to have visitors?" He waited patiently for a reply.

"Anytime, Josh, it wasn't that serious, their just watching me."

Joshua said, "What the old ticker?" George remained quiet. Joshua looks around the kitchen for a wash cloth, I'll be over tomorrow around lunch time."

George asked, "How's the Angelfish?"

Joshua laughed, "Shiny, George, slippery, big." George started laughing," Don't worry, I be back in a few days." Letting George go, Joshua excused himself For making him laugh. George interrupts," How, you going to ship it ?" Joshua rinses the washcloth off, wiping the kitchen food spoils up," I've been in bed We're working all that out on Monday." George laughed, "Monday?' Good luck!"

Joshua giggled, "I got to go George, I'll be over tomorrow soon as I can." Joshua closes fast then headed for his vehicle and favorite pub.

Wilma planned her meeting when she returned home. The entire community of psychics attended. Wilma mentioned the existence of the tomahawk. Slowly with a tape recorder on, the group shared the actual experience of holding the tomahawk. Wilma turned to Joe, the oldest. Joe grabbed the cheese dip, "I knew I was in for a surprise the minute it was handed to me. I drifted off to a river and watched people diving in to save my life."

Stella, next in line to talk, "What I noticed was rage. My first connection was severe rage."

Gary, next in line to handle the tomahawk said, "What I felt was invasion. It's like a house being robbed."

Wilma thought, "What I felt was a lot of emotion."

The table turned back to Joe. Joe hesitated, then remarked, "Someone was looking for a lost child."

Stella next in line said, "I felt emptiness, loneliness."

Gary next to have the floor. "This stone was a prize possession."

Wilma next to have the floor, "The first turn, I didn't connect but when I did, I was somewhere in Philadelphia, then later in someone's house!"

The table shifted back to Joe. "A lost child caused quite a fiasco. Neighbors helped by bringing rafts and canoes."

Switching to Stella, "It must have been way back during the revolution times."

Moving next to Gary, "Seems the object possessed some emotional factor, or brought out sensitivity."

Next in line, Wilma, "I felt the change or ownership through tremendous turmoil. Some people seemed almost obsessed with it."

Gary, cutting in, "Like Gold or something."

Joe waited patiently, "The lost child or loved one becomes unattainable! I felt the sorrow, then later the pursuit." He turned to Stella, "I felt the emotion of hate, fear, rage, and extreme isolation."

Gary took the floor, "If it was during the American Revolution, it was the Native Americans and the early settlers."

Wilma, in deep meditation said, "The stone must possess a sort of catalyst to the spiritual planes."

Suddenly everyone in the group stopped as if on cue. Looking at each other, they realized the potential. Wilma explained her visit to the museum with the class trip. Stumbling for answers she remarked, "This must have been how it helped that lady's kid with polio!" Wilma turned the lights back on and breathed a sigh of relief. Shaking her head she said, "That was very good. I never thought we'd get as far as we did."

Joe, the oldest, remarked, "We could use another visit."

Wilma looked angry and remarked, "I can't get that boy fired, and us thrown in jail!"

Gary looked back to Joe, "Maybe there's another way. I know some people who contribute a lot to the museum."

Stella laughed, "What, are you going to threaten them for funding?"

Gary added, "No, of course not; that wouldn't work anyway."

Wilma, curiously asked, "What do you have in mind?"

Gary said, "I might get a special visit some evening with supervised attendance."

Then Stella jumped in with, "Yes, but you know, Gary we've tried doing things in the past. Sometimes outside influence destroys some of the medium."

Wilma said, "Not if they leave us alone."

Joe interrupted, "That's a lot better than sneaking."

Wilma walked to the kitchen and turned on the light and reached in the refrigerator, she said, "Gary, go ahead give it a shot. If after a couple of tries, then maybe I'll talk to Joshua."

Filling the bowl with chips, Joe remarked, "Well, good luck! I got to be leavin shortly."

Walking rapidly, Pauline began the morning routine. Thinking most of the evening about the move, she went straight up to her office. Opening the blinds she quickly headed back out through the hall to the elevator. She exited off the fifth floor. There she walked in on a dilemma! The glass case which contained the now giant Angelfish was nearly half empty! She took the water hose and quickly channeled fresh water mixed with the salt ingredient slowly into the tank. The fish were now, even larger! Pauline pulled out her cell phone. She paged Joshua. He was finishing up the east fourth floor, heard the page and picked up the intercom, "Yes, I'm right across from her, I didn't notice." Running, Joshua immediately opened the west annex door. He said, "Pauline, what's wrong?"

Pauline looked displeased, "I thought you were keeping an eye on this!"

Joshua looked in astonishment, "Honestly, I was just in here about forty minutes ago!"

Pauline strutted and checked the food log in a rage, then asked, "He was alright?"

Joshua added, "George, Yes absolutely!"

Pauline looked apologetic, "I'm sorry, when I came in the tank was half empty!"

Joshua pulled the hose from the salt mixer. Looking over to Pauline, he said, "I haven't had a chance to think this through."

Pauline looked at her watch and said, "Donna should be in by now, maybe the coffee's ready."

Joshua said, "I'll finish the floor and come straight over."

Donna arrived from downstairs and brought the coffee straight into Pauline's office. "Good morning, Miss Johnson."

Pauline giggled, "I just came in from upstairs, Joshua's coming in as soon as he's finished."

Pauline asked, "Do you know if any of our people have a C.D.L.?"

Donna paused, "You mean that Commercial Driver's License?"

Pauline replied, "I'm going to have to check on the Boston truck's tonnage."

Donna said, "I doubt if it's that big a vehicle."

Pauline reached for the creamer, "I'll call Boston soon as the world gets awake."

Joshua arrived within moments and knocked on the outside door. "Hello, may I come in?"

Pauline laughed, "The coffee's fresh."

Donna smiled and handed Joshua a cup. Pauline was mentioning some thing about needing a C.D.L.?"

Joshua said, "I thought it was just a van of some kind." Joshua, making himself comfortable, glanced at his watch.

Pauline rinsed her cup then returned to her desk. "Maybe we should just let them hire someone to come get him."

Donna walked back in and said, "Joshua, time for you to head home."

Joshua jumped up as if on cue, saluted Pauline and said, "I'm sure we can handle it. Just find out what that entails."

Pauline looked straight at Joshua and said, "I'll find out today."

Joshua walked down the steps land headed straight to the main lobby. Jeff walked toward him, they met mid floor of the main entrance. Jeff asked, "How's the home front?"

Joshua laughed, ""Well, they're getting ready for *something*."

Jeff continued his walk through to the upstairs office. Pauline, now busy on the phone called several neighboring museums. All were eager to volunteer. She seemed increasingly fatigued. Jeff entered the outer office, Donna said to him, "Pauline probably wants to see you."

Jeff laughed, "Probably? Is she free?"

Donna quipped, "Yes, go right in."

Pauline watched the door open, she said, "Jeff, come right on in."

Jeff grabbed a cup and strutted straight towards the coffee.

Pauline laughed, "You're a quick study, your old boss does the same thing!"

Jeff settled in the big, red chair across from Pauline. He laughed, "So what's up?"

Pauline said, "I'm going to find out about how to take this fish to Boston."

Jeff sneered as he looked straight across at her, "It can't be that big a deal." Pauline checked her computer screen. "I'll let you go take care of things while I check."

Jeff set his empty coffee cup down and slowly picked himself out of the deep, velvet chair. "Just when I was getting comfortable!"

Joshua made it home, slipped in the shower, set the clock for eleven and headed straight to bed. Wilma left her message around 10:30 and woke Joshua in his sleep. Tossing in bed, the alarm clock went off in what seemed minutes. Slowly rising from his sleep, Joshua walked to the phone answering service. "This is Wilma calling. When you get in, give me a call. I'm free all this week." Not bothering to call her, Joshua dressed and headed straight to the hospital. Waiting his turn in a pre visit room of the hospital, Joshua finally got to see George. George looked happy. "I'm glad you came, I almost had the big one!" he said. Not getting any response from Joshua, George invited Joshua over closer. "Here, sit down. You make me nervous." George, on oxygen pushed a button to raise his bed. George looked at Joshua and said, "I've been meaning to ask you." Slowly George pulled the oxygen out of his nose, "You ever see Chuck?"

Joshua scanned the room for a nurse, "Put that thing back in," he said. "Yeah, I saw him last weekend. Why?"

George again raising the line from his face, "Him and me were pretty tight."

The nurse now entered and said, "George, you can have that off, just let us know so we can reinsert it." The nurse slowly removed the pressure supply and finally the nose line. Feeling George's pulse first, then his head, she said, "You thirsty or anything?"

George looked interrupted, "No, mame, I'm just fine." Then he added, "When am I going home?"

The nurse looked at Joshua and smiled, "I don't think the doctor's ready for that yet." The nurse left.

Joshua slowly pulled the small chair over by the bed. Joshua grabbed George's hand and said, "You know you really had one heck of a job."

George's mind, still on the doctor said, "Yeah, well I'll tell you, that place gets dirty fast. You're in for me, right?"

Joshua laughed, "And then some!"

George understood and asked, "What's new over at the job?"

Joshua chuckled, "Did you know about the Angelfish?"

George, remained quiet, looking around with a nod.

Joshua said, "It's getting so big!"

George looked around the room and said, "I had a newspaper,"

Joshua continued, "I don't know how it all got so big!"

George back from his newspaper search said, "I wasn't listening, you say it actually got bigger yet?"

Joshua continued, "Pauline's going crazy trying to have it shipped to Boston."

George glanced back from the paper, "Too big for us?"

Joshua quipped, "Absolutely! It's barely staying alive right now."

George looked at the news and remarked, "How's the crews doing?"

Joshua said, "Well, I'm in for you. I moved Jeff to my post. Wrong answer."

George laughed, "Why's that?"

Joshua smiled, "He likes it too much! I'm going to have to push him off a cliff to get it back!"

George laughed, "What's hot at the podium?"

Joshua thinking, "Last week it was "Frogs of the Amazon!"

George smiled, "Frogs"

Joshua then said, "He's really a cool orator. He had a little frog jumping around in a glass container. It wouldn't stop jumping!"

George remarked, "How's the display going?"

Joshua frowned, "Unbelievable! Pauline's having some big state visit this week, some dignitaries" George laughed, "I was against putting it on display."

Joshua curious asked, "Why's that?"

George continued, "I thought Pauline was spending too much money. I also felt she was too aggressive."

Joshua smiled, "You're right. She's been jumping since she came in the door. You hear about the big national tour?"

George reached for a cup of tomato juice, "What National tour?"

Joshua continued, "It's the Native American displays. They held some meeting, somebody agreed to get the funding for the roof. We agreed to the U.S. tour."

George pondering his thoughts, "There's something to that stone. I used to get spooks, early in the morning."

Joshua was remembering his encounter with the child spirit.

George added, "I'd be doing the floors and it felt like I entered a realm or something."

Joshua smiled, "I thought I saw some small boy running around."

George said, "Night before last, I dreamt about some small child. He was trying to tell me something."

Joshua added, "This one was running around looking at all the stuffed animals."

George chuckled, "Yeah, don't say that to too many people! I told you the big story about my boy's letters and pictures?"

Joshua nodded, "Yeah." Joshua looked out the hospital window, "You ought to ask them to wheel you out and get a tan."

George replied, "That's right, nothing like a tan!"

Joshua glanced at his watch, "Well, I better get home and get some rest."

George grabbed his hand, "I hope to be out of here soon."

Joshua walked out and said, "I'll tell them you're getting better."

Joshua was thinking about the dream as he walked out to his car. He remembered Wilma, too and started towards his home. Grabbing the mail on the way in, he headed straight to the phone. He pushed the auto redial. Joshua called Wilma almost immediately. No answer so Joshua left a message. "Let me know when we can get together. Thanks." Running up the steps, Joshua jumped back in the shower. Within hours he went to bed. He fell asleep and started dreaming of his encounter. He was approached by the tomahawk. He slowly picked the stone up and walked towards the special exit, but a strong warrior blocked his passage. Looking back where the display was, he realized The robotic warrior had come to life also. Caught in between, Joshua charged towards the door holding the tomahawk like a football. Clearing the door, he ended up in another dimension. Walking around on cobblestones, Joshua realized he's somewhere around a small city. Walking up the street looking at the people, he realizes he's back in frontier time. As he approached a woman, she ran in the house. Walking farther, townspeople step off and stare. Entering an open food stand area, some Native Americans started talking to him. One grabbed his arm and shook his head. Joshua turned and asked, "Why?"

Joshua woke up in a heated sweat. He rushed to the mirror. He looked at his wristwatch and realized he was extremely hungry. Joshua rinsed his face, then headed straight down stairs to the refrigerator. Keeping his mind on his thoughts, he prepared a left over pork chop. Still thinking about the dream,

Joshua set the microwave and walked back towards the dining room. He pushed redial and called Wilma back again. He said, "Wilma, I caught up with you. You got my message?

Wilma laughed, "Of course, Joshua, tell me when?"

Joshua heard the buzzer on the microwave, "How about in an hour?" Wilma agreed. "Great, catch you then!"

Joshua prepared a quick meal of a half burned pork chop. Finishing quickly he started his walk to the car. Joshua was thinking about the museum starting Monday. Arriving at Wilma's, he walked up to the front door. Using the doorbell and a knock, he's greeted with a smile. Removing his sunglasses, he walked straight through to the dining room table. Wilma, aware of his interest, followed him to the table.

Wilma, looking very serious said, "You're aware that we're very grateful to you for sticking your neck out."

Joshua looked curious, "What'd you find out?"

Wilma continued, "Well, we passed it back and forth concentrating on our thoughts. Each of us had totally different experiences."

Joshua waited patiently as Wilma continued. "Over all it was like fishing in a very deep river. Each person that possessed the stone had totally different and far reaching experiences. I never felt so unsettled in my life. It's as if this stone had enormous control over our thoughts. I felt some of the rage of the native Americans during the early period" Wilma continued, "It seems the distrust became more magnified as a result of the harsh weather and growing paranoia." Wilma was pacing in her kitchen by now. Then she added, "Last week, when we shared notes, we seemed to be stumbling around on different hills. Each of us brought back a totally different experience. The tomahawk passed through so many people's ownership, all you felt was constant rage, misery, and all the bad things."

Joshua looked around the room and stumbled on a deck of tarot cards. Glancing back at Wilma, still in the kitchen, he moved the cards closer to his reach. Wilma looked up and noticed Joshua's interest. She said, "Wait, I'll show you how we do it."

Joshua was startled and pulled his arms back from the card case.

Wilma said, "Have you ever had a reading?"

Joshua smiled, "No, I've heard about them."

Wilma watched her friend lay the cards in a spread of thirteen. Joshua was reluctant at first, but participated according to Wilma's instruction. Upon completion of the tarot spread, Wilma continued about the tomahawk. "Somehow this stone became a passageway."

Joshua, said, "I had a weird dream this morning shortly after making it home from work." Wilma seemed uninterested and glanced reluctantly at Joshua as he said, "I had climbed in the display. I exited through the door that I used when while you were there. I had to play charge football with a warrior blocking the exit." Wilma now looked interested. Joshua continued, "I really wasn't myself, I think I was in the body of someone who lived in that time."

Wilma looked at the clock, "Well, what I want is a half hour viewing with the stone."

Joshua looked shocked, and his mouth fell open. Wilma raised her hand, holding back Joshua's fear. She said, "What I mean, Josh, is some of our people have friends in high places. It's so weird, you really get addicted to being around it. You seemed to get an unquenchable thirst for knowledge."

Joshua, rethinking his visit to the hospital interrupted, "I went to the hospital around noon to see a fellow coworker, he and I both swear we've had some kind of spiritual encounter."

Wilma laughed, "You probably did!"

Joshua looked at Wilma and said, "You never mentioned what all the different people experiences were that night."

"It was just weird, it felt like each one of us was in a different dimension, not just from this one but from each others experiences as well," said Wilma.

Joshua said, "I'm leaving, I got to get some more rest."

Wilma jumped to the occasion and said, "I hope you got some insight."

Joshua smiled, "Absolutely!" Walking out, he turned and said, "I want to come back sometime for another reading."

Wilma laughed, "That's not really what psychics do."

Joshua shrugged his shoulders, "Yeah, you sure seem to know what you're doing!"

Wilma said, "No, you really don't get it. We're usually called in to help solve murders."

Joshua stunned, turns around lowering his sunglasses, "How's all that work?" Wilma laughed, "I had learned tarot while attending classes in college."

Joshua was completely confused by now.

Wilma said, "I use the tarot more for entertainment."

Joshua said, "What about your meetings?"

Wilma replied, "We're all full pledged, unsolved murder psychics, a whole different field."

Joshua yawned, "I think I will get back with you on the readings."

Wilma replied, "Keep in touch!"

Joshua left quickly and headed straight home. He headed for the door and ran through the kitchen and ran upstairs.

Meanwhile, George greeted Donna and Pauline at the hospital. George mentioned his visits with Joshua. Pauline looked at her clock, "What time was that?"

George said, "Some time around 11:00."

Donna looked over to Pauline, "I guess we better wait till Monday morning."

George asked, "Something wrong?"

Donna asked, "He didn't mention anything about an Angelfish?"

George was pondering his answer. "Yeah, something abut it growing extra large?"

Donna replied, "Well, we have a van to ship it in. I got a vehicle from a local rental place." She glanced at Pauline. "We sort of hoped we might take the fish to Boston this weekend."

Pauline looked back from the window and said, "I sort of hate to bother him. If we don't move that poor thing soon, we're going to lose him!"

George asked, "How big is it?"

Donna interrupted, "It's almost to the point where it's bigger than the aquarium!"

Pauline added, "I know that's at least a 200 gallon tank, maybe more."

George added, "Maybe you can use the large tub from the basement." Pauline and Donna were listening spellbound. George continued, "Bring it up with the long bodied hand truck." He pulled his bed up to an elevated position then said, "Let the tub fill with the saltwater mix and put the water filter on the battery charge unit." He then paused. "You're probably going to have to all but empty the aquarium tank. Wrap the fish so he can't see. Use some light canvas." He paused again. "Lift it out with the ropes, it should go pretty smooth. If the boys find the fish too awkward, then they're going to have to raise the hand truck on some platform."

Pauline interrupted, "Tilt the aquarium?"

George looked over to Donna. "Let the fish sort of slide easily into the tub."

Donna shook her head, "Man, this is going to be real fun."

Pauline disturbed, "I really appreciate your insight, George, I just wonder if that's too much to ask of our help so soon."

Donna looked from George to Pauline, and said, "I'm sure Jeff wants to do the driving. I'm not sure Joshua's ready for the other part."

George laughed, "You know who would have been good for this?"

The whole group in unison said, "Chuck!!"

Pauline looked at Donna and said, "Just for the heck of it, see if he'll give us a hand."

George looked interested, "I'm sure he'll help."

Pauline and Donna were preparing to leave when Pauline said, "George, we have to be going."

Donna quipped, "I'll tell everyone you said Hello."

George replied, "Yeah, if Chuck doesn't want to help tell him he owes me one."

Pauline looked out the door into the hall and then looked back and said, "We will, thanks!"

George returned his bed to another position and reached for the remote. He slowly forced down a fresh juice. Donna and Pauline started back to the hospital parking lot.

Meanwhile, Joshua looked at his clock and decided to wake up and have dinner. Walking to the refrigerator he discovered it was empty! He ran back upstairs for a quick shower. He began his preparation for a night on the town. He closed the back door and pushed the auto start key. Joshua was embarking on his journey to a good restaurant. Passing Wilma's home and later George's, he made his way closer to the museum. The employees parking lot was empty, he continued towards the center of town. Getting stuck in traffic, he called his long time girlfriend. "Trish, this is Joshua."

Trish answered, "Josh! How have you been?"

Joshua laughed, "Actually hungry—you wouldn't be interested in eating somewhere would you?"

"Yeah, what the heck, I'll be hungry shortly," Trish said. "How soon you going to be here?"

Joshua chuckled, "I'm stuck in traffic about two blocks from our house."

Trish said, "Well, don't get unstuck too quick. I want to finish these dishes."

Traffic moving, Joshua laughed, "I'll be right there!" Joshua listened to the music on the super sport truck radio as he reached her driveway. Walking up to the back door, he quickly rapped.

Trish yelled, "Come in."

Joshua came in through the porch shed into the back kitchen door. He watched Trish in the kitchen. "Here, I'll help. Nothing like putting dishes away before you eat."

In walked Trish's mom. "Who's that with you Trish?" Slowly an elderly lady entered the kitchen hallway.

Trish looked back, "Josh meet my grandmother."

Joshua looked weird at Trish, "Hello, I'm a friend of your granddaughter."

Trish smiled and looked at grandmom. "Josh and I date once in awhile."

Joshua choking, "Sometimes things get in the way."

Trish remaining coy, "You know billiard games, late nights at the museum, things like that."

Grandmom totally amused made her way to the kitchen table. "How's that again about late nights at the museum?"

Trish and Joshua both started laughing.

Trish continued, "He has a job as supervisor, but some dude takes a heart attack and now he's on floors."

Joshua turned red and added, "It's sort of a favor."

Trish laughed, "I'd say. You talk to grandmom, I'll go get ready."

Grandmom interrupted, "How long you two going to be out?"

Trish looked back and said, "Couple days."

Joshua rolled his eyes and whispered in grandmom's ear, "Couple hours."

Grandmom looked up, "Really?"

Joshua shook his head, "Well, yea, were going somewhere to eat."

Within moments Trish was ready. She kissed grandmom and came back out through the hall. "I'm ready."

Joshua looked over at grandmom politely and waved, "Nice to meet you."

Trish said, "Come on."

Both headed to the truck. When Trish offered to drive, Joshua said, "Yeah, go ahead."

Trish pulled out darting through thick traffic. Joshua placed his hands across his eyes and peaked through his fingers. Trish asked, "You want to head towards town or someplace close."

Joshua said, "I just want to eat someplace without a whole bunch of noise."

Trish turned at the next light almost on cue and headed down a side street. "How about right here?" She veered off the road into a parking lot.

Joshua glanced up, "Yeah, I heard of this place."

Trish remarked, "I all but live here."

Joshua unloosened his seat belt and said, "Well, it's quaint enough."

Trish stretching out front of the truck, handed Joshua the keys, "They have everything you're into."

Joshua glanced around the outside and said, "This place wasn't here that long ago."

Trish opened the wooden doors, and said, "I think it was an auto parts store."

Joshua remembered and laughed, "Yeah, that's right! I use to come here with dad all the time!"

As they walked towards the hostess Trish started talking about last week's soap operas." Joshua was growing impatient and said, "Can we sit down first?" Slowly everything began to fall into place.

As the meal was being served, Trish started talking about her office job. As Joshua listened he glanced over in the adjacent billiard room. "Do you know how to play?"

Trish laughed, "Do you mean do *you* know how to play?"

Joshua returning to his meal said, "Why don't you put your name in over there with us?" Trish burst out laughing.

Joshua frowned, "What's so funny?"

Trish went into hysterics, "I could just imagine wiping out some mummy or something."

Joshua looked at her strangely, "I'm just trying to help."

Trish, tried to control her laughter, "I know—I'd be more than honored."

Trish, back under control said, "You find out when, I'll put the application in."

Joshua glanced out the window, "You're not going back out?"

Trish laughed, "No, I need a career change."

Pushing his food around the platter with his fork, Joshua began thinking about the giant Angelfish. He wondered how to approach the challenge. Joshua glanced back at Trish. Trish said, "You were way out there."

Joshua laughed, "Yeah, we have a small problem at work."

Trish said, "Go ahead."

Joshua laughed, "Sometimes little problems breed bigger ones."

Trish glanced at the waiter and said, "Thanks." Then she said to Joshua, "Go on."

"Well, we have an exhibit going on tour, an Angelfish too large for it's fish tank and a roof that needs replaced before it caves in," said Joshua.

Trish laughed, "Tell me about the Angelfish."

Joshua, holding his composure said, "Something in it's genes, something In the mixture of salt water, maybe something in the food we feed it, caused it to become, well—large! Along the lines of extra large, gigantic!

Trish started giggling, "What?"

Joshua smiled, "We have an aquarium around Boston we think will take him. We just have to figure out how to get him there." Walking over to the billiards, he continued, "You want me to stack em?"

Trish looked for the triangle, then headed toward the corner.

Trish said, "Maybe they'll come get it."

Joshua looked back at Trish, "Most of the places didn't even return our phone calls."

Breaking the balls, Trish took the first turn, "What about the display?"

Joshua remarked, "We acquired a rare Native American exhibit. As soon as interest got good, the big boys wanted it on National tour."

Trish called the pockets, "What's the big deal?"

Joshua watching Trish clean the table, "I think it's great, everyone wins. But we really spent a lot of money on remodeling." Joshua took aim at the last ball, "I suppose everything will work out, once things get back to normal."

Missing the ball, Trish put the final ball in the pocket. "You want to head back?"

Joshua looked at his wristwatch. "Yeah, I imagine we should." Joshua drove on the way home. Within a few moments he pulled up close to Trish's house. Looking at each other, Trish laughed, "You really want me to apply?"

"That's if you're not scared of mummies," said Joshua.

Trish went into hysterics, "Yes, I'm scared to death of mummies!"

Joshua glanced out the window, "I'll introduce you to the one we call Pete." Trish shivered at the thought, "I'll think about it," she said. Closing the door of the pickup she yelled, "Thank you!"

Meanwhile, back at the hospital, George was drifting into sleep, remembering Joshua's last visit. Thinking about his letters and pictures of a son long lost, he remembers the birthday parties. Entering another realm of deep sleep, George drifted back to work at the museum. Someone, bringing the floor supplies up grabbed his arm on the service elevator. "Watch your back up there, things are all stirred up." George shaking his head, walked with his arms full toward the main office. Hearing an unusual sound, George slowly approached the new display. Walking slowly through the makeshift tunnel, higher and higher towards the final display, George walked with greater and greater anticipation. as he made the last turn, George noticed a Native American warrior holding the stone. Stopping at the turn, George observed from a distance. Suddenly the presence screamed out loud right towards George's spot. Without translators, George saw the warriors rage building. Turning to run, he noticed a whole tunnel and museum full of warriors. Pushing one person straight in the face, George ran full blast for the service elevator. Suddenly a voice George recognized came through the dream. "Mr. Andrews, are you alright?" Then again, "Mr. Andrews!"

George, waking in a sweat, looked at the nurse. "I had a bad dream." Pushing the button to raise the bed, George sipped on some cold ice. The nurse, watching his movements, remained silent. George, feeling stupid, laughed, "I'm O.K." Slowly the nurse remarked, "You had us worried for a minute!"

George, looking up, "If you would have been in that dream, you'd be more than worried!"

George, drinking the last of his ice water, requested more for later. Reading a book about world news, George settled back down. Keeping his mind off the dream, thinking about returning home, he patiently waited for the nurse to return.

Meanwhile, Joshua decided to take a walk. Sporting a baseball cap and a new walkman, he passed George's home. Walking farther, Joshua passed Trish's house and kept right on walking. Street by street, Joshua slowly approached his favorite corner with the pool hall. He walked up, paid the cover charge. He heard a rock band playing noisily. Removing his baseball cap and walkman, he headed straight for the bar. Eyes not adjusted yet, he squinted looking out towards a couple sitting in a dark corner. Ordering a drink, the male sitting in the dark corner walked up to him. "You mind if I come back for a week or two?"

Joshua jumped with surprise. "Chuck, you scared me! What brings you back out this way?"

Chuck, remembering his date, "I brought one of my girl friends with me."

Pondering his remark, Joshua said, "You're coming back?"

Chuck said, "Yeah, Donna called at Pauline's request to help with the Angelfish thing." Laughing he said, "I hear you're filling in for George?"

Joshua sipped on his drink, "It's not as easy to fill the old man's shoes as I thought."

Chuck asked, "Is he out of the hospital?"

Joshua shook his head. "You better get back to your date. I think they're taking the order."

Chuck looked back a second time, "Yeah, maybe you're right. I'll call you later tonight or tomorrow."

Joshua, still tired from working midnight shift said, "Yeah, tomorrow; Sunday, that will be fine." Returning to his table, Joshua felt isolated sitting by himself at the bar. He finished his drink and slowly headed back out the door. Walking the five or six block square, he approached the museum from the far side. The evening sky showed millions of stars over the dark parking lot. Joshua zigzagged past the back parking lot and looked around himself then again across at the museum front dome, then over the river towards the city. A late night ball game and hockey players were in the park. As he walked he saw the lights on at George's house. Usually this late, everything's pretty quiet. Walking farther, Joshua began picking up the pace for the final hundred yards. Opening the back door of his home, he heard the beeper on the answering machine. Walking over, out of breath, he glanced at the clock. He flopped down in the arm chair. 1st message: "Hello, this is Donna. Just wanted to say Pauline got a hold of Chuck. He's going to give us a hand next week. 2nd message: "Josh!, this is George. Good news; they let me out. I'll see if the doc will let me come back next week." Looking out the window, Joshua returned to the answering machine. 3rd message: "This is Pauline, I got some extra help next week. Chuck said he'll give us a hand." Deleting the messages, Joshua finally reached the last one. 4th message: "This is Trish, my grandmom really liked you. Would you be interested in coming over tomorrow for lunch or maybe dinner? By the way, I liked driving your truck." Joshua deleted the messages and headed up the steps.

Monday morning came like a flash. Pauline started out by coming to work early. Donna approached the main entrance and headed straight for the cafeteria. Joshua pulled in the parking lot and noticed Chuck coming up the main street from the other side. Joshua glanced around the museum parking lot. He waited as Chuck made his way toward his truck.

Chuck blew his horn and laughed, "This ought to be fun."

Joshua nodded his head towards the other parking space. "She's here already."

Chuck paused then asked, "Pauline?"

Joshua smiled, "Yea."

Joshua walking, lit a cigarette as he approached the main sidewalk.

Chuck remarked, "Would you believe it's been six, almost seven weeks already."

Joshua shook his head, "Oh, I believe it!" He looked back to where he parked. "You have a hard time getting off work over that other place?"

Chuck shrugged his shoulders, "They're pretty good that way. Especially when I told them Pauline needed help."

Joshua looked at Chuck. "You didn't work that long with her, right?"

Chuck said, "Ah, about three weeks." Opening the huge glass doors, Chuck and Joshua watched Donna come out of the cafeteria towards the elevators.

Chapter Six

THE DISAPPEARANCE

Joshua ran across the large room and shouted, "We're coming Donna. Walking behind the counter to punch in, Joshua quickly punched his time card. Donna waited patiently for the door to open and said, "Chuck, glad you were able to come!"

Joshua ran up and relieved Donna of holding the coffee tray. Joshua glanced the work notebook reviewing the upcoming work plans and asked, "Wonder if Pauline got a hold of someone about the truck?"

Donna quietly replied, "I'm not sure, but I think there's a change in plans."

Pauline greeted her team as soon as she got off the elevator on the fifth floor. Pauline interjected, "Yeah, that's sort of true." Looking over to Chuck, "Oohh, hello stranger! I couldn't get anyone to return by e-mail!" Then she added, "The National aquarium in Baltimore offered everything."

Joshua grabbed the door for Pauline. Joshua looked back at Donna, "Are they going to supply a driver?"

Pauline nodded. "Everything. Plus they're very nice people."

Following Pauline into her office, Chuck beat Joshua to the red, velvet chair than laughed, "You get to sit here all the time."

Chuck walked in the room and found himself drifting over towards the small aquarium, like a lost soul. Pauline immediately turned on the computer and waited for the screen to come on. Looking across to Chuck, she said, "You might find it easier if you cover him over first."

Chuck was staring towards Joshua and said, "What? Oh, yeah, you're right Pauline."

Chuck said, "I think it will help a lot with it being apprehensive." Glancing back to Joshua, Joshua started laughing. "Does he always play in the aquarium?"

Pauline took the coffee from Donna and smiled, "Only when someone sits in his favorite chair!" Pauline glanced at the monitor and clicked for the sixth floor. As she zoomed in carefully on the Angelfish, she remarked, "Yeah, maybe it's a good idea we get started."

Chuck and Joshua quickly walked around Pauline's desk and stared at the computer screen. Joshua shook his head, "What about the oxygen level?"

Donna, overhearing the conversation jumped in quickly with, "Baltimore suggested using a 50/50 mix of oxygen and water."

Pauline added, "Try to keep the bag sealed. Leave an air pocket in the top of the bag."

Chuck, coming back to his senses said, "Bag?" Then asked, "Do we have a bag that big??"

Donna returned to the room after hearing the phone ring. "That was them, they'll be there in about twenty minutes."

Pauline spun around in the swivel chair and glanced at her desk clock. "Not bad."

Chuck looked towards Joshua and asked, "What time you got?"

Joshua quipped, "9:10. Chuck?"

Chuck looking back across from Pauline, tilted his head and said, "What?"

Joshua almost forget his composure and then said, "Oh, George says, there's a large tub in the basement."

Chuck rapped his muscular round fingers on Pauline's desk, and said, "That sounds like a better idea. Where in the basement?"

Pauline smiled at Joshua than looked back at Chuck, "You want to try that?"

Chuck, in a deep thought, nodded his head. "Yea, that's much better."

Pauline seizing the moment said, "I'll page Jeff to go down and get it."

Chuck looked over to Joshua and said, "We better get started." Walking out the main curator's office, Chuck looked back at Pauline and remarked, "We'll let you know how we make out."

Pauline giggled, "I wouldn't miss this for the world."

Joshua, rolled his eyes holding the door for Chuck at the outer office, Then walked down the hall Around the curb and out towards the elevators.

Chuck looked back to see if Pauline was following them. "She's pretty Into this kind of stuff.' pushing the elevator button.

Joshua with his shirt half unbuttoned smiled and said, "Yea, she never goes home." Joshua glanced back quickly, smiled and hoped she didn't approach. "You hear a noise?"

Chuck, pushing the elevator button again for Joshua growing impatient. "Yeah, they sure to be getting their money back." The door opened and Chuck and Joshua Immediately approached the west annex. Opening the double wooden doors, Chuck fixed his stare towards the Angelfish. "This is not going to be easy!" Half the fish, now exposed, Chuck added, "Good thing somebody hooked up the sprinkling water rig."

Almost immediately, Pauline and Donna swing open the double doors. Chuck glanced at Pauline, "We're going to need something to wrap around his face."

Donna looked to Joshua, "How about a garbage bag?"

Chuck turned around towards Donna, "Yea, some kind of small hoist, too."

Donna looked to Pauline, "There's a come-along somewhere."

Joshua quietly said, "It's holding up a water pipe in the main lobby, behind where the time clock is."

Pauline, holding the pager said, "Jeff, can you send somebody? What's it called?"

Chuck laughed, "A come-along."

Pauline finished with, "Jeff, the "come-along" is in the main lobby by the time clock."

Moments later, Jeff said, "Pauline, it's on the way! Pauline clicked her microphone several times in acknowledgement.

Joshua looked across the room, "How we going to keep it still if it starts to splash?"

Chuck laughed, "Work quickly!"

Pauline and Donna began laughing. Jeff entered the room and pushed the double doors open with the hand truck. "Is this the tub you guys were talking about?"

Joshua looked closer, "Oh, this one. Yea, Jeff."

Chuck looked closer at the Angelfish. What I think we'll do is wrap his eyes with some kind of colored plastic, maybe a garbage bag." Then looking towards the ceiling he said, "Hook the "come-along" on a swivel from up there."

Joshua looked at Chuck, "How about we put the fish in a bag of water?"

Chuck looked back to Pauline, "Yeah, then wrap the fish in a clear plastic makeshift bag of 50/50." Pauline nodded in agreement. "Then lower it into the tub."

Donna walked over towards the octopus and said, "Funny, it was just the Angelfish."

Meanwhile, George had been cleared to return to work. He waited patiently in Donna's outer office. A crew member noticed and recognized George and yelled in the office, "They're all upstairs getting ready to move that Angelfish!"

George, waving off the worker, said, "Thank you." Reading a museum circular, he twisted and squirmed on the waiting room couch. He heard Donna's phone ring. One line started blinking then another stated ringing on the adjacent. George was growing impatient and threw down the paper, remarking to himself "I better go see how they're making out." Getting off the elevator, Jeff noticed George approaching the double wood doors, "George! Welcome back!"

George smiled and pushed against the wooden doors. Walking in while everyone had their back turned, George watched Chuck on a large step ladder.

He was placing a swivel hook into the ceiling support studs. He tapped Donna on the shoulder, "You got it pretty much figured out?"

Donna, recognizing, the voice, exclaimed, "George!!"

Pauline, glanced for a moment back, then readjusted her eyes on Chuck. She remained silent. Joshua smiled from ear to ear and said, "Wow, that's a Quick recovery."

George, giving Joshua a frown, said, 'What you trying to say?"

Joshua laughed, "No, I'm glad you're coming back. You are coming back?"

George nodded his head all the time watching Chuck hang the "come- along."

Joshua looked first to Donna, then to Jeff who was returning with a thick, clear plastic bag. "Maybe no one else misses you," Glancing back to Chuck, then looking back again to George, "Those floors are murder!"

George tried not to laugh, but started smirking and said, 'Yeah, they sort of grow on you."

Chuck, walked carefully down the step ladder, past Pauline and shook George's hand. "Welcome back, George!" Suddenly the door swung open, George hesitantly returned the shake, "Chuck!' "It's great seeing you here."

Chuck gave George a long stare, "Yeah, we're getting there." Jeff holding the double doors hands Chuck the green bag. Inch by inch they slowly eased the clean, green garbage bag around the fish. Water started missing the tank spraying everywhere! Joshua's shirt was wet and he said, "Maybe the clear plastic first, then put the other color around the eyes."

Chuck inched the clear, plastic slowly around the fish. They began tying the rope holding lines to the twisted makeshift grips, duck taped every couple feet along the far side. Once the fish was completely encompassed, Chuck slowly filled some of the plastic and raised it totally up enclosing the Angelfish. Chuck now soak and wet glanced and shook his head, back to Pauline and Donna. "I think this is going to work. I don't think we have to worry about his vision of us." Then Chuck slowly brought all the twists to the center and wrapped the fish snuggly. He then attached them to the "come-along" hoist. After stepping back down to catch his breath, he said, "We'll wait for the bag to completely fill. George looked over to Joshua and said, "I hope the bag can hold all that weight."

Donna whispered with her hand over her mouth, "I don't think the Angel fish is that heavy."

George looked back towards the fish tank and said, "Donna, that water aint light!"

Pauline walked over and asked, "What you whispering about?"

Donna laughed, "We're arguing about the weight."

Just then, Joshua jumped on the ladder and began slowly cranking the "come-along". Looking down to the spectators, he said, "This is going to take a while."

Donna glanced at her watch and remarked, "I better go check the office."

George, stressed said, "Maybe I'll come with you."

Chuck watched them leave, laughed and yelled, "Scardey Cats!!"

Inch by inch it seemed like forever, Joshua slowly brought the bag full of water out of the enclosure. The fish remained calm. Chuck started bringing the tub closer to the fish tank. Inch, by inch, the Angelfish and the bag lifted higher and higher. The men walked closer to aid if needed. Joshua very slowly trolled the bag and fish out over the lip of the tank and closer to the tub. Smiles and jubilees quickly set in while the last of the bag began loosening in the tub and hand truck. Chuck looking back realized they were all by themselves. Then Chuck remembered the closed circuit cameras. Chuck walked over to the corner, and looked back at Joshua then peered up to the camera and clapped. He gave a double thumbs up when suddenly a voice across the intercom announced, through the entire museum, "We see you, Chuck, thanks a million!" Joshua and one of Jeff's workers held the fish. The three men made their way towards the double wood doors. Suddenly Joshua looked at Chuck bursting Out in Laughter," I didn't know we had a fan club." Outside the six floor stood a room full of spectators. Pushing from behind the tub, Joshua and Chuck reach the main service elevator. Entering the elevator on the far side of the east annex, the men slowly descended to the basement loading dock.

Chuck looked at Joshua and the other worker, "I guess you can handle it from here."

Joshua looked up while holding the far side of the plastic and said, "Chuck, thank you very much! I'll buy you dinner over at the pool hall some night."

Chuck smiled, "I want to say good-bye to the girls and talk to George a minute."

Joshua laughed, "Especially one?"

Chuck chuckled, "You have one long memory." He looked over to the men from Baltimore and smiled, "I'm coming down to Baltimore and check things out when I get a chance."

The two men laughed, "Let us know in advance, we'll give you a tour guide."

Waving to the crews, Chuck closed the elevator door and started up to the fifth floor. George walked on the other side of the floor, then started to head out to the other elevator. Chuck, recognizing him from a distance yelled across the floor, "George, wait up!"

George stopped while Chuck ran zigzag through the crowded east annex. "We did it!!"

George laughed, "That was luck. I was waiting for the fish to start Squirming or maybe the bag to break."

Watching the long line form for Native American display, Chuck smiled back at George, "That was another trying feat!"

George asked, "You still in school?"

Chuck shook his head, "Probably for the rest of my life as slow as things are going. We're on semester break."

George, now in the elevator, asked, "You going down?"

Chuck nodded, "I want to say good-bye to the girls first."

George laughed, "Good luck with school."

Chuck shook George's hand and said, "Hope you're back to work soon, with us that is, not across the street!."

Joshua waved and headed toward the curator's office. Donna walked in and burst out in euphoria, "Good job!! I'll buzz Pauline, I think she wants to see you." Pauline walked out, "I thought I heard you talking to somebody. If you ever need work or a reference or anything—"

Chuck cut her off, "I'll know where to come. I just thought I'd drop in before I left. Joshua and the crews were a lot of help."

Donna glanced at the clock, "You want to join us for a late lunch?"

Chuck glanced at the wall clock, "Yeah, Wow it got late quick."

Donna was deleting some old messages on the computer. She glanced up to Pauline, "You Mind I come along?"

Chuck interjected, "Absolutely!"

Pauline smiled and closed her main office door. As they walked together Chuck noticed the packed east annex. "You mean they're all standing in line for the Indian displays?"

Dona replied, "Chuck, it never slows down."

Chuck looked curiously at Pauline, "What's the big deal?"

As they stand waiting for the elevator, Pauline said, "It's the kid thing. new display with the surprise waiting for them around the final corner. The kids aren't aware of the robotic warrior's existence until they're on top of it."

Donna added, "Pauline's actually being humble."

Chuck, held the door exiting on the ground floor and slowly walked towards the cafeteria. Looking over to the guest speakers podium, Chuck asked, "I wonder what I've been missing."

Donna again, "Actually the speech about Neptune."

Pauline looked back to Donna who was approaching the food trays, "I thought it was Mars?"

Donna quipped, "That was two months ago."

Chuck, at the cashier register looked over to Pauline and said, "I was going to ask you something about ancient Iraq."

Pauline placed the tray on the table and said, "Shoot!"

Chuck laughed, "I don't remember the question."

Pauline rolled her eyes and reached for her lunch tray. Chuck looked at Donna passing her a coffee cup, "How you been doing?"

Donna shook her head, "Fine, very busy."

Pauline talking loudly said, "She's helped me out a lot."

Chuck watching Jeff and the work crews approach the lunch counter and asked, "Did they clear George to come back?"

Pauline, taking a bite of her sandwich said, "Yeah." Donna noticed her with her mouth full and said, "George wants a week off to shore up things around the house."

Pauline come back with, "Joshua will be happy. He doesn't like getting up that early."

Jeff glanced at Chuck and the other two and walked over slowly. "Don't I know you from somewhere?"

Chuck, just finishing his lunch looked up. It was Jeff. "That thing worked out pretty good this morning." Jeff smiled from ear to ear, "I was holding my breath."

Chuck glanced over to Pauline and then at Donna, "Somebody had important work to do all of a sudden." Donna smirked looking back at Chuck.

Chuck said, "I'm going to head out. I'll e-mail you if I think of any questions. I had a good time." On the way out, Chuck read the list of upcoming guest speakers. He waved and made his way to the main lobby.

Jeff, sitting down next to Donna said, "You don't mind if I sit here?"

Donna looked over to Pauline and said, "No, not at all!"

Jeff, who was all smiles asked, "How many more weeks do I get Joshua's job?"

Pauline and Donna burst out in hysterics. Pauline looked around the room and said, "George will be coming back week after next."

Jeff snapped his fingers and said, "It was a lot of fun."

Donna looked across the table at Pauline, "But I don't think Josh had any."

Donna again, "Did anyone put the "come-along" back on the pipe?"

Jeff answered, "Sure did. How long was Chuck with us?"

Donna, finishing her juice, "Chuck was here when I came. Probably around five years."

"He's very quick with ideas," said Jeff.

Pauline glanced at her watch, "Donna, I'm ready to go."

Donna said, "Jeff, tell everyone they did a good job."

Pauline and Donna walked out and headed to the elevators. The crowds were now heavy. Pauline and Donna waited patiently for the elevators. Pauline walked out into the main lobby and checked the "come-along." Walking back to Donna she remarked, "I don't trust him for some reason."

Donna remained quiet. Getting off on the fifth floor, they shortly made their way through the crowds and approached the main curator's office.

Donna checked the answering service while Pauline walked briskly to her own desk. Donna slowly reviewed each call. Donna checked the next message: "Gary Thomas calling—want to discuss a time to meet with you. Thanks." Pauline heard the call from the inner office, buzzed Donna and said, "You have his number?"

Donna scrambled, "Yes, right here."

Pauline immediately returned the call, "Hello, Gary Thomas, please."

Gary, busy in the outer hall took forever to make the office, in New York.

Out of breath, Gary said, "Hello, Pauline—sorry it took so long! I want to keep you updated on the National tour." Pauline remained quiet. Gary continued, "The superior fund raising and increased awareness that the National tours creates is our main goal." Pauline glanced at her desk clock. Gary continued, 'I have a check here for $175,000 towards the repairs of the museum's roof."

Pauline said, "I know I don't want to appear rude, but that won't cover legal fees."

Gary Thomas added, "Yeah, I know, well there's a lot more coming later. There's a lot of interest in National tours."

Pauline said, "Look, Gary, whatever's gong to make it work, you certainly have my cooperation."

Gary laughed, "That leads me to my next question. I want to bring a crew around a week or so early to decide what we want to take, plus bar code each item and photograph them for insurance reasons."

Pauline checking her calendar, "We're caught up for now, so whenever your people want; we'll even help."

Gary Thomas glanced at a room full of helpers and said, "How's Wednesday sound?"

Pauline smiled as Donna approached her desk. "That will be great! See you Wednesday." Pauline looked up to Donna and asked, "Something wrong?"

Donna curiously asked, "I wonder how soon they're going to take the stuff?"

Pauline shook her head, "I got side tracked, and I forgot to ask!"

Donna asked, "May I go home?"

Pauline laughed, "Yeah, sure. Anything bad?"

Donna replied, "My mother wants someone to run her to the doctor."

Pauline looked back at her desk clock, "It's 1:30 anyway. I'll cover the Desk, You go head and take the afternoon if you want."

Donna, walking out said, "We must have had forty calls when we went to lunch."

Pauline walking out behind Donna stopped at the desk and said, "Yeah, Donna, I'll screen them. Tell your family I said hello."

Donna grabbed her pocketbook and b-lined towards the outer door. Pauline, staring at John's old fishing picture waited patiently for Donna to exit. Preparing to screen the calls, Pauline returned to her own desk for her coffee cup. After turning off the computer monitor and cleaning her eyeglasses, she Started walking towards the outer desk. Sitting down at Donna's desk, Pauline moved the empty coffee pitcher off the counter.

Jeff was approaching the outer lobby. Noticing Pauline, Jeff scanned the room quickly for Donna, then asked, "Where's Donna?"

Pauline looked up curiously, "Is there something I can help you with?"

Jeff smiled, "I'm sorry, I just thought I'd ask about the empty aquarium upstairs."

Pauline looking irritated, "I would just shut it down and we'll take a look up there tomorrow. Don't get too involved with anything on Wednesday. We have people coming from New York who want to pick certain items for the National tour."

Jeff, looked serious and said, "They want the Indian displays, right?"

Pauline, hiding her emotions, "Yes, some of it. You doing O.K. with your work crews?"

Jeff chuckled, "Absolutely."

Pauline smiled and pushed for the next message. Jeff, catching a hint, said, "Well, I'll get back to work." Pauline, staring at the answering machine, waved and shook her head.

The tank truck, leaving the Philadelphia area, slowly started down I-95 approaching the airport exit. Harvey and Greg steadied the Angelfish in the back of the truck. Harvey, using his walkman, stared out the back window. Greg called home and found his wife on the telephone. Careful observation of the fish showed all was well. The driver, thinking quickly, merged into the passing lane approaching Wilmington, Delaware. Harvey shouted over to Greg, "We should be there by 6:00. Glancing out the side window, Harvey began drifting into deep thought. Slowly the large plastic bag began a downward drift into the tub. Greg first noticed it, glanced at the slack, not thinking and redialed his cell phone. Suddenly the reality hit! "Oh, shucks!"

Harvey, hearing Greg's outburst glanced back towards the fish tub. Totally overwhelmed, Harvey shouted across the hollow truck. 'Where'd it go?"

Greg jumped up, still holding his cell phone and pulled at the loose plastic. Greg and Harvey in unison, started banging for the driver to pull off. They flicked on a light in the back from the front console panel. The driver opened up the pull down door from the back. The driver yelled over noisy traffic, "What's wrong?" Harvey glanced at Greg, "The fish, it's gone!!" The driver immediately turned off the motor. Running back he tripped over a piece of road debris. Limping back to the occupants, the driver flashed a beam of light around the exterior of the tub. "That's impossible! What are we going to do?"

Harvey, shook his head, "I'll call Baltimore." Greg got a hold of his wife and started telling the story. Harvey started laughing and said, "They want to talk to you."

The driver reached for Harvey's cell phone. "I don't know—that's weird!! Yea, we're about two hours out."

Pausing, the driver looked to the occupants, "You guys sit up front the rest of the way."

Harvey and Greg immediately jumped down off the back of the truck. The driver slowly pulled down the rear door. Harvey closed the door of the cab after Greg, then looked across to the driver, "We both were supporting the plastic, when everything started to happen."

Harvey looked towards Greg in the middle of the cab, "What's your wife think?"

Greg, shaking his head remained quiet. The truck slowly made it's way closer to home. Harvey said, "It's really a weird situation! First it grew gigantic, now it disappears!"

Meanwhile Pauline finished covering for Donna. Closing up shop, she headed for the elevators. Joshua stopped in to get his last weeks paycheck and greeted Pauline in the main lobby. "How'd things go with the fish?"

Pauline, turning around, "Joshua said, "Things went pretty well. Joshua laughed, "I forgot to get my paycheck."

Pauline walked towards the front glass doors and said, "Chuck helped a lot. The museum in Baltimore offered everything."

Joshua curiously asked "I thought we were going to take it someplace Around Boston?" then waiting for a crowd to pass, "I really sort of looking forward to it."

Pauline watches Joshua push the elevator button, "We did, too, but the other place was a lot more helpful." She took a deep breath and then said, "Least that's one problem solved!"

Joshua stopped suddenly and walked towards the parking lot, "By the way, when's George coming back?"

Pauline started smiling, "This has been the focal point discussion all week. George coming back." She reached for her car keys and said, "He requested another week to shore up loose ends at home."

Joshua said jubilantly, "Yippee!" He tapped on the hood of Pauline's car and waved, then ran for his truck.

Tuesday morning came on like a lion. When Donna returned she noticed the work crews cleaning the window display cases.

Joshua watched from a distance then walked to the service elevator with a large vacuum cleaner. Pauline trotted past the workers and headed straight for her office. Jeff, held the end hose and asked, Joshua, "Did you have a rough night?"

Joshua said, "I don't know how George does all this by himself." Jeff fresh from a nights sleep, "Maybe we can get him some help, now that he's had some trouble." Joshua closed the elevator leaving Jeff standing with a mop. "We can bring it up, but George won't want any," he said laughing.

Joshua signaled with his hand as the elevator door closed.

Donna looked as Pauline arrived, "Good morning."

Pauline shook her head and said, "Not that good."

Donna looked curiously at Pauline and followed her with the tray of coffee. Donna sat in the red, velvet chair in front of Pauline, "What's wrong?"

Pauline shook her head and walked over and looked out to the parking lot. *"They-lost-the-fish!!"*

Donna remained calm. Pauline continued, "I had a call on my cell phone. I didn't bother to check till I got home." Pauline looked at her coffee cup, "Some how, the fish came up missing!"

Joshua returned home from work and noticed the answering machine beeper. Pushing the call button, Joshua ran up the steps to begin gathering clothing for a hot morning shower. Hearing Donna's voice, he rushed back down the steps. "Joshua, this is Donna calling, you get a chance, give me a call." Joshua, scratched his head with a big yawn and ran back to take his shower.

Jeff finished his morning routine and walked into Donna's outer office. Donna, was busy accessing files on the computer. She glanced up and asked, "Oh, Jeff, did you hear?"

Jeff, sitting on the arm of the couch asked, "Hear what?"

Donna, holding her composure "Something happened to the fish!"

Jeff looking intently said, "Go on."

Donna laughed, "We don't know." Stopping for a moment to listen for Pauline, Donna continued, "According to Pauline, the work crew stopped in traffic someplace outside Delaware. One of the helpers started screaming, it's gone! Both helpers holding the fish started banging on the walls of the tank truck for the driver to pull off."

Jeff, not amused asked, "How do you lose a giant fish?"

Donna turned off the computer monitor, shook her head and said, "Your guess is as good as mine!"

Jeff peeks through the doors towards Pauline's desk, "I'm going back to work, I'll drop back later." Just as he started towards the elevator, he remembered his purpose for going to the office. Snapping his fingers, he turned and started back towards Donna's office.

Pauline retuning from the main office walked out to Donna's desk, she said, "I'm going to check on some things, I'll be back soon." Just as she passed Donna's desk, Jeff swings the outer door open and walked right into Pauline.

Jeff walked to Donna's desk and asked, "Can you put some razor blades on order?" Jeff continued, "We have a wax graffiti artist making havoc on the animal display windows."

Moments later, the phone rang. Donna answering said, "Joshua, sorry to bother you. Jeff was standing nearby and shouted loud enough for Joshua to hear, "Your not going to believe this!" Pauline lifts her head annoyed from her inner office.

Donna looked again concentrating on the phone, "Somehow, something happened to the Angelfish." Donna, holding the phone out so Jeff could hear, Donna continued, "Yea, I know, aint' it weird? No, just disappeared!"

Jeff began shaking his head and smirked. Donna looked at her watch, "I better let you get some sleep."

Joshua, totally overwhelmed, "Yea, guess I better. Just think about all That work!"

Donna looked back at Jeff still talking to Joshua, "You want razor blades?"

Jeff smiled, "The kind you use to scrape windows with."

Donna said, "I'll call, they'll bring them right out."

Jeff exited almost on cue, while Donna got up to walk to Pauline's office. Listening momentarily, Donna laughed, "I'll let you go Josh." Joshua looked at his wrist watch, with a yawn, "Yes Donna, I'm falling asleep on my feet, see you tomorrow morning when I'm done the floors.' Joshua returned to sleep after a quick flick of the T.V. Slowly the day unfolded like most others. Joshua entered work around 2:30 a.m. Wednesday and found the museum in total disarray. Someone moved his cleaning supplies and never returned them. The vacuum cleaner bag was so gull Joshua had to change it. The mops were gone. The first two hours were spent on playing catch up. The only signs of life were the security patrols outside and the fish tanks on the sixth floor. Approaching the fifth floor on elevator, Joshua exited and looked for a floor mop. Walking past the window cases, he noticed the growing miles of graffiti. Shaking his head and talking to himself, he said, out loud, "Who the heck's doing all this stuff?" Walking across to the bathrooms, Joshua saw the graffiti on the mirrors as well. After leaving the rest room, he walked into the west annex. The wax scribbles became visible with each step! He immediately picked up a wall phone and asked for security. Joshua, pranced back and forth, then started walking toward the elevators. Security on the third floor, responded immediately! Two security patrol men walked off the fifth floor and flashed a beam of light towards the display cases. The female security person holding the light remarked, "Joshua, do you have any enemies?"

Joshua looked back at walking towards the octopus. "No, not at all."

Both flashing lights while walking with Joshua, the tall male figure asked, "This stuff's hard to get off?" Then pausing with a glance at his helper, he said, "You ever tried taking this off your windows at Halloween?"

The short haired brunette female burst out laughing, "No, our family usually gives candy."

Joshua, not amused reaches for her flashlight, "It must have happened at night. Somebody here sure would of noticed something."

The male guard walked down the main corridor returning with his flashlight off. A shallow click sound through out each floor marked the arrival of the large ceiling lights activated by a remote timer. The female looked patient towards Joshua then slowly continued reaching for her flashlight, "We'll go check downstairs around the rest of the premises as soon as our other crews make their post." Joshua walked behind them and shook his head, "Pauline will have a fit. Today's a big day. We have dignitaries coming." Returning to the main floor with security, Joshua approached the main entrance. Joshua said, "Just the one floor, so it seems." Then Joshua started back toward the elevators alone. Reaching the fifth floor, Joshua began his early morning routine.

Chapter Seven

GARY THOMAS AND THE COORDINATORS

Shortly, the sun began coming through the windows. Jeff reported early, and hit the time clock first. Walking towards the elevators, he's approached by security. The female, having been up all night, yawed and said, "You haven't seen anyone running around in here or anything, have you?"

Jeff laughed, fresh from a night's sleep, "Why, yes, thousands!"

The female giggled, "No, I mean like up to no good?"

Jeff said, "It's about the graffiti?"

The female smiled, "You do know."

Jeff replied, 'Yeah, I asked Donna to order some straight blades. It was all over the animal's window cases."

The female looked straight in Jeff's eyes and said, "It's all over the fifth floor now."

Jeff, shaking his head said, "I don't know how they got away with it."

The female added, "We did security spot checks all night. You see Joshua, tell him we'll keep trying. We're done for today."

Jeff nodded and walked to the elevator. Donna grabbed the door and asked, "What's that all about?"

Both rode up to the fifth floor. Jeff quipped, "Somebody's gone crazy with graffiti."

Donna looked shocked, "What?"

Jeff continued, "Security doesn't have a clue." Exiting the elevator on the fifth floor, Jeff and Donna approached Joshua. Jeff spouted out, "I'm sorry about the wax."

Joshua, really tired by now, looked over, shook his head and said, "I don't know. It's all over the place!"

Donna, in shock, said, "Pauline will be fit to be tied!"

Jeff noticing how tired Joshua was, asked, "You want me to finish any thing?"

Joshua replied, "Oh, no, I got everything, but who would do that?"

Now pointing towards the west annex, Donna and Jeff approached slowly. Jeff walked past the entrance and left Donna standing by herself. Then Jeff walked back, "It's all the way down to the end!"

Donna smiled and said, "Think I'll open up and go get the coffee real quick."

Jeff, watched his crew come off the elevators. He walked slowly towards their assembly. "You guys have any ides about removing wax real quick?"

One worker said, "They make something for that. Maybe the stripping stuff you use for the floors will work."

Jeff quipped, "Good idea, let's go try it!"

The men, not knowing the inside scoop, walked up with Jeff reluctantly. Donna closed the door on the fifth floor elevator, just as Pauline opened up the adjacent elevator door. Walking quickly to her office, she zoomed right past Joshua without a word. Joshua remained quiet and pretended he didn't notice. Jeff returned moments later with the stripping solution. Joshua giggled "You just missed her. You going to be the good news bear?"

Jeff looked back with a frozen frown and said, "Yeah, but I think I'll wait for awhile."

Joshua giggled as he dragged the vacuum cleaner towards the service elevator. Donna, now exiting the elevator, was pushing a wheeled metal cart with coffee. Looking across the floor, she spotted Jeff behind the first window display near he service elevator. Shouting loudly, Dona attracted Jeff's attention. Jeff waved his arm and ran and approached Donna. Donna looked right at Jeff and said, "You didn't say anything, yet did you?"

Jeff smiled, "Not yet, but somebody better."

Donna looked back up and said, "I'll handle it."

Jeff, smiling from ear to ear, said, "Thanks!"

Within moments, Donna approached with the wheeled coffee tray. Pushing the buzzer, she proceeded to the inner office. Pauline ran to the door, and helped Donna stabilize the tray. "Good morning, Donna."

Donna looked straight up at Pauline, "You better have some coffee."

Pauline turned, flushed in the face and asked, "Now what?"

Donna remained quiet and poured the coffee, "We have a graffiti problem."

Pauline, sipping her coffee said, "A what?"

Donna looked up and said, "Somebody's waxing up all the window displays."

Pauline lowered her cup to the table, "Is it bad?" Donna nodded her head.

Pauline sarcastically retorted, "Great!" She looked at the calendar on the computer screen and said, "We got big brass coming in today, not just the foot soldiers." She walked over to the large office bay window and looked back at Dona and asked, "Wonder if there's a quick way to remove a lot of it? Like *real* quick!"

Donna raised up out of the chair, walked quickly toward her desk; she paged Jeff, then she walked back to Pauline's desk. Pauline, sipping the last of her coffee said, "Let's go see the damage."

Walking out together, Jeff walked around the last corner towards the office door. Pauline waved in a forward motion and said, "Hey Jeff, show us where it's at." Jeff looked at Donna, but remained quiet. Jeff walked to the tourist elevators and said, "Well, it's only on this floor. It starts from the east annex floor with the animal displays, straight through to the bathrooms to the Indian displays."

Pauline blasted, "Don't we have security??"

Donna shook her head, looking at Jeff. Jeff looked at Pauline, "The work crews are trying some of the floor stripping stuff."

Donna looked to Jeff, "You told me yesterday to order razor blades. Why didn't you tell us it was this bad?"

Jeff shook his head, "It wasn't! This is all new since yesterday!"

Pauline used the wall phone to call security, "Yes, this is Pauline. Will you review the closed circuit cameras for the last two days? Yes, we're looking for a graffiti freak." Walking back out towards the center fifth floor, Pauline noticed Gary Thomas exiting the elevator. She looked at Donna, "It's starting already." Then she yelled in a friendly shout, "Over here." Pauline and Donna ran to greet him. Looking back at Jeff, Pauline said, "See what you can do."

Gary Thomas greeted them and started walking with them towards the main curator's office. Opening the inner office door, Gary and Pauline proceeded through. Gary, not wasting any time, remarked, "Pauline, I have some good news. Our board released another check for a little more money."

Pauline opened a letter with an envelope opener and glanced across the desk to Gary Thomas, "That's a little bit better!"

Gary smiled, "There's more coming."

Pauline curious, "How soon you taking the stuff?"

Gary cleared his throat, "How's today?"

Pauline reached for the coffee pitcher, "Care for some coffee? Today?"

Gary Thomas said, "Well, most of the other museums are already finished up."

Pauline looked across at Donna, "Check on Jeff, see how he's doing?" Then glancing back to Gary, Pauline asked the next question. "How involved is the process?"

Gary looking at his watch holding his arm towards the light said, "I bet we'll be out of here by 11:00."

Donna walked back in, "It's working," she said.

Gary looked a little curious. Pauline, fumbling for words said, "We had some weird experience with wax graffiti." Pauline, not elaborating, walked over to the big window, "Wow! Is that all your stuff?"

Gary laughed, "Yeah, they must be here."

Pauline looked back to Gary, "We have a crew we can spare if you need extra help."

Gary, sipping the last of his coffee, said, "No, that's O.K. We have sort of a system. We need one person to open up each display case."

Pauline looked over at Donna, "I'll have Jeff follow you through."

Donna quipped, "I'll page him." Walking back to her office, Donna noticed the outer office full of people. She asked, "You're all with Gary?"

The crowd shook their heads. Picking up the pager, Donna noticed Jeff standing in the outside hall. She shouted out to Jeff, "Pauline wants you to open the window cases, and displays for these people."

Jeff nodded his head and walked in and grabbed the master keys from Donna's cabinet.

Pauline shook Gary's hand as he walked out towards Donna's desk. Glancing at the crowd, Pauline giggled, "Yes, Gary, you have plenty of help." Then smiling at the people, she said, "Welcome to our museum." She glanced over to Donna, "Would you order me some more coffee?" Walking back in her office, she called back security. Finally Pauline received the final review. She jumped to her feet and loudly said, "Nothing!!?? I have an entourage of people taking museum pieces for a National tour. For insurance reasons, yeah, that's right, thank you." She turned on the computer monitor and watched the group appraise the first display, One individual was writing down the items, another checking a master list attempting not to have too much of one thing. A lady, dressed in a power suit, examined each item to identify time line and Native American ancestry. A fourth individual placed each item on a scanner device which placed a special barcode identifier on it. Two remaining men photographed each item and wrapped them for shipping and packaging. Slowly, like clockwork, the team with Gary approached the last Native American glass enclosure. Walking in slow reverence up the tunnel of joy, Jeff on cue, opened the trap door and climbed behind the wall of displays. Slowly the evaluators pointed as Jeff held up pottery and finally the spears. Each window having different displays, Jeff ran back to the first and handed each item chosen through the trap door. Slowly and carefully, the team made their way through the inclined tunnel of displays. Approaching the bend before reaching the final display, the whole team stared in suspense. Jeff turned off the robotic warrior and reached down and held up the Crystal Tomahawk. The main team leader looked around at each of the others, then back to Jeff and nodded with a smile of approval. Slowly Jeff made his way through the narrow inclined hallway. Passing the Tomahawk first to Gary Thomas, Jeff saluted and began walking down the inclined internal hall. Gary shook his head in disbelief, "So this is really it?"

The lady with the power suit stepped around the group and reached for the find. Slowly, with shaking hands, Gary handed the

Crystal to the lady. Holding the Crystal next to a flashlight, a prism of different colors and shades radiated from her hand! The woman, looking over to the evaluators, shook her head, then said, "I see why this thing caused so much trouble." They walked down the inclined hallway back out into the fifth floor. There, the team met Pauline. Gary said, "Absolutely incredible!" Gary Thomas, reaching for her hand, said, "I told you we'd be done by 11:00.

Pauline looked at the team, "You people want some coffee or lunch?"

The last person finally walked down the incline now holding the Crystal. First a grin, then a burst of laughter as the whole group remained amazed.

Gary Thomas turned to his crowd. "You guys want to get going?" Slowly each person responded affirmatively. Gary looked back to Pauline and said, "You should be getting the next installment for the roof in a couple weeks."

Pauline asked, "How long before we get our displays back?"

Gary looked hard at his team, "It's going to be awhile, at least a year."

Pauline laughed, I hope not much longer than that."

Gary looked back and said, "Well, it takes awhile for the tour to come back around."

Pauline, almost in tears, walked the team to the front entrance. Men with canvas covered wooden boxes pushed themselves toward the loading area. Pauline burst in tears, and quickly turned and began walking toward the first floor elevator as she realized what a big part the Crystal had played in the lives of so many people!

THE END

* * *